Blunt Spurs

The Griffin's Aide-De-Camp

Blunt Spurs

The Griffin's Aide-De-Camp

ISBN/EAN: 9783337422967

Printed in Europe, USA, Canada, Australia, Japan

Cover: Foto ©Andreas Hilbeck / pixelio.de

More available books at **www.hansebooks.com**

THE

GRIFFIN'S AIDE-DE-CAMP.

BY

BLUNT SPURS.

EDITED BY A PROFESSIONAL MAN.

Third Edition,

WITH

AN ADDENDUM

CONTAINING

HINTS ON THE EDUCATION OF A HORSE.

MADRAS:

PRINTED AT THE SCOTTISH PRESS, BY GRAVES AND CO.

FOR J. HIGGINBOTHAM.

SOLD BY MESSRS. THACKER, SPINK AND CO., CALCUTTA.
    ,,   MESSRS. SMITH, TAYLOR AND CO., BOMBAY.

1860.

MAJOR OUTRAM, C. B.

RESIDENT AT THE COURT OF HYDERABAD, IN SCINDE,

ETC. ETC.

As an admirer of your public talents and private virtues, as well as of your justly celebrated character as one of the best hog-hunters on the Bombay side of India, but as no admirer of the neglect in your stable, this volume is dedicated by your much obliged friend,

BLUNT SPURS.

CONTENTS.

PART IV.

ADDENDUM.

PREFACE TO THE FIRST EDITION.

BROTHERLY love and friendly kindness being generally shown in an inverse ratio in the purchase of a horse to what they are in any other transaction, and the loss sustained from the high price being often ruinous and provokingly vexatious, I publish the following pages, in the hope that you, as well as your noble but ill-treated slave, may mutually derive benefit from the contents.

I have never fallen in with any little pamphlet entirely divested of technical language, such as a tyro would like from its simplicity, giving plain and succinct directions how to purchase a horse for a racer, charger, and hunter, together with an easy account of putting him into condition, &c., and showing how far he might

venture to treat him when diseased. What is
here written has been gained by study from
works of others,* and what professional men
have taught me, interspersed throughout with
my own observations. Proceeding from an
undiploma'd hand, these are not supposed to
be infallible; but though errors may exist,
they will not lead far out of the right path,
and perhaps will aid a novice when buying,
and afterwards tend to prevent him ruining his
horse by injudicious treatment, more than if
he pounced on a scientific veterinary volume.
These learned books are but ill-adapted to a
person who has neither had experience, nor
given the subject any attention ; and they are

---

* This acknowledgment was the cause of my book, when in manuscript, being much depreciated, and by one of the very persons
who, no doubt, will most benefit by it. "Compile!" said he, " any
body can compile." Now, discoveries of this kind are of a *green*,
and also of a jealous hue. How are our ideas confirmed, and how
is our information got, if not from books ? All amateur writings
must of necessity be more or less compiled ; but it is only amateurs
who have studied, and reflected, and had practice on such a subject
as horseflesh, that are capable of *translating* scientific and technical
English for the understanding of their brethren. Nearly the whole
of the last part of this work, to say nothing of much of the preceding parts, will be a compilation, then, if you like, from various
professional and other authors ; but as I have had some little experience, I reserve to myself the liberty of extracting from those whose opinions approach nearest my own.

daily misunderstood, even in their most simple parts.

If I am occasionally a little censorius, re-member, this is the best mode of impressing things on the memory ; and if you are of opi-nion that the contents are very generally known, I can only say, that it is a great pity they are not more generally practised : at the same time, I may inform you, this is not written for those who do know, but for those who do not; so that for the future we may all start even.

I beg one favour—that you will not be so inconsistent as to deride the contents of this little treatise, and at the same time adopt the precepts it contains; and moreover, if you do, take care you never invite me to inspect your stud, or I will " show up" more faults in each horse than you thought existed in the whole of the Bomb Proof.

To enable you, condescending reader, who may read for instruction, to purchase a casty, sound, and useful Arab ; to keep him in con-dition always fit for work ; to take your gallop out of him without injury, or to bring him on

the turf; and to prevent your inflicting unnecessary pain when illness overtakes him, is the
object of

THE GRIFFIN'S AID-DE-CAMP,

IN FOUR PARTS.

I. PURCHASING FROM THE STABLES, ETC.

II. THE AGE, THE PULSE, BLEEDING, PHYSICK-
ING, SHOEING.

III. PUTTING INTO CONDITION. TRAINING.

IV. TREATMENT OF A FEW DISEASES.

PREFACE TO THE NEW EDITION.

The following pages have been revised and corrected by a PROFESSIONAL MAN. In a work, however, so generally correct from its author's hands, there has not been much to amend. The errors corrected were principally such as a non-professional man was likely to fall into. The Reviser has had a very extensive practice in India, extending over a period of eight and twenty years, and his position in the service of Government has afforded him the opportunity of making the peculiarities of Arabs and other horses his constant study during that long period :—while at the same time it enables him to say that with but few exceptions in India, more horses have passed through his hands professionally, than those of any other man.

He has, therefore, been able to make a few corrections in the text regarding the peculiarities of horses generally used in India, and their proper management ; also to notice characteristics which might be unobserved, by even Professional Men, with less wide experience.

This little work is now strongly recommended by the Reviser, as richly meriting the attention of all possessors of horses, (private gentlemen as well the Profession) who take an interest in their comfort and health ;—to promote and secure which many useful lessons will be found in its pages.

MADRAS, May, 1858.   D. S.

ADVERTISEMENT.

In presenting to the Public a THIRD EDITION of The Griffin's Aide-de-Camp, the Publisher desires to express his gratification at the welcome reception given to the second edition, which is now exhausted.

The fact of the ready sale which the publication has met with in the three Presidencies, not only induces him to publish this Edition, but if possible, to make the book more acceptable to the Public.

With this view, he has appended to it, with the permission of the compiler, *Hints on the education of a Horse,* printed a short time ago by a retired Officer of the Madras Army ; and it is hoped this addendum will not be considered valueless.

June, 1860.

GRIFFIN'S AID-DE-CAMP.

PART I.

PURCHASING FROM THE STABLES, ETC.

THE CASTE.

HIGH CASTE, or thorough blood, of course is the first thing to be observed in selecting an Arab for the turf, for without good caste it is all labour in vain ; but as there are different breeds, each possessing high caste, it is sometimes difficult to decide which is the better bred out of three or four that happen also to be all well built ; therefore, when it is an option between two of equally supposed good caste, do not hesitate, when buying for the turf, to choose that one shining most in running points in preference to the finer or handsomer horse ; and these points are not so universally known, and very seldom remembered, if known, when in the act of purchasing. Be quite certain first, that you really are inspecting an Arab, for there are many that are taken to be of good caste that never saw Arabia, nor sprang from Arab stock ; and though the speed which some few of these have occasionally shown, is proof that they must, by either sire or dam, have inherited good blood of some country, still, they are not to be trusted like the genuine Arab, whose pure descent and unsullied pedigree is generally graced with a shape that rarely or never deceives. There is a beautiful symmetry and harmony of proportion running through all the frame ; a superb quarter, with a high set on, well-carried tail ; a softness and thinness of skin ;* a brilliancy of eye, and an elegant contour of head ; qualities that mark the true blood, and which never exist in the numerous spurious brutes that so abound in the stables.

While these handsome points may be relied on as a sure criterion of caste, there are many that have good caste without showing it externally : these can only be proved on the day of running. Good build of itself in a great measure insures good caste,† never-

---

* Yet there are many that in the cold weather will wear a rather long coat, and be very sleek in the hot months.

† The three following extracts serve to corroborote this. I think they are also quite sufficient to refute the absurd saying, "No consequence what a horse's build is ; and if he has only blood he'll run." That thorough breeding in a bad formed horse, will generally beat half breeding in a good formed horse, must be granted ; but the slightest superiority of build in any part of the frame between two of equal blood, is known to every stable-boy to be of the greatest importance :—

Oamer, page 221. On form and performance. "For if a different formation of the parts, &c. and the degrees thereof, be not the cause of difference in the performances, why then one of these horses of the right and true blood would act alike on all ground whatever, and be just as good though made like a hog and without joints." Again, page 229. "In the nature and elegance of their constituent parts, and the due formation thereof, consist the difference between horses of the same and different countries ; or betwixt blood, and no blood." Again, page 230. "Conqueror and Othello were two full brothers, but one was a king and the other a beggar, with respect both to form and action. If then the difference in the performance of these brothers did not depend on their different formation of parts, &c. pray tell me on what it did depend, for the cause of it couldn't be in the blood, unless you will say this innate quality may appertain to one brother and not to another ; and then, I apprehend, the bystanders will say you have proved nothing."

theless, many good caste horses are seen badly formed, and many half or three parts bred, well formed.
High caste united to a running form, will never fail ;
and some horses, when led out, show such superior
blood, energy, and build, that if properly trained,
and nothing constitutionally wrong, they would be
sure to gallop : others showing *externally* only tolerable good caste, but good make ; or good caste but indifferent make, may be called the doubtful ones :
while there is a third, a numerous class, which one
may with safety declare will never run, and many of
these are handsome notwithstanding. But an ugly
horse may have as much chance of running as a handsome one, provided the different essential running
parts of his frame harmonize ; that the joints are all
equally corresponding with the size, and that the
hind parts agree in relation to the fore parts, for
" ugliness, though the opposite of beauty, is not the
opposite of proportion and fitness,"* and so it is with
the horse.

To distinguish high caste appears a very complex
affair at the imperial mart of the Bomb Proof : but,
produce me an Arab with a straight spine, and a
straight long quarter ; a muscular and handsome
dropped hind leg ; a round barrel, swelling well out
behind the elbows, with great depth of girth, and a
moderately broad but flat chest ; a very oblique and
deep shoulder ; a light neck ; a well set on lean head,
with a large brilliant eye, thin open nostril, deep
mouth, wide clear jowl, and small silky ear ;—give
me this make, with the upper inner bone of the knees
and hocks large, and hinder bone of each also large,

* Burke on the Sublime.

and the back sinews clear, powerful, and wide away from the suspensory ligament ; the whole covered with a fine thin skin, and finishing with small, but well open, short, tough feet, and I'll take the caste for granted. If added to this, he is a long horse ; five years old ; perfectly fresh ; short between the knee and fetlock ; fourteen hands two inches high ; higher at the croup than at the withers ; fine action, and a good constitution, I'll take the speed besides for granted ; for when these latter qualities of fine action, and a good constitution, are united to all the above form, the only remaining desideratum, the nervous excitability,* will then always be found, more or less, associated with it.

THE BUILD, COMMENCING WITH THE QUARTERS,

TAIL, THIGHS, STIFLE, ETC.

Four of the most desirable points for the racer are, powerful well-shaped quarters, thighs, and stifles ; and large, lean, bony hocks. The straighter and longer the spine is from the croup—the end of the loins— to the setting on of the tail, so much better is the quarter ; for the most scientific writers tell us, that

* Nervous excitability is used in contradistinction to dull temperament, yet there is a peculiar kind of docile laziness of temper characteristic of many high caste Arabs, but which, by dint of good training, put forth their energy, and shine on the turf as well as others of more choleric blood :—

J. Stewart, p. 55. " It is to be remembered, that good conformation merely gives the power to perform extraordinary exertions ; the will to exert that power depends on something else, which appears as necessary for great feats as the conformation. This energy, or disposition to work, may be too great for many purposes. The racer, indeed, can never have more than enough : it is a combination of energy with good conformation that commands eminence on the turf."

the straightness of the spine here, causing a slanting direction in the haunch and thigh-bones, enables the muscles to act to the greatest advantage, and that it is in the advantageous direction quite as much as the bulk of the muscle that the propelling power lies. Let that, therefore, be a *sine-qua-non,* that from the end of the loins to the setting on of the tail the spine must be straight, or nearly so, and it cannot be too long. A broad quarter may carry weight, but it must be long also to gallop, and the tail should be carried out straight, and carried well (it does not require always to be carried high to be carried well, but it requires to be well set on, that is, set on high up). The tail of a blood Arab is likewise generally thin, of small circumference, tapering to a very small point, and the hair on it not too bushy. " Full mane, if you like, but thin tail." Carrying it on one side can be no sign of bad caste, although it certainly looks ugly.

The thigh should be as broad as the haunch-bones; and as much as they swell out broader, they are better. A horse that is ragged-hipped, it is said, is not objectionable ; but by this is meant, that, *notwithstanding* the great muscularity of the quarters and thighs, the protuberances of the haunch-bones still project a little wider ; and not from the quarters and thighs being at all deficient in muscle, which is often also called ragged-hipped, and makes the haunch-bones look a little prominent.* Great thigh-muscle may recom-

---

* The side bones of the loins—the transverse processes of the lumber vertebræ—being short, are a cause of a horse being ragged-hipped ; and these side bones being thus short, are also the cause of a horse being wall-sided ; therefore it is that a wall-sided horse often looks ragged-hipped ; but a deficiency of quarter and thigh-muscle, which causes the haunch-bones to stick out a little, is much oftener called ragged-hipped.

pense in some degree for a slight droop in the croup ; but great thigh-muscle, added to a long and straight croup, is the make for the turf. A large hinder channel, from the anus downwards, caused by the muscles projecting, and being well asunder, is another good point, and much admired : it is a sign of great endurance.

The stifle, and all that below it, must be broad and strikingly muscular : he must be what is termed well let down in the thighs, plenty of muscle inside the thigh as well as outside, never hare-hammed ; and the muscle just above the outside of the hock, in particular, should be large.* Some horses are accounted too long in the haunches, forcing them off at full speed, but this is not against their running well. These three points, the quarter, thigh, and stifle, show the blood of a horse quite as much as the head, eye, and jaw. A muscular and elegantly dropped hind leg, having a fine elastic spring, is far more difficult to find than a casty head.

THE HOCKS AND THE HIND PARTS PROOF OF HALF

THE BREEDING.

The hock of a fresh unworked Arab is generally beautifully formed, and clean, and particularly excelling in the hind projecting bone at the point. You must never expect a runner in one who is glaringly deficient in this point. The hock should be broad also from side to side ; the bone at the *upper inner* part

---

* The part a little below the stifle being narrow and wanting muscle. See Frontispiece.

prominent. As to whether the leg for a running horse should descend straight from the hock, or incline under the body, neither should be in extreme : there is a medium. The stride is said to be lengthened by its being well bent under, yet, that there are objections, arising from the greater wear of the hock, that greatly counterbalance this. Either for a racer, charger, or hunter, a rather straight drop for an Arab will be best and handsomest. In the high caste Arab, it invariably does descend rather straight, but whether the leg from the hock is bent under or straight, the hock itself must neither turn in nor out; if the former, he will be cat-hammed, making his legs like an ill-shaped cow's, or, as the ladies say, donkey-legged ; if the latter, which is not so often met with, the toe will turn in, which is worse. For a running horse, it is an advantage if the toe is behind the stifle-joint.

A BONE SPAVIN in the clean hocks of an Arab, is generally visible enough if situated at the top of the splent-bone, that is, *on the inner side of the lowermost part of the hock.* If he should be spavined higher up, or the ligaments have been strained, it is not so easily perceived as the former, but in either case both the hocks will not look exactly alike ; and this will be quite sufficient to reject him.* A small bone spavin is often a most difficult disease to detect ; and this is not extraordinary, considering that professional men have in some instances been deceived, from not ex-

---

* A horse is not always to be rejected on account of spavin, particularly if it appears of long standing and there is no appearance of stiffness. Many spavined horses work well to the last without falling lame. For a horse of this description however, one third less ought to be given, than for a perfectly sound horse.—ED.

amining attentively. A spavin on the head of the splent-bone, on the inner side of the lowermost part of the hock, is often productive of no lameness if situated well forward, not even though it be as large as a marble; therefore this, although the most frequent seat of spavin, is not so bad as that which lies a little higher up, for here is the principal motion of the hock, and the smallest ossification always causes more or less lameness. You must discover if there is the slightest difference either in the feel or appearance of the hocks in these two places (for a horse is seldom spavined in both hocks in exactly the same manner), and if there is, pause before you conclude the bargain. Should there be any difference on the outside of the hock, blows, kicks, or hurts have most probably produced it, not strains or over work, although spavin is occasionally found in this part likewise.*

If the least swelling or enlargement exists in any part of the back of the hock, below the point, which may be detected by carefully observing if they are both alike, you must reject him also; for this will denote a strain, perhaps a curb.

CAPPED HOCKS are a great objection; they proceed from blows, hurts, or contusions from kicking, rarely, it is said, from a strain; but are apt to enlarge on work. When the hocks are but very slightly capped (for if one is capped the other is generally found so too), they may give the appearance of the bones of the points being long. Don't be deceived in this way, but feel if there is anything like a tumour there.

---

* During an experience and practice of twenty-eight years, and during which period I have had thousands of horses through my hands, I have never seen spavin on the outside of the hock, nor do I think any one else.—ED.

THE BOG-SPAVIN, a puffy swelling in front of the bend, and a little towards the inside of the joint, can never be mistaken if the finger is pressed on the large vein that runs over it, which will now sink in half an inch, and when the finger is taken away, bulge out again. If found in one hock, the other will generally have it also ; and therefore, as far as this disease is concerned, though they may appear alike, they yet look full and fat, not lean and dry, as they should do. Bog-spavin generally looks larger in the middle of the day, the cold in the morning before going to exercise acting as a sedative ; or the excited action of the absorbents during and immediately after exercise operating in keeping it down a little.*

THE THOROUGH-PIN, another small puffy swelling on the outside of the hock, nearly on a line with the point, and running through to the inside, may not prove any hindrance even in hunting ; but for a racer there should be no doubt about the hinder extremities in any way, either as regards build, injury, or disease ; they are the grand agents in progression, and a racehorse, to shine, must be nearly perfect in every thing behind. You are not to infer from this, that a horse can run because he has no defect in his hind parts, only, that he will rarely run well if he has. Formed as described under these four heads of Quarters, Thighs, Stifles, and Hocks, they will look handsome both to the eye of the novice as well as the judge ; and if, added to this, he has a decided casty head, you may take it for granted he is well bred ; but the handsomest and most casty head that was ever on an Arab is only in-

---

* Bog-spavin seldom causes lameness in ordinary work, but is almost certain to do so in very severe work, such as hunting, &c. Thorough-pin is of the same nature as Bog-spavin, and attended with the like results.—ED.

dicative of half the breeding, the hind parts must be formed as before laid down, to prove the other half.

All the good breeding in half or three-part bred horses will sometimes show itself in front, sometimes behind : for instance, put a thorough-bred horse perfect in make to a half or three-parts bred mare : one year a foal will probably be thrown badly formed behind, with a casty head and good forehand ; another year one perfectly formed behind, with an ugly head and bad forehand. The latter of these, with the good hind parts, both being of equal good blood, would be the most promising for running. But again, a half or three-parts bred horse, even possessing all good running points, will, nineteen times out of twenty, be beaten in a long race by a thorough-bred horse not so well built as himself. This is well known in England, and the same law, of course, holds good with an Arab.

THE HEAD, NOSTRILS, MOUTH, LIPS, EYE, EARS, ETC.

The head ought to be lean and bony ; the jaws wide, and not fleshy ; the channel clean, and not filled up.

The nostrils must be open and thin, or he is useless for the turf ; the best training in the world will never compensate for a thick shut nostril.

The mouth should be deep—a laughing mouth—which will allow more room for the opening of the nostril, and also give him a better mouth.

The lips should be thin and evenly closed, for the under lip hanging loose is a very unfavourable omen of his running.

The eye is never too large, and scarcely ever too prominent. A small eye should be objected to, as being more liable to disease, and symptomatic of cross blood. I warn you to look well into the eyes, so very many bear the milky marks, the result of inflammation. Whenever you find one with a cloudy appearance round the edge and close to the white, or one with white marks streaked across the centre, or one which on a close examination appears a little smaller than the other, or puckered in the lids, depend upon it there has been disease, which is likely to return. Recollect a horse's eyes are not placed like a man's : if he is blind with one eye, he is unable, without turning his head round, to see any thing on that side with the other. The slightest derangement in the eye may at times prevent him using his speed to the utmost. Should any speck of white be observable near the centre of the eye, it has been caused by some blow or hurt, and may interfere with the passage of the light through the pupil : you should therefore distrust it, for it is a very ugly blemish at all events, and reduces the value considerably. Some few others bear a resemblance to the green glass eye : there is as much difference between the clear, transparent, bright, healthy eye, and this glass eye (which is written as arising from a loss of power in the optic nerve, and generally incurable,) as there is between a polished diamond and a piece of window-glass. Shying is occasionally connected with some little alteration in the organs of vision, imperceptible to us who are not oculists.*

* If you blow a soap-sud bladder between your thumb and fore-finger, and hold it up to the light, you will discover a kind of purple variegated streaks on the surface : these colours you will often see over the horse's eyes by narrowly inspecting them, keeping the head in a greater light than the body, as just within a stable door. I do not know their cause, but imagine they have no business there.

The ears of a genuine Arab are small, and the hair inside is silky : they never have that tremendous curling in of the points so proverbial among bad Persian and country-bred horses. Lop ears are quite as ugly as those that curl in, but a large lop ear, if only well shaped, rather peaked, and not large round at the points, with a thin skin, is no such sign of bad caste ; it appears to belong to a peculiar breed.

The glands below the ears are sometimes found swollen ; and if much so, may be a serious detriment.

A small head on a large horse, or large head on a small horse, are of course equally out of proportion ; a trifle either way is perhaps immaterial, if only lean, with the large eye, broad forehead, and hollow jowl ; yet, a head possessing these and all the foregoing good points, may still, from some peculiarity of conformation, not altogether please the eye, or be a very handsome head ; but one void of these requisites can never be termed a blood head. A " cut short" head, with a slight indentation about half a foot above the nose, is a great favourite with some judges. I like it too.*

THE NECK.

The neck of an Arab I never knew too light or too long, though it is often quite long enough. Take care especially that it is light, and that the upper surface is not too thick : it should be very muscular

* This is the Nedjed head, a capital description of horse for a roadster or hunter, but the Oneisa, which has rather a large head is a horse of much greater size, stride and enduring qualities, and therefore a much superior horse for the turf.—ED.

towards the bottom, but enter the chest above the
points of the shoulders ; if it does not, you will have
neither speed nor lightness of action : it must also
curve a little where the head is set on, or he will pull
against your arm, and feel heavy in hand, consequently this will never answer for a charger or hunter, and
it is nearly as bad for a racer. There must be no
superfluous thickness on the upper part of the shoulder-blade : the division of the neck and shoulder must
be distinctly marked ; any extra bone at the upper
part of the shoulder-blade, filling up the line of de-
marcation between it and the neck, always makes a
horse go more or less stiff, and this is particularly
observable in thick necks ; yet, there must be sufficient
muscle below to prevent the neck being a "loose
neck." If he has a neck like a deer it is ugly, and
does not afford so free a passage to his breath : the
deer necks, however, with all the flesh set below, are
not so bad as those where the upper surface is thick,
and it is all set on above. Ewe necks, if only slightly ewed, and light, and not entering the chest low
down, are rather favourable than objectionable for a
racer.* The rounder a neck is the better ; and if
only shallow from mane to under surface, there is no
fear then of its being too muscular from side to side.
No thick neck is fit for the saddle, and a bull-neck is
fit for nothing but a bullock-garree.

THE WITHERS AND BACK.

High withers you will not always find, but they
should undoubtedly rise a full inch higher than the

* Darvill, vol. ii. p. 10. I have a great aversion to a high-crested race-horse.

top of the shoulder-blade, or if you like the expression better, as high withers are not at all necessary for the turf, the top of the shoulder-blade must be a full inch below the top of the withers ;* and if the withers are wide at top he will generally carry weight better than if rather fine. After the fall of the withers the spine must run straight, without any ups or downs, or arches, to the croup at the end of the loins, that is, to the centre between the haunch bones ; and from there, as mentioned before, it must be carried out straight to the tail. If the spine has any of these arches the back will be galled by the saddle, and if there is a depression at the back of the saddle, where the back and loins join, it shows weakness. A depression also where the loins and croup join, "the hind quarters looking separated from the back," is twenty times worse. After the fall of the withers the spine is often straight, yet gradually ascending ; this is an advantage, provided the ascent is continued to the end of the loins ; and if from thence it is gradually carried on to the tail, he will, notwithstanding a good height of withers, look higher behind than before, which is favourable.† The straightness of spine is essential : a horse at full speed, with his head and neck thrust out, gallops as horizontally as possible : a hollow backed horse scarcely ever runs well. Pur-

---

* I once saw an Arab—a deformity—with the top of the shoulder-blades higher than the withers, yet he was hog-hunted.

† William Osmer. Fifth edition. Treatise on the Horse, p. 222. "If the forehand be more lofty than the croup, he cannot run worth a curse." How ridiculous it is to see a London horse-dealer placing the horse, when brought out for inspection, with the fore-legs on the highest ground, making him appear of that build as if he would slip his girth. A well-built horse should merely have a nice rise in the withers, but the above abominable position ruins the appearance, making the whole backbone from the withers to the tail gradually declining backward like the formation of a cameleopard.

chase none for the turf, therefore, but what may not be inaptly termed a horizontal horse.

It is actually requisite to have some length of back for the turf, and *provided* the quarter is long, the shoulder oblique, and the spine straight, there is not much fear of the back being too long. A long quarter, a moderately long back, and a rather long neck, must necessarily make a tolerably long horse, which is the form desired for a racer. A tall, short horse, is not found to keep the pace up so well as one that is longer. The length should therefore be great from the point of the shoulder to the hindermost point of the quarter ; and then, if with this long quarter added to a good oblique slanting shoulder, the forelegs are planted well forward, and the hind-legs properly dropped, there will be observable that "shortness above and length below" so much sought after ; in other words, there will be a long horse with a short back. The reverse of this, a short horse with a long back, is shown in the frontispiece. So, the true meaning of a long horse being length from the point of the shoulder to the hindermost point of the quarter, it is very possible to have a long horse with a short neck also, which, if light, and with a curve where the head is set on, will do admirably for a racer : or to have a short horse with a long neck, which is more adapted for a charger or hunter.

THE SHOULDER AND CHEST.

The shoulder must run back with a good slant ; and then, if the withers rise a full inch above the top of the shoulder-blade, it will not be found too heavily laden. It has been asserted, by both Europeans

and Natives who have been best conversant with the
Arab, that nothing denotes the superior cast more
than that extreme obliquity of shoulder, and certainly nothing denotes the make more.   When the shoulder is very oblique, how short the neck appears
below from the back part of the channel to the chest ;
and how long above from between the ears to the
withers !   What superb conformation !   An unex-
pected trip easily throws a horse with a straight
shoulder down, and he generally hangs very heavy
in hand as he tires.   The straight-shouldered horse,
if shining in other points, may pass handsomely for
draught in a carriage or buggy, but will never answer well for the saddle.   From the top of the blade
to the point it should be long, very long, for that
will compensate for a little deficiency in the oblique-
ness ; and the space from the point to the fore-arm,
or leg, particularly short, in order that the legs may
stand well forward ; and the chest should be moderately broad, in order that these forward legs may
not be too close together, but while it is broad it
must also be flat ; not concave and hollow, but flat,
and not overloaded in front.   A round full chested
horse will do very well as a carriage-wheeler, but
not for the turf.   The great, broad, rounded and
projecting hang-over chests, with the fore-legs often
inclining under the belly, are continually called fine
chests, but they are as bad as bull-necks.

THE DEPTH OF GIRTH, AND CARCASE.

The depth of girth cannot be too great, and the
carcase, which should resemble a barrel, and not be

flat-sided, should swell out well under the elbows ; then, with the moderately broad chest, you will be sure to have what are indispensable, good large lungs. A carcase that is flat-sided is equally bad for running as for appearance. The depth of girth is a point that admits of measurement, but then the chest must sink deep between the fore-legs, or else very high withers alone may contribute more than their proper share to make a large girth : sixty-four to sixty-five inches will be very good for an Arab of fourteen hands to fourteen hands one inch ; but if you have an eye for a horse, you will tell at once if it is good, or not. There should also be some distance between the last false rib and the haunch-bone, that the hind legs in the gallop may be thrown well under : this is allowed to be an excellency in the racer, though it detracts a little from the strength.

Horses, whose carcases are light, and legs rather long, " showing too much daylight," have been run down far more than is necessary : they are only objectionable for heavy people. When there is good build otherwise, a small round carcase, if it only swells out behind the elbows, need never be objected to by a light weight, for it rather adds than detracts from the beauty, and they are often splendid runners. A large carcase ; a large circular barrel, with deep ribs, deep in the fellers, must have large broad flat legs to carry it, or they will quickly fail.

THE ELBOW AND FOREARM, ETC.

The elbow, the bone at the top of the forearm, must be large and not turn in : the top of the forearm must be decidedly swelling and muscular : the length of

3

the forearm from the elbow to the knee cannot be too great, in order that the distance between the knee and fetlock may be proportionably short : these are three indispensable points, but the two first are seldom sufficiently scrutinized. A horse with a thin forearm and corresponding lanky thigh, cannot possibly run, nor stand work either.

THE KNEE, AND BACK SINEWS, AND SUSPENSORY LIGAMENT. THE SHANK-BONE, FETLOCKS, ETC.

The knee must be broad and flat : *the upper inner part* should present a striking width, or it will look round, which is ugly, and does not betoken strength. If there is the slightest bony excrescence in front, it may interfere materially with his running, and which firing and blistering will often fail to remove ; and if there is any puffy swelling, it is worse than the bog-spavin. The hinder bone of the knee cannot be too large, so that the leg may not be tied in, that is, that the back sinews may be wide away from the shank-bone ; and these back sinews should feel smooth, strong, and well braced, like a piece of catgut tightly covered with fawnskin. The back sinews cannot always be told by the feel ; they must be carefully inspected at each side, for sometimes, while they feel smooth, strong, and wiry, there will be an evident difference in the size about the centre ; a very slight bow—a sure sign of having been injured. The suspensory ligament, the centre rope, must also feel and look, like the back sinews, fine and wiry. There is, however, a distinction between smallness immediately below the knee, and that lying in which deforms the legs, and it consists in this. Some of the best Arabs,

even while the hinder bone is of good size, are yet
small below the knee, but equally small at the fetlock ; this is no imperfection, but merely renders such
horses a little slight, and in this sense is not very
good for the turf, and a great objection to weight
certainly ; but one that is small below the knee, or if
not very small, yet gradually inclining broader towards the fetlock, is not only most unsightly tied in,
but is one of the worst faults a racer, or any horse
can have ; for when the back sinews are thus tied in,
the legs are very liable to become crooked, and fail
in hard work ; besides which, this last description of
tying in is, like the small eye, a strong sign of mon-
grel breeding. A horse that is slight, slight as before
described, all the way down, and short between the
knee and fetlock, will be quite as strong as one that
is broader below the knee, yet longer between the
knee and fetlock ; but great breadth immediately below the knee, in addition to shortness between the
knee and fetlock, is needed to make this part perfect
for a racer. An English groom of some experience
that I knew, used to say, " Always be mindful of
the scientific maxim : when purchasing or betting, if
you feel a doubt, and have an option between two
horses, always decide in favour of that one with the
largest three essential bones ; the hinder bone of the
knee, the elbow bone, and the bone at the point of
the hock."

The shank, when viewed in front, must look fine,
and of small circumference. There is no surer sign
of hard work than the shank, when viewed in front,
looking round and large. A curb or spavin may
come by a strain, but the roundness of shank I here

allude to—a thickening of the skin and cellular stuff beneath, quite independent of the bone—is produced by nothing but sheer hard work. Some few blood horses, exceptions, are born rather rounder in the shank-bone itself than others, yet it is bad ; and even this roundness in the bone itself is very ugly, and looks like work ; but even one whose shank bones are naturally rather round, will become rounder still much sooner than one whose shank bones are naturally flatter. Plenty of muscle above, large back sinews below, but small flat shank bones, solid like ivory, is the blood horse, and horse for endurance or speed.

A splent, if situated about the middle of the shank bone, is of no great harm, save that the price of a horse, if bought for appearance, is much diminished by the unsightliness of a piece of bone on the side of the leg, a lump there, from its prominent situation, offending the eye more than a large spavin. If found just below the knee, it may interfere with the motion of the joint, and if on the inside, it may be the cause of the speedy cut. If near the suspensory ligament, it also sometimes affects the free action of the leg ; and if extending on to the back sinews, it too often causes lameness. In all clean fresh blood legs, there are three different parts distinctly visible : the small, round, flat-looking shank bone, the suspensory ligament, and the back sinews ; and these are clearly free from all lumps, and bumps, and bony excrescences whatever ; the only natural prominence being the end of the splent bone, about the size of a pea, two inches above the fetlock.

The hair about the sides of the fetlock is sometimes a little ruffled : if you feel carefully, you will probably find he has been slightly fired. At other times the hair will look of a lighter colour ; when, if you get him in a proper light, you will probably find he has been blistered. Ask the reason, and you will be told, he was fired for nothing, just as a preventive ; or if blistered, merely for fun. Look on these as screws, and deduct at least seventy per cent. in consequence ; for a man who is cruel enough to fire for nothing, or to blister for fun, will not hesitate to palm off on you a bad and patched-up leg.*

The small scars, or shortened hair from cutting, either behind or at the sides of the fetlocks, are easily seen. If cutting arises from the toes turning too much out, it is, of course, incurable, for " a goose will always go like a goose," and it renders a horse much more unsaleable than a loss of hair from girthgall or sore back, both of which are looked on as most serious objections, as, the hair once off, the spot is so easily galled again, that the horse has frequently to be laid up every other month.

At the inner side of the fetlock, as often as the outside, there is sometimes, in the otherwise cleanest legs, an ossification.† I have seen this twice passed over

---

* Some sporting novices say, a fired leg is worth two others ; it never goes. A fired leg, it is true, will often stand training when its fellow fails ; the reason is plain : the horse favours the fired leg, and the other one has to stand the extra work ; consequently, the good leg goes first, but the bad one has caused it ; besides, there is good authority on record, that a leg never moves so freely after having been fired. It is astonishing how much a horse can favour a leg, without its being noticed by ordinary observers; and it has been remarked that ladies' horses generally fail in the near fore-leg first : these dear creatures always must have the horse lead with the off-leg, therefore it does not get its fair share of the stress, though the foot may get more battering.

† This enlargement is sometimes caused by displacement of the sesamoid bones, in which case it invariably causes lameness when the horse is put to any thing like hard work.—ED.

by a judge, though it was as large as an acorn : the feel and the difference of appearance of the two fet-locks, on nearly a front view, is sure to distinguish it. Ossifications at the sides of the fetlock, like spavins, are sometimes large, without causing lame-ness ; but they are invariably productive of some slight stiffness, though not discernible to every eye. If the enlargement is just above the inside of the fet-lock, and on the suspensory ligament, lameness will generally quickly ensue on work.

Immediately above, and in front of the fetlocks, there is also frequently seen a kind of dent, the fet-lock looking as if there had been too much stress on it ; and so there has been. This may be produced in a slight horse by a single month's riding of too heavy a man, though it will take many months, with rest and bandages, before it resumes its primitive clean-ness. When it accompanies the large rounded shank-bone, the chances are, he has been long shamefully overweighted, as well as overworked ; and horses in this way, though neither standing with their fetlocks knuckling over, ready to " bite the dust," nor having windgalls, are often more or less groggy, and you run the risk of some latent internal disorganization about the joints of the foot, which sooner or later will produce one of those lamenesses that " come of themselves." You cannot reasonably expect to dis-pose of a horse again with these large rounded shank-bones and dents, except as a baggage-horse.

WINDGALLS are a most annoying eye-sore. As un-fair or overwork produced them, so they will increase on work. If they are not large, and no roundness of the shank-bone accompanies them, and you are

not particular as to appearance, he may be well worth
half price : never purchase, however, a horse for the
turf, that shows by such evident signs as all these,
the combined effects of bad legs, mismanagement,
and overwork. To the former sagacious maxim of
the three essential bones, my stable acquaintance im-
pressed on me another injunction, which I hand to
you, with advice to keep it uppermost in your memory :—" Never fall in love with thick ankles." A fresh
horse, he said, like a French danseuse, is always deli-
cately clean at this much-admired part.

THE PASTERNS, ETC.

From the fetlock to the hoof should be rather long,
but not over-slanting : the pasterns of many Arabs,
when long, are sometimes too sloping, the fetlock
nearly touching the ground. The short pasterns,
even, I have seen too oblique ; and then, though the
limb should be otherwise powerful, the beautiful
springy action will be lost in a month by the riding
of the least heavy weight ; yet, on the other hand, if
too upright, the fault is far worse, for the knuckling
over will then assuredly soon commence on work, and
when it does, he will often evince an evident anxiety
to make his nose a substitute for a fifth leg. The
pasterns of a horse, for a heavy weight, should be rather short ; but for a light rider they can hardly be
too long, *provided* they are properly placed. They
should look small,* round, and smooth ; if there is
the slightest enlargement, you may suspect a ring-bone.

* They ought to have plenty of substance however.—Ed.

The easiest and surest way of detecting a ringbone, is to place a couple of fresh young colts (and
they are quickly got at the stables) beside the one you
are buying ; then feel each all up the centre of the
pastern ; and also at the side close to the hoof, about
two inches from the heal. If ringbone is formed in
either of these places, there will be an evident difference in the feel, which should make you sceptical as
to the soundness, for ringbone is not uncommon at
the stables among the newly arrived horses, both old
and young.   There are two ligaments that run down
on either side the pastern, and it is the centre of the
pasterns between these ligaments* that will show a
fulness and hardness ; or, if the ringbone should be
at the side of the coronet, about two inches from the
heel, you must discover it by the difference, which
you will if you search narrowly, first feeling one
horse, then another.   The centre of the pastern between these ligaments about two inches above the
coronet, quite on the seat of ringbone, is sometimes a
little swollen, the consequence of having been fastened with a rope there ; but this, though common
enough among country horses, seldom arises from this
cause with Arabs.   I knew a cunning fellow, who
purchased a new arrival from the boats with one of
these swellings on the off fore pastern, which unluckily turning out a ringbone ; he cleverly tied a rope
round it, so as to take the hair off a little, and searching
out his cousin, a great connoisseur of country-breds,
sold it him for nearly double what he had paid.   Be
cautious then of your friends, for ringbone often pro-
duces no lameness till it spreads on the joint.

* These ligaments, in some flat-shanked, wiry-limbed, clean-pasterned
horses, occasionally stand out very prominent, like a piece of thick cord.

The forelegs must stand straight, as you may na turally suppose : you will not be griffin enough to purchase crooked legs. They should look moderate- ly wide at the chest, gradually approaching each other at the fetlock. If they stand fixed wide apart, " pinned," like a horse labouring under inflamed lungs, it is almost as faulty as if they were crooked from the knee downwards ; but in the latter case, the knees look a trifle too forward, in consequence of the legs being a little bent backward ; he does not in fact stand straight on his forelegs, and therefore you should take the hint here, as well as in the capital crime, the knuckling over of the fetlock joint ; for they al- ways become more crooked on work. These unli- censed pins are sometimes defended on the plea of the horse having been born so, but one that was born crooked is surely quite as bad as one that has been worked so. The leg at other times, from the finish of the knee, has a slant forward instead of backward, the knee appearing too much straightened, bent a little back, calf-kneed. This is a malformation, but never proceeds from work, like the former, neither is it of a hundredth part the consequence ; indeed, some persons prefer a slight slant forwards, so as to be sure there is none backwards. If your own eyes are straight, and not askew, you ought, when standing about a yard distant at the side, to discover either of these defects at a glance, however slight they may be.

The legs are sometimes bowed, and a bow-legged horse generally dishes, and one that dishes will never run. Dishing action should not be called bad action, but rather floundering, or crooked action : bad action is when the legs are not lifted sufficiently high, nor propped sufficiently forward.

The feet are not to turn out, nor in : if the former, he will be liable to cut ; if the latter, it is equally bad, for the weight either way is most unevenly distributed. The point of the toe should be found exactly under the point of the shoulder : dropping your stick perpendicularly from the point of the shoulder will tell you this in a second, if your eye does not. As much as it is behind that, so much is the weight thrown too much forward ; and as in this case the chest will look either like the chest of a dray-horse—called, a remarkably fine chest ; or the legs will slant backward under his belly, which is as bad ; so will he be more likely, especially down hill, to fall. This you may likewise naturally suppose ; for when standing upright on your own legs, and inclining your head and body forward, a push behind will easily upset you.

THE FEET.

The hoofs of a genuine Arab are rather small. You will seldom find them too small, *provided* the hinder part of the quarters are the broadest part.

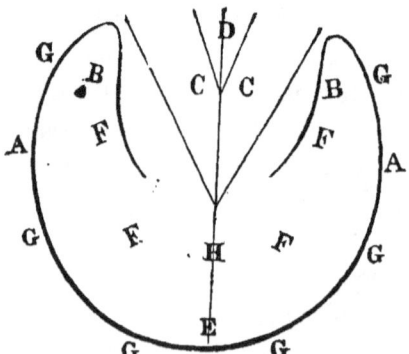

A A, the hinder part of the quarters ; B B, the bars ;

C C, the frog ; D, the cleft ; E, the toe ; four F's, the sole ; six G's, all round, the crust ; H, a line drawn across the centre, showing the outside bottom of the hoof, is more circular than the inside. If the hinder part of the quarters is not the broadest part, then the foot was either never perfectly formed, or has become contracted from want of paring,* bad shoeing, or disease. If the hinder part of the quarters should be as broad as the forepart of the foot ; the frog a good width ; the bottom of the foot properly concave ; and the hoof in front, from the coronet down to the toe, rather upright, this will be the next most desirable form to choose, for you need not expect to get a perfect foot. If the frog should be small, and the heels much wired or pinched in, you must judge from the firmness with which he brings his heels to the ground whether the wiring-in has made him at all tender : if you think it has, or if you are in doubt, reject him ; for this wiring-in proceeding so far as to cause tenderness, which quickly runs on to lameness, is the true chronic founder ; and though, by six or eight months' laying up, the heels may probably be opened again, the tenderness will still remain.

Should the foot be small at the coronet, gradually enlarging downwards like a sugar loaf, it denotes a weak foot : this kind of foot does not look so bad when lifted up, showing often a fine large frog ; but the sole is a little too flat, and the heel a little too low ; the horn often too brittle, continually chipping away at the nail holes,† and the crust being thin, it is easily pricked in shoeing. The foot at the coronet.

* Paring.—ED.

† It is also subject to sand-crack.—ED.

when the horse is standing, should not look small, but nearly as · large as it does at the bottom.

If the horn is not smooth, but ruffled, or wrinkled round the crust like an oyster-shell, it is frequently curable, if not very bad ; but the foot may possibly have suffered severely from fever, or be one of the natural weak feet. Whether a foot with these inequalities of horn can be safely purchased, must depend upon the strength with which the animal treads, and whether it is properly formed in every other respect ; if not, you will do well to reject it ; for should there be nothing internally wrong, it will take a long time, even with great care, before the horn will grow down smooth.

The heels of the crust should descend nearly straight to the ground, not slanting and shelving forward : they should run well back to the heels of the frog, or the foot will lengthen out ; and all feet which lengthen out, not descending from the coronet to the toe, as perpendicularly as the angle of 45°, are more or less weak. But the most to be dreaded foot is that which, while it gradually inclines to this horizontal shape, has also a slight hollow about midway, either in front or round by the quarters, with the sole flat ; such a foot is good for nothing save dissection, notwithstanding the frog should be broad, and the horse at the time not lame : a long and horizontal spine is very fine ; but have nothing to do with a long and horizontal foot. The sole, however, is often flat without any lengthening out of the foot, and so thin that it bends like a piece of whalebone. One or two months' gentle riding, is generally all such a foot will stand before it descends quite on a level with the crust. When it sinks lower still, down to the convex pumiced foot, it is, of course, worse ; but this is merely like a difference of choice between a wooden leg or crutches.

Do not neglect to see that both feet are exactly the same size, for this is as often heedlessly passed over as the difference in the size of the eyes. The two hind feet must correspond likewise ; but not being so liable to contraction, they seldom get out of order. If after all this you are still at a loss to comprehend what constitutes a good foot, keep the heels as open and the foot as hollow as the hind ones ; then you will not be far off the proper form.

White feet are considered objectionable ; but recollect, a white foot, properly formed and shaped, is far superior to a black one badly formed, and that white hind feet are not of much consequence.*

Examine attentively the warmth of the feet ; but this must be done early in the morning, by eight o'clock, before the horse has been exercised, to be of any avail. If one is warm whilst the others are cool, there has been a strain of the coffin joint, or there is something else wrong internally ; but the lameness, in some of these cases, is often so very slight, that you will not discover it till after one or two ridings.

You should observe also, whilst eating grass in his loose stall, if he places one foot stretched out before the other : if he stands decidedly in this position, one foot too much under the body, and the other pointed out nearly a yard in front, you may suspect there is

---

* Horses with white feet are more subject to cracked heels in wet weather, and if not properly dried after washing. The crust also is generally more brittle.— Ed.

something wrong, either a recent hurt, or, more probably, some old-standing tenderness. A dealer in England will prevent your seeing this, by not placing such a horse in a loose stall ; but in India it is generally boldly exhibited ; and I once heard the cause equally as boldly accounted for. The buyer asked, "what makes him stand in that awkward position, with one leg pointed forward ?"—" Oh," replied the seller, " that is merely in consequence of the shortness of his neck ; he could not reach his grass easily otherwise,* many of the Arabs have short necks." The innocent victim, who was a native of the Scilly Isles, appeared quite satisfied with this answer, and giving another look at the neck, said, it appeared to his eye of very good proportion, and concluded the bargain. This was one of the worst kind of the long, horizontal, flat-soled feet.†

THE TESTICLES, ETC.

Look up at the testicles : they should be small and closely hung up. Swollen testicles are very common, and may prove a considerable drawback to his speed. The testicles, even when not enlarged, are sometimes

* This is sometimes however actually the case, particularly in leggy colts.—ED.

† I have myself had two horses with perfect feet ; one had been shod for two or three years ; the other was a colt, and never shod. The feet of both these were small, but very wide at the heels ; the horn was of the proper depth, neither too high nor too low at this part, and of that fine greyish black, Oxford-mixture colour. Neither of them without shoes, over hard ground, moderately ridden, ever went tender or made a false step.

Some persons, who have paid dearly for purchasing a horse with contracted heels, instead of running into the proper opposite, one with open heels, search for nothing but a large spreading foot ; hence their second bargain is nearly as bad as their first ; for a large spreading foot is almost always a weak and a flat foot : moreover, a large spreading foot is most unfavourable for speed.

diseased. I don't know if this can be detected by the feel, or appearance of them, but a horse's value in India is diminished fully one-third by being gelt.*

" A small yard in a horse," says the native adage, " is an infallible characteristic of high blood; the foal he gets, will certainly be good." There is more truth in the first part of this sentence than in most of their sayings. As to the latter, it must depend, of course, on the kind of mare he is put to.

If you are purchasing in the highways and byways, you may inspect the vein of the neck, and also the chest, to see if he has been often bled or rowelled (lower the neck to the ground to detect the small swelling from bleeding) : these are operations that are generally performed for disease, though the former too often when there is no need for it.

THE COLOUR.

The best colour for an Arab is the grey, roan, or white,† and next to this the lighter kind of chestnut, but the former are rightly preferred ; for, caste, bone, shape, freedom from diseases, hardiness of constitution, and good feet, are certainly, generally, more conspicuous in something of the grey colour. In

---

* This is now found by experience to be a mistake. All the Cavalry horses in the Madras Presidency are now geldings, and found to do their work as well, if not better than entires.—ED.

† A writer from Edinburgh says, " It is a remarkable fact, that an Arabian of a dark grey colour was never known in India as a winner. Bays, chestnuts, and silver greys are always to be depended on. I am, &c. &c. Thomas Brown." This must have been my old friend, Mr. Green, whom I am about to introduce you to, at my last page ; for a letter signed Zeal replies, Mercury, Pyramus, Renegade, Emilius, Bundaola, Sackcloth, and Harmonica, were all iron-greys.

the Persian less so, the grey, chestnut, and bay,
having the good qualities about equally distributed
between them.   Some of the Arabs say, the highest
caste horses are generally bay, and they ought to
know best.   I speak of what come to India.   " A
good horse cannot be of a bad colour ;" but there is
a great deal of fancy in colour, some *outré* people
preferring a dirty white, or dun, piebald, or tiger-
marked.

ARRIVING THIN.

Many of the horses arrive in the boats quite skele-
tons, and badly hide-bound.   You must not be de-
terred from purchasing these.   The head, jaws, channel, nostrils, mouth, lips, eye, and ears ; the breadth
of the haunches ; the straightness of the spine from
the fall of the withers to the setting on of the tail ;
the position of the legs; the three essential bones; the
large square knee, wiry suspensory ligament, and
clean back sinews ; none of these are affected by a
horse being thin.   The belly may hang like a cow's,
the ribs may stick out, the neck may have lost its
crest, and the quarters may have sunk down to a
frightful hollow : the thigh, stifle, and forearm will,
however, yet show a little muscle, if there ever was
any ; and all that frightful hollow at the quarters will
fill up to its proper blood-form in a very few months,
if the spine bone here is only straight, and not drooping ; the neck also will regain its crest, and the belly
draw up, as the horse gets into condition : but if,
added to this thinness, there should be any dropsical-
like swelling under the chest or belly, the breath foul,
the flanks perceptibly moving with a rise and fall,

and the pulse above fifty, you must consider well the risk you run : it may be only slight fever, or temporary derangement caused by the boat, bad feeding, &c.; but there may be, also, some radically bad disease lurking.*

Most horses from the stables cough a little at first, but the whole catalogue of diseases of the lungs and air-passages, excepting chronic cough, are comparatively rare in India. If the cough is very short, like that of an asthmatic person, or very loud and stertorous, either will denote some chronic derangement, and it will be on the safe side to reject him : (I have seldom passed over a valuable horse myself in consequence of this, but merely deducted something for the risk ;) and if when one nostril is closed, the breathing is not clear in the other, it will denote an ulcer in this passage, and he should be rejected also. Pinching the windpipe is the only ready mode of exciting a cough, if the walk and trot fail ;† but all dealers will not stand much of this pinching, for it is very possible to bring on a cough that never existed. It must be the last thing resorted to when purchasing : you should previously make up your mind to take the horse, if satisfied with the sound of the cough.

* Most likely disease of the lungs.—ED.

† This is a most barbarous practise, and one which I would never practise or allow. If a horse does not cough when sharply trotted and cantered, you may make pretty certain that the lungs and air-passages are clear and all right.—ED.

MANNER OF GOING.

Having finished your examination, view him in a canter. He should go wide behind* and close before, skimming the ground with his two fore feet, like a true daisy-cutter ; but whether in the gallop, trot, or walk, he must on no account step short ; the feet must be lifted with a kind of spring, and brought firm and flat to the ground. There never was a truer passage in a book, than that the safety of a horse depends a great deal more on the manner in which he brings his feet to the ground than on that in which he lifts them up.

You should not conclude your bargain yet, till you have mounted. The dealers, if you are a light weight, will always allow you a five minutes' walk, trot, and canter, in front of the stables, and that is as much as any man ought to ask, or get. If the fore feet are not lifted light, quick, and airy, but feel to stick or dwell long on the ground, he has been overweighted, and his action ruined, or there is some· thing wrong in the chest, or feet.

PRICE.

If you are now purchasing for the turf, you will pay from eight to fifteen hundred rupees, according to age, caste, shape, &c., and your own knowledge of making a bargain. You should never exceed fifteen hundred for an untried horse, however promising he

* If the hocks turn out, and the toes turn in, described under hocks as most faulty make, he will of course go wide with his hocks ; that is, if he goes at all, which is doubtful : but hang such wide-going as this !

may look. Many of the best racers on this side of India, that were not particularly handsome, or if handsome, not high, have been bought by judges, and some by luck, for there is a great deal of that, for from six to twelve hundred.

If you are purchasing for the parade, and get all the points described under the following head of Charger, with fine high action, fourteen hands two inches high, high caste, handsome, and stylish, four or five years old, and perfectly fresh and unblemished, you get him cheap at fifteen hundred. I should be happy to obtain such a one for that sum, even if he were slight.

If you are not so very particular, and can excuse an ugly head, a small eye, a filled up narrow channel, a bent fore-leg, a small hock, a drooping quarter, a straight shoulder, a bad neck, indifferent action, or any other defect, you ought to suit yourself from eight hundred to a thousand ; and if you can excuse blood, or take a Persian with one or two of these defects, you will have no difficulty in procuring it for five hundred.*

If you go still further down, and take a screw of high caste appearance, with a gummy leg, a blind eye, a wapping spavin, a neatly fired ringbone, or a foundered foot, there are plenty to be had for two hundred, though they are often priced at two thousand, in the hopes of your making an offer. You will find, however, many of tolerable good caste and make, five years old, fresh and free of wind-galls, fourteen hands high, well adapted for hunting, from

* On the Madras side, Persians can generally be purchased at from three to four hundred rupees.—ED.

four to seven hundred rupees, but you cannot expect a fresh sound horse of height, caste, and appearance, for so small a sum.

The price of a high caste, well built, fresh Arab, of five years old, is enormously increased by a little height ; for every inch you will have to pay five hundred rupees. If fourteen hands one inch of this description can be bought for one thousand rupees, fourteen hands two inches, with the same qualifications *in every respect*, would be fifteen hundred rupees ; fourteen hands three inches with ditto, would be two thousand rupees. And the increased height is well worth the extra money ; for a large high caste, faultlessy formed, and fresh Arab of this age, is as difficult to find as a large diamond.

Two horses, very nearly resembling each other, may be very differently priced : take for instance, two of valuable caste and build, one having rather a straight shoulder, the other an oblique one ; or one rather a thick neck, the other a light one ; the latter, all other points equal, would for the saddle be worth fully double the former. So also a blemish, though not detracting from the actual utility, will often reduce a handsome horse from fifteen hundred rupees down to one thousand rupees ; in the same manner as a dab of grease or paint will ruin the value of a dresscoat : the coat may be still as useful, but not for appearance.

Recollect, a horse's price is not according to the vulgar error, " what he'll fetch," for many a ruined horse, with a good name, often fetches more than his original worth, when fresh ; and *vice versa ;* but the real intrinsic value of a horse consists in what you would have on a fair average to pay for such another, as good and unblemished in every respect, in the country in which you may be.

ADVICE.

Notwithstanding my endeavours to put the foregoing before you clearly and simply, I much fear, five or six days after your purchase, you will discover you have overpaid some twenty or thirty per cent. The brass, and plausibility of some rogues, in selling a deformed, useless, or diseased animal is incredible. If made like a cow, and showing the ill-breeding of a country horse, they will name to you some known good running Arab that had an ugly exterior, which is nothing at all to the purpose. A horse in his *tout ensemble* will often have an ugly appearance, and yet evidently show blood, and possess most of the best running points ; one, however, whether handsome or ugly, that does not possess them, will never be a first-rate. If the legs are crooked, or the feet long, another runner will be named that had these faults, and they will affirm positively, it was in consequence of these defects, not in spite of them, and from their other very superior qualities that they happened to run well. If the shank is as large and round as a pint bottle, they will put their hand down to demonstrate to you the circumference, saying, " There's strength of limb !" A bunged, windgalled leg will become clean and wiry ; a bull-neck will fine away ; a herring-gut will turn into a beautiful barrel ; a heavy shoulder into a light one ; and a contracted and long foot will both open and shorten, when he is properly shod ; in short, a brute will in a month be perfection, if you will only hand over your rupees. All this spluttering balderdash proves, either that they known nothing at all about a horse, or else that they are trying to deceive you : the former is the most charitable supposition, and, no doubt, the correct one, though a very large share of the latter is always mixed up with it. When, therefore, you hear arguments so truly nonsensical, and thinly-veiled as these, the sooner you unfold your knowledge of human nature, if you have none of a horse's, the richer you will find yourself in pocket.

Another deceptive mode of talking, shallow enough certainly, but peculiar to the Bomb Proof,* is in this way :—When the stride is found shortened and clumsy, from having been overweighted by riding or carrying heavy burdens—a very common occurrence —the answer is, " Oh, that was done in Arabia ;" or, " he was always so." Well, if overweighted in Arabia when he was young, and the action injured in consequence, the chances are a hundred to one against his ever recovering it, unless a very powerful horse, and always after ridden by a light weight of seven or eight stone : and if he was by nature always so, why, then of course, it is incurable. When the eyes are dim, or cataracts forming : " Oh ! that's only from the heat of the stables." When the legs are injured, and the back sinews all bowed : " Oh ! that's only from the heel-ropes, or a tent-peg :" just as if it made any difference to the purchaser whether the eyesight was injured by the heat of the stables or a pitchfork ; or the legs ruined by a tent-peg, or a sledge hammer.

---

* Stables where the Arab dealers keep their horses.—Ed.

Again, if a colt is produced that is badly formed :
" Oh ! he's only a colt, he'll alter in another year."
To be sure, all colts alter, but if he is well-formed
at three years old, he will be well-formed at twenty ;
and if badly formed, and want of due proportion at
three years old, he will be the same as long as he
lives. Now, unless you have been educated at Don-
caster, or dubbed yourself a judge, self-constituted,
as I have done, I strongly recommend, especially if
you are a New Arrival, and have any regard for
" your order," (letter of credit, I mean,) to ask some
friend to accompany you in your rambles through
these stables. Should you purchase from " gentlemen judges," the only chance of escape you have, is
candidly to confess that you are only in the elemen-
tary instructions of the " Griffin's Aid-de-Camp," and
then it would be ungenerous and unfair indeed to
deceive and take advantage of you; but if you are a
judge, (a question I always like to ask, if I can do so
without giving offence,) then you have no right to
complain of being outwitted : you dubbed yourself;
the more shame for you to acknowledge being so
quickly dismounted.

Remember, however, that though a good Arab may
be found without all the points I have described, a
bad Arab will never be found with them ; and also,
that a horse may be of the highest caste, and yet
have no great speed, in consequence of some faulti-
ness of build, or being more adapted for the purposes
of parade. A charger, racer, and carriage-horse,
cannot be all of perfect build in one and the same
skin : you cannot expect to obtain all these qualities
in one horse, though they are much more nearly procurable in the Arab than the English breed. A

draught horse seldom makes a good riding horse ; you must make up your mind what you want, and . be thankful if you get it.

For any purpose except the turf, always choose make before blood. A three-part bred Arab, of the proper form, will be preferable for either charger or hunter, to better caste faultily built ; and for the carriage, half-bred, if well made, will also be better than more blood with less shape. An unexceptionably formed Persian or half-bred, will always bring a fair price ; but a well bred, if faultily formed or deficient in appearance, will often be objected to, unless he has speed.* Yet, let no man presume to quote from my book who has not well learnt by heart

THE GRIFFIN'S CATECHISM.

What gives a horse endurance ?—Blood.
What gives a horse speed ?—Ditto.
What gives a horse beauty and symmetry ?—Ditto.
What gives a horse a thin skin ?—Ditto.
What gives a horse a straight croup ?—Ditto.
What gives a horse large thighs ?—Ditto.
What gives a horse a well-formed large hock ?--Do.
What gives a horse a light neck ?—Ditto.
What gives a horse a large eye ?—Ditto.
What gives a horse a wide jowl ?—Ditto.
What gives a horse a thin open nostril ?—Ditto.
What gives a horse a deep chest ?—Ditto.

---

* Of late years, many horses with an English caste about them have found their way into the stables, and are called Arabs when well built, with a fine quarter, open jowl, and large eye ; and Persian when otherwise. The opinion seems to be, they are Arabs, or Persians, or some mixed Eastern breed ; but some few certainly look as if they had a dash of English blood in their veins.

What gives a horse a fine forearm ?—Blood.

What gives a horse a flat shank-bone ?—Ditto.

What gives a horse a wiry limb, and large back sinews ?—Ditto.

What is the real meaning of blood ?—Blood.

Blood is shown in Premier and Perfection, pp. 52 and 53 ; Half-bred, in Water Proof, p. 53 ; and No Blood, in the Frontispiece.   If you are so dull of comprehension that you cannot understand the meaning of it from all these drawings, assisted by all the foregoing explanation, confine yourself to a tattoo or screw ; you were never born to display Perfection.

To decide upon the exact quantity of breeding every individual horse may possess, is another affair.   The numerous shades of difference from the lowest caste up through the half and three-quarter bred to the highest caste, complicated as they are rendered by a greater or less degree of good and indifferent build attached to each, makes that impossible ; it can only be known to a certainty by the breeder, where the pedigrees have been accurately noted down from generation to generation ; and in India, so long as all pedigrees are taken upon trust, these intermediate shades of distinction must always remain a matter of opinion ; but I do not hesitate to say, that if you are unbiassed, one month's study and reflection of the first part of this book will, as far as this blood or caste, and the build are concerned, enable you to purchase for yourself without disappointment.

A high-caste Arab, for a Racer, Charger, or Hunter, should therefore possess the following points :

RACER.

Long quarter ; straight spine ; well set-on tail, and not too bushy.

Broad across the haunch-bones, but broader at the thighs.

Large and muscular stifle.

Large and broad lean hock, with the bone at the point long.

Lean head ; broad forehead ; large, full, bright eye; open thin nostril ; deep mouth ; evenly-closed lips ; wide jaws ; clean channel ; and small erect ears.

Neck, rather long and light.

Withers, whether high or low, should rise above the top of the shoulder-blade.

Back, straight, and rather long.

Long and slanting shoulder.

Short arm, and legs well forward.

Moderately broad and flat chest.

Great depth of girth.

Some distance between the last false rib and the haunch-bone.

Round barreled carcase.

Large elbow-bone.

Long and muscular forearm, that there may be shortness between the knee and fetlock.

Broad square knee and large hinder bone.

Suspensory ligament and back sinews strong, wiry, and far apart.

Shank-bone flat ; small round in front.

Pasterns long, but not too oblique. The point of the toe under the point of the shoulder.

Sound, well-shaped, black fore-foot ; rather upright in front of the crust ; never lengthening out more than the angle of forty-five degrees ; open heels ; sound frog ; and a concave sole.

CHARGER.

Long quarter ; straight spine ; well set-on tail, and not too bushy ; but, for a handsome charger, the tail should be carried rather high also.

Broad across the haunch-bones, but broader at the thighs.

Large and muscular stifle.

Large and broad lean hock, with the bone at the point long.

Lean head ; broad forehead ; large, full, bright eye ; open thin nostril ; deep mouth ; evenly-closed lips ; wide jaws ; clean channel ; and small erect ears.

Neck rather long and light ; but a fine crest, and well-carried head, are indispensable.

Withers should be high for a charger.

Back must not be too long, or he will never pull up properly on his haunches, without which he cannot be a good charger.

Long and slanting shoulder ; but it should have a little more substance than the racer's, so that, with high withers, added to a good girth and fine chest, the saddle may keep back in its place ; for the charger that does not carry his saddle well is a nuisance.

Short arm, and legs well forward.

. Moderately broad and flat chest.

Depth of girth not actually requisite to the same extent as in the racer. A good caste Arab is never very deficient in this.

Not much distance between the last false rib and the haunch-bone. A charger should be well ribbed home. Being well " coupled up" is a sign of strength and endurance.

Round barreled carcase.

Large elbow bone.

Forearm quite as muscular as the racer, but no harm if there is a trifle more length between the knee and fetlock, for a charger must lift his fore-feet well up, and not move like a daisy-cutter, or over stony ground he will soon come head over heels.

Broad square knee, and large hinder bone.

Suspensory ligament and back sinews strong, wiry, and far apart.

Shank-bone flat, small round in front.

Pasterns should not be so long, nor quite so oblique as the racer's. The point of the toe in its proper place is most essential.

Sound, well-shaped, black fore-feet; rather upright in front of the crust ; never lengthening out more than the angle of forty-five degrees ; open heels ; sound frog ; and a concave sole, are indispensable. A racer on soft turf might get on better with an indifferent shaped foot : have any fault in preference to an indifferent one for a charger. A bad foot can be worth nothing to either.

HUNTER.

The nearer he comes to the description of a Charger the better. There is no necessity for his being so high or so handsome. Hog-hunters generally prefer small horses. Great strength, however, in all his limbs, with a moderately broad and flat chest, and circular carcase, is essential.

The neck must have the curve where the head is set on ; the mouth deep, and the jaws wide, that he may be light in hand.

The back should be short* (yet not a too short horse), but the spine straight.

The withers must be as high, and shoulder as slanting, with as much substance (not thick and cloddy) as the charger's. These two points, with a fine chest, are most requisite, both in the charger and hunter, that the saddle may be carried in its proper place. The charger is always kicking, and his tail becoming galled by the crupper, when the saddle presses forward, and the hunter, in a leap, not having a crupper, may have the saddle and driver thrown on the withers, and fall topsy-turvy in consequence.

The distance between the knee and fetlock need not be so short as in the racer ; for the hunter (though not required to have the high action of a charger) must lift his legs well. This is a point, however, that is seldom found too short, and in a racer never. As high caste and excellence of build can very seldom be obtained, and quite as seldom afforded, attend,

In the Hunter, first to the fore parts : the well set-on head and neck, slanting shoulders, well placed forelegs, and good, open, tough feet.

In the Racer, first to the cast and the hind parts.

In the Charger, as you value your neck and comfort, attend to every part. Money here is well laid out : he should be faultless : his name Perfection, and his mottto, *Fier, mais sensible.*

The annexed drawings will serve as a good index to the foregoing description. The second is a beautiful model of the proper form of a Light Dragoon Charger, and an excellent cut as a general runner of all races. The **Racer** and **Hunter** may look very different to the same class of horse in **England**; but though the points should be the same, the **Arab**, in consequence of his stature, which in some of the best runners has not exceeded fourteen hands one and a half inch, and from his having inherited nothing but his native blood, assumes a very different appearance.

A cavalry horse must partake of something of this second form; for a charger with a long back and straight shoulder, that cannot be brought on his haunches, is as ridiculous as a racer with a bull-neck and a camel's hind quarter, that cannot be got into a gallop; both being about as useful to answer their trades as a Newmarket carrier-pigeon without wings; and yet, such are continually purchased by Mr. Green and his brother; and the former not unfrequently sent to the light cavalry. Another description chosen for troopers, is the low Persian, or Gulph horse, often without any breeding at all, sometimes having a roach back, and consequently deformed quarter, drooping to the elegant angle of fifty degrees; such a brute can neither be useful nor ornamental for any purpose. A half-bred Arab, or well-formed Gulph horse, of fourteen hands one inch high, may do very well as a charger for a light weight of eight stone; but a good Kattywar, with his handsome crest and high action, is worth a hundred Gulph fourteen hands one inch tattoos.* Size, strength, and activity, with

* Kattywar horses generally possess good action, but are often underlimb-ed, and by their high action soon batter and bung their legs.—Ed.

fresh strong legs, tough feet, and open heels, are the grand desiderata for the cavalry.

Breeding the cavalry horse is foreign to my present purpose, but no man should be entrusted to pair horses and mares, until he understands something of the proper build of both, and is also fully aware of the undoubted truism, that " Like will produce Like." The keeping a bad horse costs the Honorable Company's government quite as much as a good one, indeed, more ; for the curious-shaped animals that are sometimes sent as colts for troopers take five times as long to break in as proper formed ones would ; and even then, they are always laming themselves, or annoying their riders. There is no more difficulty in breeding good shaped horses than bad ones, if the breeder has only a little knowledge how to pair : blood is not required ; half to three parts bred is abundance of blood, but make is indispensable. Some few *lusus naturæ*, under the most scientific management, will, of course, be thrown ; it is beyond the power of man to prevent these occasional freaks of nature ; but nine times out of ten, if the horse and mare are adapted to each other, four-fifths at least of the good form and good qualities will be inherited. A bull-neck will run through a dozen generations, and a stallion with a bull-neck should never be bred from. A thick neck, in an otherwise fine horse, may be bred from solely for draught for the artillery, but a downright bull-neck should be shot. A straight-shouldered stallion, if otherwise good, may be bred from, for straight shoulders are required for draught ; and if the shoulder has only good depth, and crossed with an oblique-shouldered mare, this point may occasionally alter sufficiently for the cavalry ; but not so cer-

tainly as if the obliquity was on the side of the
stallion. A wall-sided stallion, if not very flatsided,
and otherwise good, may be bred from, for if put to
a well circular-barreled mare, the carcase will always
improve : the Godolphin Arabian was wall-sided. A
drooping hind-quarter, if only muscular, may be bred
from, for if crossed with a straight-crouped mare the
quarter will never be bad.* No small carcased, or
narrow-chested, or lanky-thighed horse or mare should
be bred from ; and no horse or mare with a very long
back, or badly set-on head should be bred from : I
am speaking as to breeding for the cavalry. Regarding the head itself, I should not care what it was
like : the less brains a troop-horse has the better ; but
I would not breed from a stallion with a small eye,
neither would I ever breed from one with a very large
yard. Every stallion must have harmony of proportion united to general substance, and never be over-
laden at the top of the shoulder blade-bone ; and every
brood-mare must also possess these qualifications,
besides being particularly broad in the haunches.
Another great error that is committed, is in the difference of the size of the horse and mare. Not more
than an inch and a half difference in the height
should ever be allowed, and even that is too much,
unless the manager has proper discrimination with
regard to the form : for instance, put a very fine, substantial, well-built stallion of fifteen hands to a rather

---

* I would never breed from a stallion faulty in any respect. I would always breed from faultless stallions, and endeavour to correct the faults in
mares which I was obliged to breed from. The better plan however is to have
both sire and dam as faultless as possible, for unless that is the case, one
can never be sure of the progeny. Never breed from either a horse or mare
that has hereditary blemish of any kind, such as spavin, curb, or ringbone,
or turning in or turning out the toes. In fact every defect possessed either
by the sire or dam is hereditary.—ED.

slight but yet well-formed mare of fourteen hands
two inches and a half; the chances here, with make
on both sides, are ten times as much against a sym-
metrical produce as if the height had been the other
way, and a very fine, substantial, well-built stallion
of fourteen hands two and a half inches had been put
to a rather slight but yet well-formed mare of fifteen
hands: these last may, with some little propriety, be
termed nearly even-sized horses. The only true
method of increasing the size of the Indian horse,
and at the same time insuring symmetry, is never
to allow more than an inch and a half difference
in the height, and only that under the restrictions
just mentioned. An indifferent point in the stallion
must also always be met by a very superior one
in the mare, and *vice versa ;* but the cardinal points
of both must be perfect, or there will be no improvement in the breed worth speaking of. This is attended with no difficulty, and very little expense, when
choosing half and three parts bred horses. There are
hundred to be had: good feeding and proper care of
the colts and fillies would then in a very short time
amply repay an establishment. English, Arab, and
Kattywar horses and mares, judiciously chosen and
crossed, would, in five generations, or thirty years,
yield a breed that would pay a hundred per cent. ;
but when a huge, faulty stallion, whether thorough-
bred, passing for thorough-bred, or half-bred, is put
to a coarse, country, drooping-quartered, and perhaps crooked-legged mare, and this mare two or three
inches smaller than the stallion,* what can be ex-

* Professor Coleman stated in his lectures (I have not seen it in print), that
trying to increase the size of the Indian horses by crossing with the large
English stallions was ruination to the breed, and that no well-proportioned
foals could be expected.

7

pected ?   It would be contrary to nature to find a
good produce.

A half, or three parts bred*horse, may often be
found with all the good points of a thorough-bred,
save three or four, and the want of these three or
four shall indubitably prove him no thorough-bred.
In lieu of the large brilliant eye, thin skin, small, flat
shank-bone, and large back sinews, substitute a smaller eye, a thicker skin, a larger round shank-bone,
and small tied-in back-sinews; who will then believe
him thorough-bred?   Or, to take other points, in lieu
of the clean, wide jowl, thin open nostril, deep mouth,
and large muscular hind quarters, substitute a closed
fleshy jowl, a thick shut nostril, a heavy-lipped mouth,
and hind quarters, deficient of thigh muscle ; and who
will then believe him thorough-bred ? With faults
like these, he must gallop a mile and a half in very
good time before you will obtain thorough-bred price.
Even one single faulty point will frequently enable a
good judge to detect a flaw in the blood.   And this
brings me to a question I have often heard mooted.
When two horses are brought out and sold, each
showing externally every point of thorough breeding
and good build in exact equal proportion, and both
of equal energy and equal supposed good constitution,
how is it that one turns out far superior to the other,
and how is it to be distinguished ?   To distinguish at
the time of purchase between two so exactly equal is
impossible ; but supposing every point was allowed
by the best judges to be exactly equal, and we could
positively know that the constitutions of each were
exactly equally good and strong, still, in India we
are ignorant of their blood—of their line of descent :
and even if we know that as correctly as they do in

England, still the solution of the question is impossible ; but there may exist a closeness of fibre about the one, and a finer cementing together of the different parts of the frame, which scientific dissection might detect. The living proof in these cases, although we must wait a short time for it, is nevertheless a true proof, viz., the greater speed and *endurance* shown on the turf after each has had six months of proper training. Where you have the running build, and every other external visible point in equal good proportion, and the training, riding, &c., equally good, then the turf, and the turf alone, furnishes the only living proof of the better blood, and this blood, this latent energy for work, is comprehended with very good accuracy by persons who unite experience to a knowledge of the structure of the horse.

Another abstruce question is, why this superior blood loses itself in a greater ratio when crossed with inferior blood in good build, than with good blood in inferior build, when build itself is one of the best proofs of good blood ? This does hold true, but only to a certain extent : that highly-finished interior mechanism of some internal parts, in whatever it may consist, does, beyond a doubt, in many horses with external indifferent conformation, excel in point of endurance that of inferior blood in a better external conformation.* But some parts of external conformation denote blood more than others ; for instance, take one horse with every point perfect, and then change his large brilliant eye to a small one ; take another with every point perfect, 'and then change

* No horses without blood however good their external formation may be, an or do possess enduring qualities.—Ed.

his straight forelegs to crooked ones, or make the chest too narrow : the former proves more a loss of blood, the latter more that of build ; and the odds would be three to one in favour of the latter for a race.   All these little minutiæ are of material consequence to breeders of horses, or men on the turf ; but practice, added to study, and the possession of a good "eye for a horse," can alone give them.   As beginners ; do not devote too much time to any speculative points, but first pay attention and learn the *externals :* the foal with any bad blood, will, to a certainty, when grown up, show some external visible flaw, such as a small eye, thick closed nostril, bad ear, small back sinews, &c., or very probably three or four of these. The points that denote pure caste, or thorough blood of long descent, are given at p. 3, together with the other requisites that enable a horse to gallop ; but every good point therein enumerated is rarely attainable.

PREMIER.

PERFECTION.

"Fier, mais sensible."

WATER PROOF.

OUTLINE,

Showing different parts of the horses, also the seat of diseases.

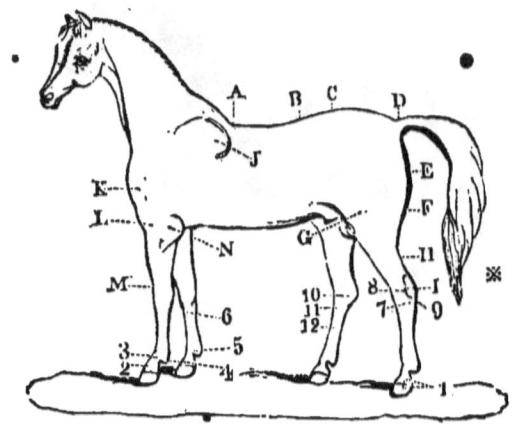

A to B, the back ; B to C, the loins ; C to D, the croup ; C to E, the quarter ; E to F, the thigh ; G, the stifle-joint ; G to H, all that below the stifle ; C to H, taking in the thigh, stifle, and all that below it, is sometimes called the whole quarter ; I, the bone at the point of the hock ; J, the shoulder-blade bone ; K, the point of the shoulder ; K to L, the arm ; L to M, the fore-arm ; N, the elbow-bone.

1, the place of the side, or lateral cartilages ; when they ossify they lose their springy feel, and become hard as granite; they are then called side-bones ; by some, ringbones ; 2, the seat of ringbone in front, just above the coronet, seen in the fore as often as the hind pasterns ; 3, the place enlarged, from being tied round the pasterns, close on the seat of ringbone ; 4, the place often seen ossified on the outside of the pastern ; 5, the place often seen ossified on the inside of the pastern ; 6, the place that enlarges from sprain of the back sinews ; 7, the seat of bone-spavin on the inner side of the lowermost part of the hock ; 8, the seat of bone-spavin, a little higher up, and more towards the back part of the hock; 9, the seat of bog-spavin; 10, the seat of thorough-pin ; 11, the seat of curb ; 12, the place that enlarges from sprain of the back-sinews of the hind leg, seldom met with.

* I would place 7, 8 and 9 on the inside of the hock—9 much farther forward, between 7 and 8, and 10, 11 and 12 on the outside of the hock, which would give a much better idea of the seat of these diseases.—ED.

PART II.

THE AGE.

THE teeth are forty in number : twenty-four grinders, or double teeth ; twelve nippers, or single teeth ; and four tushes.

THE COLT'S GRINDERS.

The colt, at his birth, has eight colt's grinders, four above and four below ; that is, two above and two below, on each side of his mouth.

At a month old he has four more colt's grinders, two above and two below ; that is, one more above and one more below, on each side of his mouth.

These are subsequently shed, in the same order as the nippers.

At one year old four more grinders come, two above and two below ; that is, one more above and one more below, on each side of his mouth.—Not shed.

At a little before two years old four more grinders come, two above and two below ; that is, one more above and one more below, on each side of his mouth. —Not shed.

At about four years old four more grinders come, two above and two below ; that is, one more above and one more below, on each side of his mouth.— Not shed.

Change of the Colt's Grinders for Horse Grinders.—
At two years and a half old four colt's grinders fall
out, one above and one below, on each side of his
mouth, and four horse grinders come in their stead.

At three years and a half old four more colt's
grinders fall out, one above and one below, on each
side of his mouth, and four more horse grinders come
in their stead.

At four years and a half old four more colt's grinders fall out, one above and one below, on each side
of his mouth, and four more horse grinders come in
their stead.

THE COLT'S NIPPERS.

The colt, at his birth sometimes, but always at a
fortnight old, has four front colt's nippers, two above
and two below, in the front of his mouth.

At a month and a half old, he has four middle
colt's nippers, two above and two below, one on each
side of each front nipper.

At eight or ten months old,* he has four corner
colt's nippers, two above and two below, one on each
side of each middle nipper.

Change of the Colt's Nippers for Horse Nippers.—
At two years and a half old, the four front colt's nippers fall out, and four front horse nippers come in
their stead.   When they are well up, he is three.

At three years and a half old, the four middle colt's
nippers fall out, and four middle horse nippers come
in their stead.   When they are well up, he is four.

---

* Generally at nine months.

At four years and a half old, the four corner colt's nippers fall out, and four corner horse nippers come in their stead. When they are well up, he is five.

These colt's nippers take about four months falling out, commencing two months before the half year, and finishing two months after it. From the day the last corner nipper falls out the colt becomes a horse, and the filly a mare.

THE TUSHES.

At three years and a half old to four years and a half old, the four tushes come, two above and two below; that is, one above and one below on each side of his mouth, and never change.

The mare has seldom any tushes.

MARKS THAT SHOW THE AGE.

At six years old, the marks in the two front horse nippers in the lower jaw are worn out.

At seven years old, the marks in the two middle horse nippers in the lower jaw are worn out.

At eight years old, the marks in the two corner horse nippers in the lower jaw are worn out.

REMARKS.

As the teeth of horses grow very differently, and the marks are retained much longer in some than in others, it requires a little careful inspection of a few different mouths to enable you to decide at all correctly. The common rule of concluding that a horse is six, when the marks in the two front horse nippers in the lower jaw are worn out ; that he is seven, when

8

the marks in the two middle horse nippers in the
lower jaw are worn out ; that he is eight, when the
marks in the two corner horse nippers in the lower
jaw are worn out, will occasionally deceive you, if
taken solely as a guide ; for a horse that is always fed
on dry grain and dry grass, wears out the marks
quicker than one that is always fed on soft grain and
green grass. The groove in the inside of the tushes
that gradually fills up as he advances in years, varies
so much in different horses, that it is no better a guide ;
for in some colts they come before three and a half years
old, and in others not till after four and a half : in some
horses they are very little blunted at the points at
twelve, and in others they are blunted at eight.* The
length of the teeth is no surer a test, for they are sometimes found short at twelve, and long at ten.

If a horse that is known to be ten or eleven years
old, has the marks remaining in the two corner horse
nippers in the lower jaw, it is sometimes concluded
from this that he has been bishoped. If at this age
the tushes should happen to be sharp at the points,
and the teeth also short, like a young horse, it no
doubt would be a good opportunity to endeavour to
deceive us by bishoping a couple of marks in these
two corner horse nippers, if they should be worn out ;
but the stain on such a tooth, somewhat similar to that
burnt on the bone handle of a knife to give it the resemblance of tortoiseshell, will often expose the cheat
of itself. A little round hole, made with a pointed
iron, as well as the mark of a file, with occasionally a
very small particle of the outer side of the tooth chip-

* It is seldom you are deceived in the tush. I have aged many thousands
of horses, always taking the tush as a criterion, and have seldom been much
out. — ED.

ped off, is sometimes distinguishable at one of the " on my honour" stables* at Bombay. I have, however, seen a troop horse of eleven years old with the marks remaining in the corner horse nippers, the tushes rather sharp, and the teeth rather short, giving to him the appearance of a seven-year old horse ; but the teeth were not quite so straight down in the mouth as they ought to have been ; they projected a little obliquely forward, and they were very yellow : this furnishes a better criterion in these doubtful mouths.

To discover the age, therefore, examine carefully, first, the marks in the teeth ; secondly, if the tushes are small and sharp, or grown round and dumpy ; thirdly, the length of the teeth ; and, lastly, the position and colour of the teeth.

Up to six years old, there is not much difficulty in deciding ; and from six until eight, if you balance all these four rules, not taking the marks solely as a guide, you will generally tell within six months. After eight, it is all guess ; yet, when the tush is round and blunted, and the marks in the two upper front nippers are gone, you may conclude he is turned of nine, though marks should remain in the lower jaw ; but the upper front nippers are, now-a-days, also sometimes bishoped, and I have seen a horse of sixteen sold for a seven-year old. At ten, the marks in the two front horse-nippers in the upper jaw ; at twelve, the marks in the two middle horse-nippers in the upper jaw ; and at fourteen, the marks in the two corner horse-nippers in the upper jaw will sometimes, at these respective ages, also wear out regularly ; though these cannot be depended on like the lower jaw : but a

* Figging is also very common here.

horse whose teeth are at all long, and at the same
time yellow, and projecting a little obliquely forward,
you may be sure is no chicken.   At ten years old, the
lower horse-nippers also begin to lose their oblong
shape, so that at fifteen they are nearly triangular from
the front of the mouth backward. *(See sketches below.)*

As a horse grows old, the pit above the eye deepens ;
but this will also be found sunken in one that is much
emaciated, and it is thought to be observable in those
that have been got by old stallions.[*]

The comparative ages between horse and man have
been estimated at about the following comparison :
one year of the horse to every four of man being reckoned from the age of two up to that of ten, and
after that less.   Thus,

A horse at 2 years is as a boy of 8 years.

,,	3	as	12.
,,	4	as	16.
,,	5	as a man of	20.
,,	6	as	24.
,,	7	as	28.
,,	8	as	32.`
,,	9	as	36.
,,	10	as	40.
,,	15	as	50.
,,	20	as	60.
,,	25	as	70.
,,	30	as	80.
,,	35	as	90.

[*] It is invariably the case, even from foal-hood.—Ed.

THE PULSE.

IT really is unpardonable in some freshmen taking on themselves to decide on the complaint of a horse, and then recommending a treatment for him, without ever feeling the pulse. It is cruel to abuse, and half destroy a horse's constitution, in the dark, in this way. There can be no difficulty in " catching" the pulse, if you put your two forefingers under the upper part of the lower jaw, and press the artery very gently against the bone. If the channel is not clean, but much filled up and fleshy, a hard pulse may feel softer than it actually is ; but taking out your watch will always tell you if it is too quick ; and, after feeling one or two horses under disease, you may be able in some degree to allow for this thickness of skin and flesh.

Thirty-five to near forty is the standard pulse* (young colts two or three quicker) ; and when it beats about this number in the minute, going off with a full bounding feel, it is the pulse of strong health in a strong constitution. Fort-five is too quick ; thirty, too slow. When the pulse is under forty-five, there can be no active inflammation that will not quickly show itself.

When it is weak and not full, it bespeaks more or less of debility, according to other symptoms that may be present.

When it rises to sixty, there may be fever, or some local inflammation, according as other symptoms are present.

---

* This is correct as regards English and other large horses, but in the little Arab, the healthy pulse is from forty to forty-five, and in young colts two or three quicker.—ED.

When at the number of seventy, or eighty, or more, it is hard, and yet small and wiry. It denotes inflammation of the bowels, if the other symptoms are present.

When it is oppressed and indistinct, feeling as if there was too much blood in the artery, it denotes inflammation of the lungs, if the other symptoms are present.

When the pulse is irregular or intermittent, stop-- ping a second, then going on again, it denotes great danger under disease, if other bad symptoms are present. The intermittent pulse is sometimes pro- duced intentionally, by giving digitalis, or other poisonous medicines.

BLEEDING

should never be resorted to till the disease is clear- ly ascertained.

When you bleed from the neck vein, the first six inches near the head must not be punctured, nor lower down the neck than a foot.* Any spot between six and twelve inches will do. The vein branches off about six inches below the jaw, and the best spot for bleeding is two inches below that.

If you have never bled a horse before, or the vein does not show sufficiently full, smooth it down and press upon it below with the fingers, then tie the cord round the neck† and lay the fleam along the course of

* I would never bleed lower down than two inches from where the vein branches off, which is nearer four than six inches below the jaw.—ED.

† A cord ought never to be tied round the neck. It is not necessary, and is likely to make the horse restive. By pressing the fingers on the vein, it will rise quite sufficiently for any one to bleed who knows how to do it. I have bled thousands of horses and never on any occasion used a cord.—ED.

the vein, never crossways, gently fixing it without
penetrating the skin. Having blindfolded him, do
not shut your eyes and jerk the fleam when you strike,
like a boy pulling the trigger of a gun, or you have
no more chance of hitting the vein than he has the
bird ; but, keeping your eyes fixed on the fleam, give it a
sharp but not a severe knock with a blood-stick or
tent-peg.

Some people cannot bleed, which is unfortunate in
case of inflammation. Perhaps you may be more
successful with a lancet. Having first tied a piece of
cloth round the bottom, or holding it tight between
your forefinger and thumb, that it may not go in deep-
er than the fleam would, insert the point gently into
the vein, and ram it in a little upwards, so as to make
an orifice full half an inch in length.

The beauty, and the great effect, of bleeding a
horse in the neck vein, particularly under inflammation, consists in taking a large quantity of blood in a
short time ; therefore both veins in these cases should
be opened at once, and the larger orifice the fleam
makes the better. No fleams from Mr. Long, or any
good maker, are made too broad-shouldered ; if made
too deep, the artery underneath may be penetrated,
and the horse lost. Having got the quantity of blood
you want, do not let the flow stop quite suddenly, or
air may get into the vein and half kill him ; but loosen
the cord, if one has been on, gradually ; then close the
wound immediately, and that without pulling the skin
from the neck, by which blood is apt to get underneath and cause a bad swelling ; pin the two edges
together, taking care not to include any of the hair
between the lips of the wound, with the smallest possible pin, or needle, which is better, not an inch and

a half skewer ; and do not forget to tie the head up
for an hour, and to see that he does not rub the part
afterwards, or inflammation and loss of the vein may
follow.   The pin should be gently drawn out two
days after, first cutting the horse-hair or thread tied
round it with a pair of scissors.   If the blood does
not flow sufficiently free and quick, keep his mouth
in motion by putting your fingers in at the corners, and
throw hot water over the loins, if needed, or put a
sheepskin or half-a-dozen jhools over them.

Take care that your fleam and lancet are clean, and
not rusty, and always ascertain how much the koondee
holds that is to receive the blood, or you may take
away a gallon and a half for a gallon, which I have
often seen done.

The blood should fall in a stream into the middle
of the koondee, or nothing can be judged from the
colour of it afterwards ; and it must rest undisturbed
in the shade for half an hour, which is about the time
it takes to coagulate.   The appearance, however, the
blood puts on after its coagulation, and the coagulation being slow or quick, is so exceedingly complicated
an affair, and influenced by so many causes, that no
criterion as to the degree of inflammation can be gained by it, at least by us ; the great thickness of the
buffy or sizy coat at top being present in a state of
health as well as under disease ; and often none at all
existing, though the blood may be darker, when the
inflammation is greatest.   When, however, the blood
has become solid, after being drawn in a full stream,
and is found with or without this sizy coat, yet at
the same time thin or watery, it will, perhaps, more
correctly denote that it ought not to have been taken.

When bleeding is necessary, you will find it under the proper head ; so, if you take on yourself to bleed for imaginary purposes, you deserve to suffer for it.

In taking a large quantity of blood from a horse labouring under any inflammation, always take care there is a good soft bedding in case he should faint. The pulse will first falter ; and he will generally begin to droop and stagger a few seconds before he falls, which, of course, must be the signal to desist, and then ease him down gently, if possible. The faintness will go off in a few minutes ; but he must be left to rise at his own pleasure.

Bleeding from the forearm vein, inside the forearm, and from the thigh vein above the hock, should be done with the lancet, it not being driven in so far as in the neck vein. Bleeding from the eye vein, two inches below the inner corner of the eye, must be done with a very slight puncture, or the point of the lancet will be broken against the bone.

To bleed from the toe, you have only to cut away the sole underneath at the toe, where the crust and sole join, until blood comes. When the sole is cut away underneath with the drawing-knife, take a fresh sharper one, or a clean " searcher" to cut through the vessels. If you cut deep enough, you will generally get the quantity of blood you want. A little tow or cotton is then to be stuffed into the hole, and tar over it, and a bandage wrapped over all for four or five days.

9

PHYSICKING

takes six days : two for preparation ; the day it is given, and the day on which it operates ; and two more to return to the former diet : but on an emergency, or when the dung appears softened, four days may be sufficient : one for preparation ; the day it is given, and the day it operates ; and one more to increase to the former diet.

Whenever a does of purgative physic is to be given to a horse in consequence of being out of condition, or previous to being put in training, or when in training, or coming out of training, it is most necessary he should have bran mashes, instead of his grain, and very little grass for the previous day, or two days, whether the physic is to be aloes or oil, a ball or a drench. If he will not eat bran mash, he must be well stinted of dry grass, and a little green (cut the previous day) given. There is a peculiarity of structure about a horse's inside, that, unless he is properly prepared and carefully looked after under physic, you not only will do no good, but, on the contrary, you will throw him some weeks back, and even run the risk of losing him ; for it is surprising how suddenly a horse will sometimes "go out" under a dose of physic improperly given. You should endeavour to give your physic, for any of the above purposes, of that strength that not more than ten extra evacuations will be produced. Some horses are easily operated on with a ball of four drachms of aloes ; others require a large dose of seven. At one time in the year, a horse will sometimes purge with five drachms, that another time will not feel the effect of six. Four to six drachms of Mr. Sprague's or Treacher's aloes are

generally ample for any Arab horse, if properly prepared and properly exercised; but eight drachms may
fail to purge, without proper precautions and exercise,
and yet easily produce inflammation and death. Some
horses, again, will purge in twelve hours ;* others not
for thirty-six. The best and safest purge for a novice to give is a drench, and that drench composed
of aloes and Epsom salts, or oil and Epsom salts : thus,
if you think five drachms of aloes is required to purge,
give three drachms, and five ounces of Epsom salts
(two and a half ounces of salts for one drachm of
aloes), dissolved in three quarters of a pint of warm
water, adding one ounce of salad-oil and a quarter of
a drachm of ginger ; or, if oil is to be given, a pint of
linseed-oil and five ounces of the salts. These aloetic
balls prove occasionally most raking to the bowels of
an Arab horse, and a large dose of them is always attended with risk.† The above drench may be safely
given, even when bran mashes are refused, provided
the horse has been muzzled at night and the other
directions duly attended to ; and, with a clyster of
salt and water on the same day, it will, with proper
exercise, purge effectually, and rarely disagree. The
following directions will guide you how to treat a
horse under physic. Suppose it is to be given on
Wednesday morning :—

Monday.—Give four mäps, that is, one bazaar seer,
of bran mash for his first feed at eight in the morning,
and only one pooly of grass after it. Four ditto at

---

* A little Arab I once had charge of used to purge in ten hours, though
the physic was given in a ball ; and in fifteen hours it had generally set.

† I always prefer a ball to a drench. It is much easier given, and does
not annoy the horse one tenth part so much as giving a drench. If your
aloes are good, properly prepared, and of proper quantity, with a drachm of
powdered ginger to each ball, it will never do harm.—ED.

one o'clock and only one pooly of grass after it.
Four ditto at evening's feed, and then allow him to
eat grass until 9 o'clock, when the muzzle is to be
put on for the night. Give as much water as he likes
· to drink, but no more grass than this. He should
have an hour and a half of walking exercise, both in
the morning and evening, for which he may be ridden ; or if strong, and in good health, may be gently
trotted.

Tuesday.—Exactly the same as Monday, with another bran mash at nine o'clock, before being muzzled.

Wednesday.—At day break let him have the physic, always washing it down with two drachms of
common salt in half a pint of warm water, whether
it is a ball or a drench ; this facilitates the " working,"
and may prevent the horse feeling sick. Give five
mäps of bran mash for his first feed at eight in the
morning, but only a mouthful of grass after it. Five
ditto at one o'clock, and half a pooly of grass after it.
Five ditto at evening's feed, and one pooly of grass
after it, when the muzzle is to be put on till nine
o'clock, at which hour he may have another bran
mash, before being muzzled for the night. The
more water that is drunk the better, but on this day
the chill must be taken off, whether it is the hot or
the cold weather. Walking, or very gentle trotting
exercise, morning and evening, the same as on Monday and Tuesday.

Thursday Morning.—The physic, during exercise,
will perhaps begin to work ; if it does not,* you must

---

* If it has not commenced operating by this time, give a clyster of warm
water and Europe brown soap. This with exercise will generally cause it
to operate freely.—ED.

feed exactly the same as the day before, for sometimes it will not operate for another ten or twelve
hours. A mash and a little warm water, and another half hour's trot, will often bring the purging on ;
and, when it does come on, he may have bran mash
again, a little dried green, or a pooly of grass, and
water with the chill off. If only two or three evacuations take place, give more warm water and another
trot, which will carry it off. But, though the medicine should fail entirely to act, you must not adminis-
ter another dose, for fear of producing over-purging
or inflammation. Some bran mashes must still be
continued, with but little grain, for the following
forty-eight hours ; and then, after an interval of another four days, making exactly a week from the time
the first dose was exhibited, a stronger may be given,
preparing the animal the last two days as before.

Should the physic have been a drench,* precisely
the same rules are to be followed throughout ; but
the purging will in this case commence on the evening of the same day, or about sixteen hours after it
is given. Whenever it does commence, he may have
bran mash, grass, and water with the chill off. You
can give these mashes warm, but there is no occasion
for any extra clothing ; and, if he has not been accustomed to any clothing at all, do not put any on, unless the weather is damp or cold. If he has been
standing outside, he should, during these six days,
be brought under cover ; but never dream of putting
him into a shut up, close stable, like many of those
in Bombay. Such is far more hurtful and dangerous
than leaving him outside.

* Have a drachm of aloes more than you are going to give, finely powdered,
so as to be ready in case of spilling.

If the dose you have given was not a mild one,
which it ought to have been if you were not aware of
your horse's constitution, and he should purge more
than ten times, give immediately a quart of luke-
warm finest bajree, or wheat-flour gruel, with two
drachms of gum arabic dissolved and put into it, and
repeat this every two hours till the purging stops, or
he has once dunged a little thicker. He is not to
eat or drink a particle of anything else till this takes
place, but remain quiet in a loose stall with a muzzle
on, and allowed to lie down on his bed. If he will
drink the gruel, let him take a couple of quarts each
time ; if not, drench him with one. A horse should
not have a dozen watery evacuations, when the intention is merely to promote condition or prevent
illness, or, the object for which the physic is
given will be defeated. This fine bajree, or wheat-
flour gruel, and gum, will soothe the bowels, and in
the course of six or eight hours generally stop the
purging. Should it not be found sufficient, and he
should still purge on to the number of twenty times
and more, it will be time for you to look to OVER-
PURGING, in a subsequent page of this volume.

When the physic has done working, whether it has
been a ball or a drench, two days more are still required before he can resume his former grain, and be
put to work ; for the too rapidly filling of the stomach
and bowels immediately after physic, often proves as
dangerous as giving the physic without preparation.
Two maps of bran mash, and one of ground grain,
can be given at each feed, and one pooly of grass after it, and at night he may eat away at grass till the
muzzle is put on at nine o'clock : the water must have
the chill off, as before. The next day the grain may

be increased to two mäps at each feed, and the bran mash reduced to one : the water may now be given cold, and the muzzle left off at night.

I have particularized everything under this head, because I have been witness to numerous horses being greatly reduced in flesh, and also to severe gripes, and even inflammation and death taking place, solely from neglect of the above precautions. If you deviate one iota from these directions, or do not see that they are minutely attended to, and your horse should sicken, and the prescription under Class I. of Part IV. fail to cure him, do not blame the Aide-de-Camp.

TO MAKE BRAN MASH, AND BRAN TEA.

Mash.—Pour boiling water on sweet fresh bran, stirring it about ; then cover it up until it is cold. Some horses dislike bran, especially if it is stale, or has been given them dirty at some former period. A seer mixed with their gram, at each feed, two or three days before you commence preparing for physic, is a good way of accustoming them to it. If he should refuse to eat the bran mash on either of the two first days, you may put half a mäp of soaked gram in it, but none on the day the physic is given.

Bran Tea.—One gallon of boiling water to be poured over every four mäps of bran, and strained off when cold. The bran is quite fit to be eaten afterwards.

TO MAKE FINE GRAM, OR WHEAT FLOUR GRUEL.

Mix two mäps of the finest flour with six quarts of boiling water in an earthen koondee : put it on the fire for eight or ten minutes, stirring it about. If merely mixed with water, it is liable to clot in the stomach and do harm, especially when given in over-durging ; for this last case it must therefore always be made with the hot water, and properly boiled ; or keep at hand some previously made thus : boil two or three pounds of dry wheat bajree, or gram flour, tied up in a cloth like a pudding, for four hours : it will keep for months, and a piece being broken off, and mixed with boiling water, it is ready at once. No animal, and no man either, has so nice and delicate a taste for drink as a healthy horse ; and if the water is the least smoked, or the gruel should get the least smoked when on the fire, or the koondee it is put into the least greasy or dirty, or even, perhaps, if the koondee is quite new, he will be sure to smell it, and most proba-bly refuse to drink ; and, if he has not occasionally had gruel before, will very likely never afterwards volun-tarily swallow it : now, as this is of consequence, in-asmuch as gruel is very necessary at times for a horse recovering from sickness, it behoves you to take care and offer it him clean. Many horses will turn their heads away even from clean gruel, when under physic, that at other times would drink a dhool full.

MUZZLE.

Let your muzzle be at least eight inches deep, with two large holes, both full two inches in diameter at the sides close to the bottom, for each nostril ; and the top of it large enough to put your hand in on each side. It is barbarous to see the way in which some horses are half suffocated with a little hard muzzle tightly drawn over their mouths. Do not choke him either with the neck-strap : see that it is well and fast buckled, but not drawn tight round the throat. The neck-strap of the head-stall is also often tied or buckled so tight, that the poor animal is half throttled, and, not being able to speak, loses his whole night's rest in consequence.

DRENCHING.

In drenching a horse either with gruel or physic, a common soda-water bottle, or a thick English wine-bottle, with a piece of leather sewed tight round the neck, to prevent accident from the glass breaking, is cleaner than any thing else. Put the neck gently into the mouth just above the tush : if he is a quiet horse, and it is properly given, he will swallow down the most nauseous dose with as little trouble as a child takes its pap. If very restive, you can have it put into a thick leather bottle, which a Moochee in any bazaar will knock up for you in a few hours.

PHYSIC BALL, AND DRENCH.

Ball.—Finely powdered aloes, and a quarter the quantity of kidney mutton fat, that has been well boiled down.* Make into a long ball, or two, if it should be large, adding a dozen drops of oil of anise-seed, and some calomel, if required. Wrap it up in tissue-paper, oiling the same with linseed-oil at the time of giving, for a ball cannot be too soft. A hard ball takes double the time to dissolve, besides the danger of its sticking in the gullet, and choking the animal. If

* I prefer honey or treacle to any kind of fat.—ED.

10

the aloes be soft and difficult to powder, mix in the mutton fat and warm them together over a fire.

Drench.—Put the aloes and Epsom salts into a pint bottle, pour three quarters of a pint of hot water over them, shake until *well dissolved,* and, when cool, give.* †

When calomel is required over night, previous to a ball or drench on the following morning, it is to be mixed up with a spoonful of linseed-meal and ghee, and given at five or six o'clock, on an empty stomach, before taking his walk. The bran mash and a pooly of grass may be eaten afterwards, at evening's feeding-time, and then the muzzle put on for the night.

ALTERATIVES.

Nine to ten drachms of best aloes, one drachm of calomel, and thirty drops of oil of anise-seed, made up with linseed-oil, and a tea-spoonful of linseed meal ; or, as under " PHYSIC BALL," and divided into eight balls, one to be given every morning at daybreak, and one also every evening about five, when he goes out for his walk, will answer this purpose, when they are requir-

---

* Some horses will hold a drench in their mouths for ten minutes without swallowing it.

† When aloes are given in solution, they should always be prepared as follows, aloes in small pieces one part, distilled water seven parts, proof spirit one part. Dissolve the aloes by means of the water bath, that is, put the aloes and distilled water in a bottle. Put the bottle up to the neck in boiling water in a pot or chattie and allow it to simmer over a slow fire for two hours, and when removed add the spirit. The dose, as a purgative will vary from four to six fluid ounces —ED.

ed ;* but an alterative drench morning and evening, of one drachm of aloes and two ounces of Epsom salts for each drench, is sometimes preferable :† a drachm of Turkey rhubarb may be added to each drench for a thin horse. The same care is to be taken as under "PHYSICKING." He must have bran mashes instead of gram from the day the first ball is given, and be muzzled at night ; the water always with the chill off, and only one pooly, or the same quantity of dried green grass after each feed, except in the evening, when he may eat grass until muzzled, at nine or ten o'clock. If he is thin, half a mäp of soaked or boiled ground gram may be added to each mash. Good walking exercise morning and evening, but no *wet* green grass, and no washing under physic. If they do not operate twelve hours after the last is given, and after you have given a trot, continue them on until they do ; but clyster first, with one ounce of soap and two drachms of aloes ‡ in a gallon of warm water, or the horse may be severely over-purged from the effect of the whole taking place at once.

When calomel is required in combination with alteratives to a greater amount than a drachm, it should be mixed in the four first balls, to prevent any chance of salivation.

---

* I have always found the following an excellent alterative. Aloes one drachm, calomel ten grains, powdered gentian root two drachms, thirty drops of oil of aniseed, or tincture of ginger, made into a ball with treacle or honey. One to be given morning and evening. When the bowels become relaxed, discontinue the ball for a day or two, and then go on with it again.—ED.

† I would never give alteratives in the form of a drench. It is by far too annoying to the horse.—ED.

‡ The aloes are not necessary.— ED.

If your horse will not eat bran mash, which is most probably your own fault, do not give laxative alteratives.*

GENERAL ALTERATIVES.

Three drachms of black sulphuret of antimony, three drachms of sulphur, two drachms of nitre, and half a drachm of ginger, made into a ball with honey or ghoor, and given every night for a week or ten days, the horse eating partly-boiled food, and receiving only gentle exercise, is the best alterative for improving appearance when no particular complaint exists. It is also good for preventing plethora.

___

SHOEING.

VARIOUS kinds of shoes and nails cannot be constructed in India : there are neither proper forges, nor proper persons to superintend them. The pattern here given is easily made, and will be found to answer well for either a Racer, Charger, or a Hunter, and be less productive of injury than a broader web at the toes, which, being never sufficiently beveled out, is consequently apt to press on the sole, besides being more liable to pick up stones. There is no occasion to discard it when it becomes old and thin at

* A one-pound powder-canister once full, piled up, is about equal to a miip, or kutcha seer ; but whenever a map or seer of ground gram is mentioned, it does not mean a kutcha seer of whole grain taken and ground, that would be upwards of a kutcha seer and a quarter ; for eight miips, seers or powder-canisters full of unground gram, will make eleven when ground. A pooly of grass is about two pounds,

the toe ; the older the better, if only strong ; and wearing thin at the tòe is no disadvantage.*

If this shoe is properly made ; the crust that it rests upon evenly rasped ; the sole properly pared ; and the foot, during the intervals of shoeing, always kept properly stopped and moist, you will most likely be

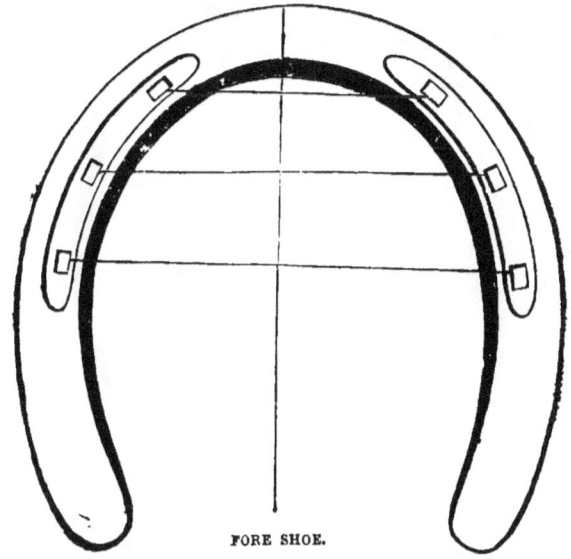

FORE SHOE.

able to avoid contraction : if you fail in any of these, you will have contraction.

* Some of the French shoes are bent up at the toes when first put on, in the shape of men's wooden shoes; but to be able to judge of the comparative merits of different forms of shoes and nails, requires great study and great practice. Whether you adopt that which I have recommended or not, keep the heels open. In France, my horse's heels never contracted, and in England they never contracted : in the former country they were generally shod under the superintendence of a government veterinary surgeon, and in the latter at the celebrated Mr. Turner's : neither in India have my horse's heels ever contracted, and here they have always been shod with this kind of shoe.

A pattern of the fore and hind shoe is lying at Dady's, in Bombay, which will show the groove, as also the form of the nail, and how the nail-holes are to be punched ; and by which you will see if the nails are properly pointed ; so that the Nolband will have some difficulty in pricking the horse, even if he tries.

It is five-eighths of an inch broad all the way round foom toe to heel, and one-fifth of an inch thick all the way round from toe to heel. There is a groove sufficiently large and deep to receive the small oblong

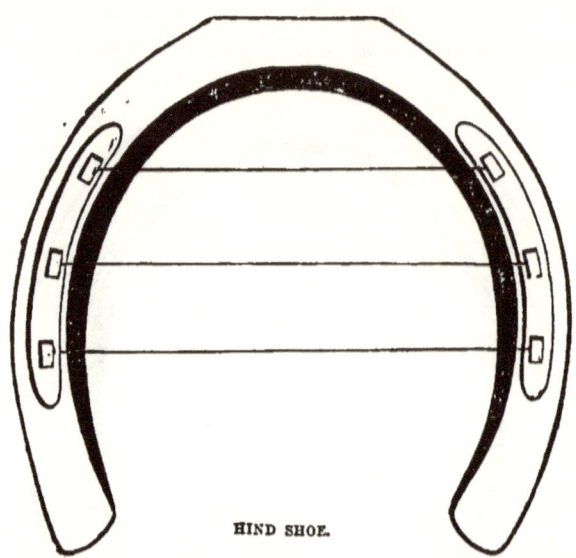

HIND SHOE.

heads of the nails, which are to be driven in even with the shoe ; and this groove is well away from the edge of the shoe, so that the nails shall be driven nearly as far in as where the crust and sole join— "just between wind and water"—and brought out about three quarters of an inch high up in the hoof. From the nail-holes on the inside, it is scooped out, beaten out, beveled off, or filed away, to admit of a pricker being passed under to clear out all sand and gravel, and so that it shall not press on the sole. The inch at the heel that is not beveled off is to rest where the bar and crust join, not quite touching the frog. There arc six nail-holes, three on each side ; and the nail-holes are to be punched with the Nolband's common punch, firstly on the inside, lastly on

the outside ; by which means they get a slanting direction outwards, and there will be no danger of the
foot being pricked. These nail-holes must be punched while the shoe is hot, or the iron, which is rarely
of the best quality, will split. Always see that the
nails fit the holes before you put the shoe on ; for if
the heads of the nails are not small enough to go into
the groove, or the groove not large enough to receive
them, they will be broken, and the shoe come off.

A horse with straight pasterns, on a very hollow
foot, may have it made a little thinner at the heel than
at the toe ; and if the foot is black, strong, and well
open, another nail may be put on the outer side for
hunting, &c. ; but, out 'of some hundreds of feet, I
have found the outside very nearly as often contracted as the inside. The hind shoe has the nails rather
farther back, and the toe is a little squared.

The weight of this shoe is about six ounces, and by
reducing the thickness a little it will weigh about five
ounces, which will be a proper training shoe. It must
not project the least beyond the heel, but be there
nicely rounded, or the hind foot in the gallop may
possibly come in contact with it, and the horse be
thrown, or the shoe wrenched off. The ground surface of the toe of the hind shoe should also be filed a
little, to take off the edge, as a further precaution.

CUTTING THE HOOF.

The foot having been soaked in water to render it
soft, the sung-turash is to be used very sparingly—not
at all for a flat foot ; for if too much of the bottom of
the crust is first taken off, there m ay not be sufficient

horn left in the sole to make it properly concave :
then with the drawing-knife cut away the horn, till,
by the strong pressure of your own or the Nolband's
thumb, you can feel the sole bend up towards the corners, as well as the fore-part : this is the guide for all
feet worth the expense of shoeing. If more is cut
away, the horse will be tender, perhaps lamed : if less
is taken off, he will require shoeing again in a fortnight.
When the foot is not softened before going to the
Nolband's, either by cow-dung stopping for the two
previous days, or by being soaked in water two
or three hours before shoeing, or by cloths wrapped
round the coronet, and warm water poured on them
for that time, a great deal too much horn may be cut
away before the sole will yield. A fine flaky foot will
often show of itself the proper quantity to be taken
off; but others again would suffer ; besides, the hoof
being moistened, adds to the nails taking firm hold,
and prevents the horn splintering ; the foot, moreover,
is shod in half the time, and the Nolband saved from
a gash in his arm. The horn between the bars and
the crust having been cut away with the drawing-
knife, a full sixth of an inch of depth must be left up
in the corner where the bar and crust join. Never
cut away the horn between the bar* and the frog,
but cut away a little of the very hindermost part of

* For mercy's sake ! learn where the bars are, for the manner in which English farriers, as well as Nolbands, cut them away at this part is disgraceful.
The English farrier calls it opening the heels ; and I have seen them retrograde
into this most destructive method of cutting, a few months after losing the
supervision of a veterinary surgeon. The bars are the finish of the crust, of
harder horn than the sole, and a different shade of colour ; they never run down
straight, but curve, as shown at p. 26 in the description of feet ; and the place
for opening the heels is not in the middle of the bars, where the Nolband sideways scoops them half way, but opposite the heel of the shoe, *behind* where
the bar and crust join.

the heel, just the last quarter of an inch, so as to allow
the heel of the frog, where the cleft is, to expand, and
prevent the horn bending in there. Neither cut the
frog unless it is ragged, excepting towards the toe ;
and only there, if it should be hard and higher than
the heel.* Lastly, file till the crust and bars are even,
leaving the frog, if possible, the eighth of an inch higher, so that it shall be just within the level of the shoe.
The toe should always be shortened as much as it
will admit of, and any unevenness in the wall rasped
smooth. There should be room enough for the edge
of a knife-blade to play between the shoe and the
crust at the heel when on ; and the shoe at the heel
should extend the eighth of an inch beyond the crust
on the inside, as well as the outside. You need not
fear that this will be a cause of cutting : a horse cuts
with the quarter, sometimes with the coronet ; his legs
must be very faultily placed to cut with the heel.
The natural well-formed foot, also, is a smaller
half circle on the inside than the outside, as shown
at page 26 ; and this form is, of course, to be pre-
served.

THREE-QUARTER SHOES AND TIPS.

Three-quarter shoes I dislike, for I think they
lame as many horses as they cure of contraction :
they lame, because they are rarely put on good feet,
but on those that have contracted heels, in the hope
that the heels will open without the horse being taken out of work ; but it is only strong black heels

---

* If the frog is deficient in height, after the heels have been lowered, tar
must be daily laid over it. If naturally too high, which is not so often the
case, it may be slightly pared.

11

that are tough enough to stand hunting, or battering
on a hard road, when the shoe does not come well
home.   They seldom have much beneficial effect on
contraction, because the heels are never sufficiently
lowered when a three-quarter shoe is worn ; and if the
heels, when the pasterns are long, were to be sufficiently lowered, too great stress would be thrown on
the back sinews, unless more horn at the toe is pared
away, as I am about to explain, under Tips.

Tips are equally objectionable on this principle,
and more so if the horse is to be worked (though not
quite so liable to get imbedded in the foot).   But
when a brittle hoof is laid up from contraction, a tip
with two nails on each side, close to the toe, will
save the crust without any impediment to the heels
opening ; yet there are two errors universally committed in India in putting on a tip.   The heel of the
tip is always too thick ; it should slope down to as
fine an edge as a dinner-knife blade, and the horn towards the toe should have as much extra pared away,
after the foot is finished cutting, as directed under
" CUTTING THE HOOF," as the tip is thick ; then the
horse is not thrown in the slightest degree more than
natural on the heel, which is of great consequence
with an oblique pastern.   Secondly, a tip should always be narrow.   A horse on soft turf, or Bombay
sands, may be trotted, or gently cantered, or put in
the lounge, with benefit to contraction, and no fear
of strain, when tips are made strictly in this way :
and if put on good strong black feet, with open heels,
they will prevent contraction taking place, and answer
very well for ordinary riding, or even for hunting, in
some of the sandy soils of India.

PART III.

PUTTING INTO CONDITION.

STABLING AND CLOTHING.

HAVING made your purchase from the stables, whether as a Racer, Charger, or Hunter, the same system is to be pursued in order to put him into strong healthy condition, externally and internally ; and, from the day he comes out of the Bomb Proof, never let him enter a shut-up stable, but picket him in an open pendal, or under a tent. You are not in England now, and you will reap the benefit of this by-and-by. From about the 1st November to the 1st of March, one unlined cumly is necessary at night, when picketed in either of the above ; but never more than a dungaree one, if he is, where he has no business to be, in a close shut-up stable. There is no medium with some people ; they either advocate shutting their horses up in a dark and hot stable, thereby doing their best to introduce half a dozen English diseases ; or else picket the poor brutes out in the open mydan the whole year long, caring nothing about the thermometer for six months being at 130 degrees in the sun, whose rays penetrate their very brains ; while, at other seasons, the rains pelt down on their unlucky backs unceasingly for twelve hours, and sometimes for twenty-four, without their being exercised during this time ; thereby producing fevers, rheumatisms, bad surfeits, and inveterate mange. The man who pays fifteen hundred rupees for his nag, generally adopts the first of these, the hot and dark stable, by way of taking care of him ; the man who pays five hundred, the open mydan, by way of allowing the poor brute to take care of himself ; either way impairing their constitutions, and making them miserable.* A stable in all the warm latitudes of India should be nothing more than an open thatched or tiled pendal, fifteen feet high, and made into loose stalls of twelve feet square each. During the hot and rainy months also, if the ground is not damp, make his bed outside ; the insects in some places may be more numerous, but it is cooler. If at a cold station, and one side of the stable closed up, let it be the north-east side, and open to the south-west. Should you be anxious to ascertain whether it is the proper temperature, and clean or foul, sleep in it yourself for a couple of nights ; and if you find it close and uncomfortable, so will your horse.

A small jhool, merely covering the back, and not even meeting under the belly, is but half a jhool. Jhools, whether to keep the horse warm, or to keep the rain, the sun, or the flies off, should all be made on the same principle. A fourth-inch broad band should tie or buckle across the chest, to prevent it slipping backward ; the hinder part should cover the thighs nearly down to the hocks, a large hole being cut for the tail ; this in the cold weather prevents the wind from rattling along the belly ; but, when the

---

* The Bombay cavalry are always picketed outside, and this is called a *state of nature.*

jhool is made of thick numbda, it is better to have the hinder part of lighter stuff. In the hot weather, when made of dungaree, this form alone keeps the flies off the inside of the thighs and testicles, and it never interferes with the motion of the legs. Whether made of heavy or light material, it should double well under the belly, and have two ties of inch and a half broad tape, one piece a little behind the withers, and one in the middle of the back, both fastening on the near side, just under the ribs. The breast-piece must be separate, or the horse can never have the free use of his legs ; and it should always be worn with the body jhool. An extra piece, a foot square, should also be put on the back, when a roller is worn. The neck and head piece in one, when required, must fasten with tape over the withers on to the body-jhool, but not too tight, or it may tear from off the head when lowered to lie down or to eat.

Fly-flappers should always be worn from the 1st of March to the 1st of November.

When you use a tobra, let the mouth be the smallest part and not the bottom, or a lot of the grain is lost on the ground by the horse throwing up his head.

THE FEET, PHYSIC, ETC.

Having picketed your horse where he can breathe fresh air, and at the same time be safe from a stroke of the sun, send for the Nolband, take off his horrible shoes, have the soles properly pared, the horn rasped smooth, and let him be walked on the sands unshod. Give a little bran mash in each of his feeds of ground gram ; as much water as he likes to drink ; but not

much grass.   Continue this for a week or ten days,
and then prepare him for physic.   This is the only
time I shall urge you, without a very good reason, to
give physic ; but on first coming out of the stables
(if he has not been physicked since he came out of
the boat, which you should inquire, for many of the
dealers are great physickers) he will be safer ; and, if
thin, get into condition quicker by a mild dose.*
Prepare him, therefore, as directed, and give over
night a drachm of calomel, and at daybreak the fol-

* J. Stewart, p. 48. " Hundreds of horses have been ruined or destroyed
by the first journey they have made after being purchased.   The buyer has
been ignorant, that, to command even moderate work from a horse, he must
be prepared for it very gradually, and by a systematic course of treatment."

Horses never thrive well in Bombay during the rains.   If purchased from
the stables in April or May, they should be physicked and sent off to the Deccan by the 1st of June : the benefit will be great, *if properly* looked after.

A short time since I heard the following dialogue between two of my brother amateurs, one a civilian, the other a militaire.

Civilian.—Are you fond of physicking horses ?

Militaire.—No, I never yet physicked a horse, and never would. I never
knew any good come from physic.

Civilian.—Well, I differ from you.   I never had a horse come into my possession, I did not immediately physic ; and ever would. If I had fifty, I would
physic them all to-morrow.

Now, there are some individuals in almost every camp holding exactly these
opinions : they never give a thought, nor care a button, whether the horse requires physic, or not : they are persons who have never seen a stable properly
managed ; have most likely never had a valuable horse, and most certainly
never ought to have one.   One always physics, because it is his custom to do
so : the other never physics, because it is his custom not to do so.

But worse than the above are some of those fresh-landed sportsmen, who,
with pockets well lined, have, previous to embarking, obtained a slight insight
into their grandfathers' or uncles' great studs, and therefore they would have
us believe they must intuitively have great knowledge of horseflesh, like the
strolling boys that played the jews-harp, saying, they must be good musicians
for their fathers belonged to the town band.   These people commit more cru-
elty, havoc, and ruin in one year than their careless or less wealthy brethren do
in a dozen ; and I never knew one that could harden the flesh and get a horse
good wind, and at the same time preserve the legs clean, and the heels open.

lowing morning a drench,* deducting a drachm of
aloes for the drachm of calomel.† If your medicine
is not made up at Mr. Treacher's or Mr. Sprague's,
at least learn that the aloes is good; as that brought
from the bazaar contains from a third to one half of
dirt. Never attempt to allow for this by giving a
larger quantity, or you may be much deceived, since
two drachms too much may irreparably injure the
bowels of a weak horse, perhaps send him out of this
world. Two days after the physic has set, if he should
have been purchased thin, hide-bound, having the
lampas, a staring coat, and looking dull, as these are
all merely the symptoms of a deranged inside, take
ten drachms of emetic tartar, five drachms of ginger,
and five ounces of nitre ; mix these up with honey or
ghoor, divide into ten balls, and give one every morning at daybreak. Continue a little bran mash at
each feed with his ground gram, and let the gram be
steeped in hot water ten minutes to soften it, or
change the food to boiled oorud, which is an excellent fattening grain on these occasions ; or give some
boiled barley at each feed with his bran and soaked
gram.‡ There is no necessity to muzzle him every
night you give these balls, unless he is a foul feeder

* As before stated I much prefer giving the physic in the shape of a
ball.—ED.

† See "PHYSICKING." Never venture on more than one dose in order to
put your nag into condition. If that does not effect all that is required for
this purpose, when no ailing exists, twenty will not ; there is something else
needed besides purgative physic. Eight drachms of purified bazaar aloes,
such as you may get and purify yourself, I find equal to about six of those
procured from Mr. Treacher or Mr. Sprague. Twelve drachms of unpurified
bazaar aloes I have given without effect : they are very apt to bring on gripes,
bloody urine, and inflammation of the bowels.

‡ In boiling or steeping grain never put more water than it will soak up, or
a large portion of the strength of the grain goes into the water that is thrown
away.

and eats his bed, and then it should never be omitted until his stomach regains its natural tone.   When
they are finished, put a drachm of black salt, finely
pounded, in his gram at each feed, and in a few days
double it, and then treble it; nothing being more
palatable, or better suited to recall the appetite of a
horse recovering from sickness than this.   Green
grass, or lucern, but never with the dew on it, (it
should be dried twenty minutes in the sun after cutting,) should also be given in moderate quantities, if
procurable ; if not, sliced carrots ; and he should be
walked, or ridden at a walk, morning and evening,
according to his strength.   It is want of care during
the first month with these thin horses ; giving them
eight seers of hard grain when they cannot digest
half ; putting them into a canter when they are
scarce fitted to be mounted for a walk ; omitting
physic, or giving it too strong ; and allowing them to
continue gorging on all day and night at dry grass,
that disarranges their inside, and renders it so difficult to bring them round again into anything like
order.   If you have attended to the foregoing, and
evident improvement has not taken place in a month,
but he still looks dull, and feeds badly, and you can
discover no rheumatism, no fever, no worms, (examine well the pulse, mouth, teeth, &c.) persist strictly in the above way of feeding, and give every morning at daybreak, for a fortnight, some of the beer-
tonic, p. 109.* Let him, also, always now drink some
warm gram gruel, sweetened with a lump of ghoor,
when he comes in from his walk in the morning, and

---

* This is an excellent tonic, and although I would never give a drench when
a ball can be given, yet I would not hesitate to give this, when such kind of
tonics are required.—ED.

a little also on return from his walk in the evening. This simple treatment will benefit him greatly ; and when the ribs are well covered, the flesh on the quarter, and the belly of moderate size, he may be called in condition externally—a sort of dealers' condition, having an appearance ready for sale, though, of course, not ready to be violently galloped—one, however, which undoubtedly is far preferable when making a purchase, to taking a skeleton, inasmuch as some few horses really do exist that never can be made fat, and you would be so far certain you had not got hold of one of these ; besides, it is half the way to real condition, and is a state you should always advance your horse to before you attempt to put him in condition internally ; for, by commencing work too quickly before you have ascertained whether there is any latent ailing about him requiring a different course to be pursued, you may be thrown back three or four months.

HOURS OF FEEDING AND WATERING.

The usual feeding hours in India are morning, noon, and evening ; and as that is a good system by which horses get even quantities at regular hours, and go out with their stomachs empty, (riding times being morning and evening,) it cannot be advantageously altered : for noon, however, substitute one. The hours of nine, one, and seven are a better division than nine, twelve, and seven ; and do not allow him to eat grass at nine and one for more than an hour and a half after each feed, when it should be invariably all swept away. The use of salt for preserving health ; two or three drachms in each feed is granted, and should therefore continually be given. If the black salt is used, a smaller quantity will suffice.

Water is usually given twice a-day ; first, after morning's feed, and again between three and four o'clock.   They will often thrive very well on this, and if offered it at other times, even in the hot weather, will frequently refuse to sip any ; but a horse that is out of condition, or one that is to be trained after he is got into condition, will be better if water is allowed oftener.   Give a dhool, about three gallons, half an hour before the morning's feed,* and another half an hour after it ; a dhool at half past twelve, half an hour before the one o'clock feed ; and another at half past three.   In the evening, when he comes in from walking, and is cool, offer half a dhool more, but do not let him drink more than this at any one time. Horses that are only watered twice a day will often drink a bhæstees large dhool twice filled, six gallons each time ; some will drink more, which, with their bellies full of gram and grass, I have seen produce most violent gripes.†   Never allow the dhool to be used for any other purpose than drinking, and then the older it is the better.

---

* I altogether disapprove of watering before feeding. * It dilutes the gastric juice, and consequently weakens its action in digesting the food. I prefer giving a small quantity immediately after feeding, about a gallon, and the remainder in about an hour afterwards. I would always water three times a day.—ED.

* (Unless the horse has been long without water, and very thirsty, I would then give a few mouthfuls.)—ED.

† Watering immediately after feeding on barley is said to often bring on gripes and inflammation : this is far truer of wheat. A too sudden change of food, from gram to barley, and then watering immediately after, may bring on gripes and inflammation ; but then the sudden change of food is as much the cause of the disease as the watering after. Watering immediately before or immediately after any grain is unwholesome, and to some horses dangerous, and after gram quite as much as after barley. Horses of delicate stomachs, indeed all horses, should be watered half an hour before, and half an hour after morning's feeding, to prevent the food swelling in the stomach too much.

A good gora-walla, well looked after, will clean your horse quite as well as an English groom ; and twice in the day, at eight in the morning and half-past three, with a rub down and slight brushing when he comes in from exercise in the evening, are the proper times. During the months of March and October, or when he is changing his coat, dispense with the curry-comb, if thin skinned, and use only the hand-rubber and brush. Moulting, in all hot latitudes, is very slight, yet some horses are a little weak in consequence : a bran mash should be added to the gram every evening if this is the case, and a little sweet gram-flour gruel given in the morning. The hair of the mane and tail is often greatly disfigured by the curry-comb and hand-rubber, making it all scraggy, and giving it the ugly and dirty appearance of mange. Never permit the curry-comb or hand-rubber to go within three inches of either the mane or the tail, and then the hairs of the mane from the near side, that hang over to the off side, will be equally long with the rest ; and those nearest the root of the tail will be also long : the hair destroyed in one day by a slovenly mode of cleaning, will take a whole twelvemonth to grow again to a proper length. The comb is often in fault too, from the numerous teeth in it* have it of thick, strong bone, but file away every other tooth, not leaving more than six, including the corner ones ; and then the hair will neither be broken nor pulled out. The mane and tail being in nice order, add

---

* I would never use a comb to either the mane or tail. The brush properly used, will keep them in much better order.—ED.

much to the appearance, and often materially facili-
tate the sale of a horse.   The manes and tails of all
horses, excepting the Cavalry, are combed to the off
side.

When brought home in the morning, after his walk
or canter, at whatever season of the year it may be,
never allow him to be taken into the pendal till he is
quite cool.   The wisping with grass, the instant the
saddle is taken off, must then be liberally performed ;*
first over the saddle-place, till every hair is dry, and
then all down the legs to the hoofs, until the fetlocks
feel warm from the rubbing ; this will often prevent
swelling of the legs : but, if the legs are begun with,
the saddle must not be removed ; or, the back being
neglected, the first minute it is taken off may give
cold, or produce warbles.†   At this grass-rubbing, it
is always better to have a couple of gora-wallas employed, if at hand, and which is imperatively necessary if the horse has been in the rain ; but, that over,
he may be left as safe till the gora-walla is ready to
begin with the curry-comb.‡   During this cleaning
leave the legs from the knee downwards alone, till he
is watered ; or, if you like, till half an hour after that,
when the grain is given ; then lay on the hand-rubbers, and afterwards brush all smooth.   Wash his

---

* I would never take off the saddle or even loosen the girths till the head
and legs are thoroughly cleaned, by which time the horse will have become
cool, and not so likely to take cold when the saddle is taken off. Immediately
·it is removed however, wisping should be sharply performed till every hair
is dry.—ED. .

† If the above is properly attended to, there need be no fear of cold, or
warbles.—ED.

‡ I disapprove of the curry-comb for Arabs. I would never allow them to
be touched with one. The rubber, brush, and hand-rubbing is quite sufficient
to keep them as bright as a glass.—ED.

feet and heels lastly, if they must be washed; but, unless they are dirty, it is quite unnecessary. That
abominable English custom of washing a horse's legs
when he first comes in, and that often in cold water,
tends to produce windgalls, cracks in the heels, and
contraction. In the cold weather, it is true, it is
generally done with warm water ; but the rubbing and
scrubbing to dry the heels, and then the draught of
cold wind they are exposed to in a stable, is apt to
produce cracks as well. In India, once every other
day, when he is finished cleaning, at four o'clock in
the afternoon, is quite often enough to wash his legs :
the chill should be taken off the water in the cold
weather.

Should you be lately from England, you perhaps
have as great an aversion to wash your horse's body
as you have a predilection for washing his legs.
Some grooms have, I know, a great dislike, even in
the height of summer (the only time it is asked), to
wash a blood-horse all over : they think it looks strange,
and fancy it spoils his coat. The poor post-horse
gets the advantage here, only that he frequently goes
in hot. Do not be prejudiced : you are now in India,
and, for three or four of the hot months in the year,
your horse, especially if he is a high caste one, should
be taken to the river three times a week, about noon,
before he has his one o'clock feed, and washed all
over : he enjoys a lie-down in the water ; it refreshes
and invigorates him greatly. In May, and the very
hot months, if he perspires about twelve o'clock, half
an hour before sunset should be chosen, and let him
have his walk afterwards. Always take care that he
does not remain in above ten minutes, and that he is
rubbed down dry, and moved off in as short a time.

Independent of this, the mane and tail should be washed once a week in lukewarm water and soap, (trotting well afterwards in the cold or rainy weather :) it keeps the scurf away, and makes the hair grow. The inside of the ears is a part so little thought of, that large scaps sometimes form there from the sticking of clots of dirt. Every morning and afternoon, when the cleaning is finished, these should always be nicely wiped out with a wet towel, taking care that no water drops into the ear.

GETTING out of order.

If you have purchased your horse fat, in good external condition, and during the time he is being put into internal condition, by stronger exercise, &c., he should unexpectedly get stale, and cease to improve ; if his skin should become somewhat hide-bound ; his coat lie rough ; small surfeit-bumps arise on his body ; his mouth have the lampas, &c. ; should he, in short, get into that lubberly state, like a " ship in irons," evidently wrong, and neither go backwards nor forwards, you have been keeping him in a hot, shut-up stable, or, you have not duly attended to all the directions here laid down. Whatever has been the cause, treat according to " PUTTING INTO CONDITION," commencing with the mild drench of aloes and salts, followed by a week of the beer-tonic, p. 109, if rather fleshy, three or four of the ALTERATIVES, p. 74, should succeed to the physic, previous to giving the beer-tonic ; but never think of bleeding ; no, not if he is as fat as a hog.

Some persons have great objection to gora-wallas riding. If you have any kind of a decent gora-walla, and not above seven and a half stone weight, or eight and a half for a strong horse, he will, by one month's instruction, do as well to ride, at a walk, as if you had Jem Robinson. Give an old saddle, and see that it is placed well backward, clear of the shoulder, and kept there by being lined with plush ; or, if necessary, by a crupper ; and take care that the stuffing is quite free of the back bone, so that looking under the pommel you can see daylight right through, or the back may be galled, and you will accuse your gora-walla of your own neligence, and be crying out, "this comes of gora-walla riding !" Let him be ridden also with a small light mouthing-bit, and make the gora-walla keep the head well up, not by pulling at the bridle, but by pressing the heels to his sides, and occasionally giving him a touch behind with the bagdoor, one end of which is to be fastened to the ring of the mouthing-bit, the other end being in his hand, to guard against the horse running away if by accident he should fall off. This will preserve his mouth, prevent his ambling, make him put out his fore-legs, and go light in hand, and be proper walking exercise ; while the gora-walla will not be too tired to clean him well when he comes in. There is not half so much danger of your horse falling down when the gora-walla is on his back, riding in this way, as when he is slouching by his side, allowing the head every minute to come within a foot of the ground. A horse should only be led (except in training) when he is too sick, or too weak, or too tired to be ridden ; and then, if it is the cold weather, the jhool in the morning's walk should be kept on; but walking exercise at other seasons of the year, with clothing on, when the thermometer is ninety, or more, is enough to put any horse " in irons."

DANGER OF OVERFEEDING.

Condition is not the work of a week; it will often take half a year for a horse that is thin, or fresh from the stables, and if you attempt to fatten too quickly by grain, before the strength will admit of your giving proportionate exercise, the stomach, unable to digest a large quantity, will be weakened; thus the grain will often pass whole, and the horse fall off instead of improving, or he will grow dull, heavy, and gross. And even should he be able to digest all you give, this raising of the condition too quickly is very apt to produce fever, or inflammation of the bowels. It is always dangerous to allow an idle horse to overfeed on grain, it brings on scouring; besides, flesh gained at this risk adds but little to strength. There are some horses also that will keep plump on eight seers, and yet not thrive on twelve.

Continual increasing and decreasing of grain is likewise very bad. Feeding a thin horse on ten seers a-day, then reducing it suddenly to half the quantity, and then increasing it again to ten—all this irregularity is destructive to getting into condition; yet I have seen a man, when training, act not very differently from this, but I never heard of one winning, unless it was a donkey race.

97

Mixed boiled food is often absolutely necessary to recover lost flesh ; and, when given only once a day, the evening is the proper time. One mäp of coltee, one of oorud, one of barley, one of bran, half a one of linseed-meal, with three drachms of salt, or six ounces of ghoor, according to the horse's taste, all put into hot water, and boiled for twenty minutes, with one mäp of dry ground gram, and one of sliced carrots or turnips afterwards added, make an excellent evening's feed, and one which is very refreshing after a long day's hunt.* This kind of supper, however, is often refused, unless the horse has been a little habituated to it, or if the cooking-pot it was boiled in was the least greasy or dirty, or perhaps from dislike to one of the articles. Any change of diet, any thing new, must always be introduced by little and little, or the sensitive and dainty appetite of a horse will be sure to take disgust. Potatoes, or yams, should only

---

* Coltee, oorud, moong, and methee are the grains for boiling, and sometimes barley also. Coltee requires more boiling than either of the other three, but none of these should ever be given raw. Bajree and mhut are not so good for boiling; they are better in their natural state, and ground gram also, unless particularly hard, or the horse sick. Bajree and mhut are always mixed, as bajree alone is too heating ; and mhut alone gives the gripes, especially when it is mixed with rats' dung.

Wheat is the most nutritious of all grain, but at the same time the most liable to disagree. The strongest-stomached horse could not bear a change to an entire wheat diet under four or five months, and then it is very unwholesome. Barley is the next most nutritious grain, then oats, then peas, and lastly, beans. It appears singular that beans, which in England are deemed absolutely requisite to a horse at hard work (not to train on), and which are known to put on the hardest flesh, should contain less nutriment than the other grain ; and it appears equally singular that lucern, the value of which we all know in India in fattening a horse, should be the least nutritious of all the grasses ; but so it is.

13

be steamed, and turnips only parboiled ; but these had
better not be given in large quantities raw.   Carrots
and beet may be given with impunity, and very
wholesome they are ; begin with a little.   Turnips,
carrots, and linseed-meal, when continued for any
length of time, improve the skin and coat considerably.   In the hot weather, two or three of the large
radishes, called moolee, may be also given daily,
stalks and all ; but the natives term them cold and injurious, if water is drunk immediately after them.
A seer of methee, boiled, and given at each feed, in
lieu of one of the seers of gram, is also very good in
some cases ; for this grain has a double advantage, being very nourishing, and its adhesive quality preventing its being swallowed too quickly.   Giving large
quantities of ghee, ghoor, and trash of this kind, is
disapproved of ; and very properly so : but to a horse
displaying all his ribs, a seer of bajree flour, six ounces
of ghoor, and a wineglass of ghee, baked up together
into a large thick ap, with half a drachm of ginger and
two drachms of anise-seed, and given after the morning's feed, and the same again after the evening's feed,
if he can only be induced to eat it willingly, will
rapidly help to cover them.   Ghee is often very old
and rancid ; so, if disrelished, try it without the ghee,
or with nice fresh butter.   Sugar-cane, sliced, is also
most nutritious and wholesome ; but too many things
are as bad as too few ; you must select those that
best suit his taste.   Chaff will sometimes be found
very useful.   A pound of dry grass, a pound of
barley or wheat-straw, boosa, and four pounds of
lucern, chopped up small, and given after each feed ;
or his feed of boiled grain, bran mash, sliced carrots, &c., may all be mixed in the trough with half

the quantity of this chaff; and the other half given afterwards.

After a horse has picked up in flesh, and is capable of being ridden for mornings' and evening's exercise, he must not be allowed to get gross. A horse, after four years old, should never be too fat, any more than he should be too thin. Feeding also too much or too long on boiled food, chaff, sugar, &c., is bad; it must always be discontinued as improvement takes place, for it makes the flesh too soft, and may possibly have something to do with engendering worms; and the same benefit will not be derived from it as if given only during the times of thinness or sickness.

A horse that has been long thin and out of condition, (if the emaciation is not caused solely by starvation or overwork,) always needs a *mild* dose of physic, previous to being fed on boiled mixed food. The " ALTERATIVES," p. 74, are generally best adapted to this case, provided the owner will only see his horse properly mashed, to prevent the chance of over-purging, and thereby doing more harm than good.[*]

* Caveat Emptor, p. 19. " I fed him for a month on chopped clover, bran, and malt, fermented by a little yeast. This is the way to pickle a horse for a friend !"

The above kind of feeding, continued incessantly for eight or nine weeks, lies on the fat in an extraordinary manner. The belly does not become large; on the contrary, there will generally be a nice, round-looking carcase, from the great nutriment contained in the food, and its easiness of digestion; but the whole barrel, as well as the neck, become thickly laden with gross fat. In England, where the generality of horses are geldings, and the neck consequently thin, the bellies being also often of large size, a little of this benefits the appearance; but to Arabs, who are almost all entire, and whose necks, with the exception of the high caste, are seldom over-light, too much feeding on such fattening stuff ruins, instead of improving, the appearance.

EXERCISE.

The system to be adopted with regard to exercise must be regular ; and it is to be gradually and never suddenly increased. Having now improved and become strong, he should have a canter during his morning's exercise three or four times a week, and any green meat that he has been feeding on changed to dry grass ; but three weeks must be allowed before the change is wholly completed. Increase one máp of ground grain every fortnight, and let the exercise be proportioned to this gradual increase of grain, and

NATIVE REMEDIES FOR IMPROVING, FATTENING, AND GIVING A HORSE AN APPETITE.

FOR IMPROVING.

The Ralib, called Hulwaee Udruk, to be given only in the cold season.

Take of ghee, pounded turmeric, green ginger, and methee, two seers and a half each ; put the ghee on the fire first, fry the turmeric well in it ; then throw in the methee and green ginger, and let them fry thoroughly : then mix five seers of brown sugar in that, and add ten seers of milk. Work the whole up into a confection, and give a quarter of a seer once a day after watering. Increase it by degrees to a seer. It is a perfect elixir, and, if given throughout the cold season, the horse will be a world of beauty.

FOR FATTENING.

Give turmeric, for six weeks, that has been steeped for twenty-four hours thus : mix one-eighth of a seer of turmeric with milk in which it has soaked for twenty-four hours, and give it once a day, fasting. Increase the quantity gradually to a quarter of a seer.

The seer for the above, means the native puckah seer, which is nearly two pounds. The cutcha seer is nearly a one-pound measure.

FOR GIVING AN APPETITE.

Take equal parts of mustard, bhang, salt, and kichree, (kichree is rice and dal,) with flour just sufficient to mix the whole in. Weigh, and give about ten drachms once a day, after he has finished his feed, keeping him reined up for a quarter of an hour afterwards. This is also good when the bowels are flatulent, or when at exercise they make a rumbling noise, like a mussuk of water in the inside.

All these are useful at times, provided they are given in moderation, and nothing whatever ails the horse, but only simply wanting flesh, or appetite. If taken willingly, of course the better.

not the grain to the exercise : he is now only being put in condition, so, if he gets thin, decrease the exercise ; but do not increase the grain too quickly. Some horses will get fat and keep in condition on very little grain ; so much the better. By the time his appetite and digestion can contend with ten, eleven, twelve, or thirteen seers of ground grain *per diem*, (thirteen seers of ground grain is about ten pounds,) according as he may be a large or small horse, and a large or small feeder, he ought to be in strong healthy condition, externally and internally, which is to be thus defined : when he is fine in coat, and that fineness has been gained by the free use of hand-rubbers and brushes, and not by warm jhools, or hot stables ; when he is firm in flesh, the flesh well up on the quarter, and he carries a good carcase ; neither tucked up under the flank, nor let down like a cow : when he is high in spirit, produced by kindness, and regularity of feeding : when he is fresh on his legs, and they are as clean and unblemished as on the day that he was foaled : and when all this has been brought about while he has been kept in an open pendal, so that with one extra head and body covering put over the single blanket, he could go on a march, or be hunted, and sleep in the open mydan, in the cold weather, without showing or feeling the slightest bad effect from it. This is the acme of perfection of condition.

HOW TO KEEP CONDITION.

As continual gentle exercise is the surest way to preserve health and prevent disease, so never omit, when unable to ride yourself, to let the gora-walla mount for an hour's walk, both morning and evening, giving some of the grain boiled every other night; this, when a horse is idle, or only at ordinary riding, being the chief part of the secret in keeping that plump appearance over the quarter : but, if even for upwards of a month he has nothing but walking-exercise, reduce the grain, if he is fat, and feed partly on green food ; and be cautious that the change from any soft feeding, to dry feeding, and from common exercise to hard work, is always gradual, or the digestive organs will be weakened, and the legs will swell. When a horse is suddenly put to work, after being fattened on boiled food, lucern, &c., three moderate gallops will often take off all the flesh he has gained in as many months, making him ill besides.

Dry hard grain and dry grass are as injurious to a horse's body, when standing for weeks without exercise, as boiled food and green grass are to his legs whilst hunting. Turning out to grass, as they do in England, to eat nothing but green grass, or laying up altogether, in India, to eat nothing but boiled grain and green food, has long ago been proved destructive to condition. We have no opportunity in this country of doing the former ; and the latter should never be resorted to, unless sickness or great poverty demands it. Too large a quantity of bran, such as bran mashes in every feed, is also very improper, and very lowering, if continued even for a fortnight only, to a horse in health. Bran mash is the diet of the sick, or lame horse, or occasionally to give at night mixed with the grain, when the dung is in small hard balls ; but the dung in general is far too soft in India.

Never muzzle at night, unless you have some reason for it, such as preparing for physic ; the horse
being a bed-eater, &c. ; and in the latter case something should always be given in the middle of the
night, or an hour before daybreak. The system of
fasting from nine at night till nine in the morning,
to please the fancy of the owner, is ruinous to a
horse's inside.

Never allow of stimulants or masallahs indiscrimi-
nately; and particularly avoid them whenever the
least symptom of illness, or falling off in condition appears, for they are destructive at the commencement
of many illnesses, although most salutary in other sta-
ges ; therefore, give them only when out in cold or
rainy weather, or during hard work; on which occasions the pint of Hodgson, sweetened with an ounce
of ghoor, adding half a drachm of ginger, finely grat-
ed, and one drachm of anise-seed, whilst on the fire
warming, is the finest cordial of any.

Never fail to have the feet pared once in every
twenty-five days, if they grow quickly, or thirty days
at most ; and the first day you observe the least con-
tracting of the heels, take off the shoes and treat for
" Contraction."

Never picket your horse with two tent-pegs six feet
apart, unless he is a weaver, or you are about to shoot
him ; two close together are far more secure, and he
is less liable to hurt himself : and if you must use heel-
ropes, let them be very loose at night, or many an
hour's sleep will be lost from fear to lie down. I
have seen many horses thrown completely out of
spirits, and some out of condition, solely from this
cause.

Look after your horse yourself : make much of him always on mounting and on dismounting ; and *see* that he is made comfortable in his stall : by this means a bad-tempered horse will grow fond of you.*

CHANGE FROM STABLING TO THE OPEN AIR, HUNTING, ETC.

As walled-in stables are now universal in every cantonment, and as little probability exists that you will alter those attached to your habitation to that form of structure most congenial to a horse's health, you may easily suppose, that when brought from one of these warm stalls to sleep in the open air in the cold weather, and no precautions taken, illness of some kind, as a matter of course, will follow. A warm bed-blanket, head and body piece, wrapping well under the belly, should always be put under the ordinary jhool on these occasions, and the horse kept close under the tent-walls, out of the wind : this, with half a masallah at night, and taking care the gora-walla mounts at day-break, or before, (but without taking off more than the upper jhool,) for a good hour's walk, will be found the best preventive against those colds and coughs, which bring on a staring coat, debility, loss of flesh, and general bad condition.

If unexpectedly taken out during the monsoon, and rain should fall during the night, change the jhool, give a small masallah, and trot him for a quarter of an hour *immediately* the shower is over. A single

---

* Lawrence, vol. i. p. 279. "The tempers of horses, like those of their masters, are various, endowed with a greater or less proportion of intelligence, sagacity, and feeling ; and it is but too often the beast evinces the greater degree of rationality."

light black Deccan jhool, *unlined*, (the best description of jhool there is next to the bed-blanket,) should always at nine o'clock during the monsoon be put on all horses unaccustomed to the open air, for though it may be close and hot, and no rain fall, yet it is generally damp. Keeping thick jhools over the body during the heat of the day to guard against the scorching sun is very pernicious, but a light dungaree one, padded half an inch thick with cotton, along the spine, is proper, and should always be worn when out in the sun, in the hot or rainy season. The shade of a tree, however, should be searched for : it is cooler and more agreeable to a horse than even stable or pendal ; and hog-hunters should not forget this, for the continual exposure to the fiery sun throughout the day damps the spirits of many horses considerably. No one, but a native, can keep his hand upon a horse's back for ten minutes between the hours of twelve and three in those months, when picketed in the sun, without burning or blistering it : you may imagine, therefore, the effect on a high caste, thin-skinned horse, and tormented by the flies to boot.

Hunting a horse for two or three months on nothing but green food, only cut the day before for his forage, —not at all an uncommon occurrence,—or even half green and half dry, is as much the cause of those rounded shank-bones and gummy ancles, as being taken out of an idle stable, and suddenly put into training exercise, without gradual inurement. Hunters are often fed too much and too long on green food ; racers may also be included. Considering that a few days' green meat is often wanted to recruit the strength after a severe cold or other illness, no horse kept solely for racing or hunting should have more than

14

ten weeks' regular soiling throughout the year, and that at two different periods. As training usually commences in October, the month of April, or early part of May, and that of June, or early part of July, will be judiciously chosen as the most proper season, during which time the grain should be decreased nearly one half, and the exercise never exceed a trot. The hunter can have his in Auugst, September, and October, when the grass is long and rich, and the boar allowed to rest; very little being given during the months he is hunted. Green grass at coming in, during the first fall of the rains, is very weak and washy; but lucern, kept half buried in water, is equally good throughout the year.

To retain a horse, then, in hunting or hardworking condition, he must be kept chiefly on hard food : he should have a three-mile gentle canter every other day, and always be exercised, mounted, every morning and evening. If wanted after breakfast, allow but little water after finishing his morning's grain, and less grass, so that he may go out with both stomach and bowels tolerably empty. Feed and water in moderation (a gallon of water and a seer of ground grain, with a mouthful of grass, will be moderation,) if you halt to take your own tiffin ; give first a small cordial drink, if the least fatigue is apparent; and, even whilst hunting, always allow two or three go-downs of water at any river or tank, if he thirsts for it; this little will not hinder his galloping, but will prevent faintness. Invariably walk the last mile to cantonment, that he may return home cool, but never feed until he has been in an hour, and well cleaned above : then *see* that he has a cordial drink, masallah ball, or some gram flour gruel ; likewise that boiled food according to his liking is made, to be given *after*[*] he has eaten about two mäps of dry ground grain ; that a small dhool of water is offered half an hour before the dry grain is put into the trough, and another half an hour afterwards : *see* also that his legs are well malished while eating it, and that a good bedding is placed under him, in a loose stall. These little attentions after severe work are a horse's rights : he is sagacious enough to comprehend and appreciate them, and will amply repay you—if your ugly conscience does not— by cheerfulness of going the next time you require his services. When the fetlocks and feet are so dirty as to require washing, let it be done in warm (not too hot) water, and *see* that the legs are well dried and malished afterwards. If he refuses his food, it is most likely from your neglect of him after dismounting, and not the distance, unless you completely galloped him off his wind and brought him home hot : in either case, foment the legs in warm water, make a large soft bed, let him drink if inclined, and then muzzle for two hours, when he will probably have regained his appetite.†

* The soft food at this late hour will produce a quick and wholesome distention of stomach, which will induce sleep, and prevent his standing two or three unnecessary hours to produce it by eating dry grass, which, at this late hour of night, is as bad for a tired as for a weak-stomached horse.

† There is one time that masallahs, or cordial drenches, prove excessively hurtful. When severe distress is occasioned by a long run, and you find that your horse can with difficulty go forward, give a drench on the spot, if you have it, loosen the girths, and lead gently home ; but by the time he reaches his stall he will be feverish, and cordials or stimulants then may do serious [har]m. A seer of steeped ground grain in a good bran mash, sweetened by a [lum]p of ghoor, a drachm of emetic tartar, and two of nitre being put in it, will, in this case, with a large bed and loose cool stall, be the quickest and safest restorative, repeating the same on the following morning. A clyster of salt and water must also be given on arrival at his stall.

As to the considerate Christian, who, after a hog-hunt, or long day's journey, will carelessly hand his faithful steed over to an ignorant syce, perhaps to be tied up and left in the not unfrequent position of a bullock at the slaughter, the hind-legs being tugged a foot too far backwards, and the head pulled down to the tent-peg, and he march off to fill his own greedy stomach—may nought but hot beer and tough meat welcome his palate for dinner, and the night-mare, in a buggy bed, be his only nocturnal repose!

" THE HORSE TO HIS MASTER.

Take care of me a mile out, and a mile in.
Up the hill spur me not,
Down the hill push me not,
On the plain spare me not,
In the stable forget me not."

MASALLAH BALLS.

3 drs. caraway-seed, $\frac{1}{4}$ dr. mustard.

2 drs. cardamom-seeds, $\frac{1}{4}$ dr. cinnamon.

1 dr. ginger, 1 dr. black pepper.

2 drs. turmeric, 2 drs. anise-seed.

The whole to be finely pounded, and baked up with gram flour and ghoor, into a thick ap. A little ghee or fresh butter can be added, if the horse is fond of it. Some of the light pleasant stimulants will frequently be eaten with a relish, if the horse is accustomed to bread and they are given fresh.

When a horse drops exhausted, bleeding three or four quarts is recommended, giving also a pint of wine or beer, to enable him to crawl home after an hour or two of rest. When home, treat as above, with bran mash, emetic tartar, &c.

CORDIAL DRINKS.

Any one of the above, given in half a pint or a pint of warm beer.

Two wine-glasses of brandy, gin, or rum, and three ditto of hot water.

Four wine-glasses of port or sherry, and two ditto of hot water, mulled with nutmeg, &c., just as you like it yourself.*

BEER TONIC.

2 drs. gentian, 2 drs. anise-seed, 1½ dr. turmeric, ¾ dr. ginger, ½ dr. black pepper, in a pint of beer. One half of each article, in only half a pint of beer, is the proper strength to begin with after illness, increasing to the full dose in a week.

For a horse whose dung always remains soft after the grain has been reduced, and there is no apparent reason to account for it ;—but not to be given until he has first had a mild warm drench of physic, and been afterwards fed for a fortnight on partly boiled grain, with a little gruel always added to his water,— this will frequently harden the dung into balls of itself; and then the following ball or drench, given every other morning, when gradually brought on again to dry grain and dry grass, will help to keep it so. Ball : 1½ dr. gentian, quassia, or chreeate, ½ dr. catechu, ½ dr. ginger, $\frac{1}{12}$ dr. bhang, $\frac{1}{12}$ dr. opium.

* It is a bad practise accustoming a horse to cordial balls or cordial drinks. It is like a man accustoming himself to drachm drinking, after a time he cannot do without them. I would never give them but when a horse is in a state of exhaustion from overwork, or when requiring cordials and tonics when recovering from sickness.—ED.

Drench : this, mixed in half a pint of beer, or in one wine-glass of brandy, and three of hot water. These relaxed constitutioned horses should, every other evening, have their grain boiled, and not be fed wholly on gram.

A pill, the size of a pea, is often given by natives in cases of fatigue, or in gripes. The pill is thus concocted, but it requires a native to make it, who has been taught how to prepare it, and then it will keep for years :—Six drachms of solid arsenic, and six quarts of onion or moolee juice are put in a pot, and placed on the fire for eight hours, till all the juice is absorbed. About one drachm of the arsenic is lost in the residue, and the remainder is made into sixty pills ; each pill, therefore, contains about five grains of arsenic.

The following is also given by them when a horse is fatigued, and necessitated to continue his journey on the following morning :— $\frac{1}{11}$ dr. opium ; 1 dr. bhang ; 1 dr. alum ; 2 drs. googul ; 4 drs. turmeric ; 4 drs. ghoor, made into a ball with bajree flour.

NATIVE MASALLAH BALL.

Ginger......... $\frac{1}{2}$ seer.
Mustard....... $\frac{1}{8}$ do.
Black pepper. $\frac{1}{4}$ do.
Asafœtida,....   6 drs.
Garlic......... $\frac{1}{2}$ seer.
Kala jeera.... $\frac{1}{2}$ do. ; the cumin seed, or like it.
Kucha methee $\frac{1}{2}$ do. ; the fenugreek do.
Umbee huldee $\frac{1}{4}$ do. ; a turmeric-coloured zedoary.
Gora waj...... $\frac{1}{4}$ do. ; also called butch ; the orris-
                              root, or like it.

Kootke........ $\frac{1}{4}$ seer ; a febrifuge, a small round
stick.

Underjow..... $\frac{1}{8}$ do. ; a small long seed, like the
oleander.

Bungrekan... $\frac{1}{4}$ do. ; a white, mineral-looking substance.

Gulloo setwah $\frac{1}{4}$ do. ; also called iskung, the root
of a tree ; colour,
yellow.

Lindee peepah $\frac{1}{8}$ do. ; a long pepper.

Jerkatolah. ... $\frac{1}{8}$ do. ; a kind of flat bean.

Palas papra... $\frac{1}{8}$ do. ; a very thin flat bean, crimson outside, pale yel-
low in.

Ajowan........ $\frac{1}{8}$ do. ; a very small seed, half the
size of a caraway.

This is enough for twenty balls.* These ingredients should not be all made up at once, but kept
pounded, a little being mixed up fresh with ghoor,
when wanted ; then, it will often be eaten, if the gora-
walla keeps his fingers playing in the angles of the
mouth : or, as there is nothing bitter or nauseous in
it, a small quantity may be baked up in a large ap.
If forced down, the balls must be soft, in the shape
of an egg, but not more than two inches in length,
nor more than three quarters of an inch in diameter.
When a balling-iron is used, it should always be covered with leather, and the tongue very gently held.

---

* These masallah balls I would never give. If a horse requires any thing
of the kind, the cordial ball or cordial drinks at pages 108 and 109 are much
better.—ED.

TRAINING,

THAT is, for the turf, is the highest artificial state of existence the horse has to endure ; and artificial means must be resorted to before any horse can possibly be brought on the course in a fit state to run a contested race with a chance of winning ; but there is no necessity to follow in the wake of admitted errors, much less to practise absurdities, or to block up the animal's nostrils every night at nine o'clock with that confounded little muzzle : when the muzzle is required, let it always be of the shape and size before directed.

Near one fourth of those that are put in training, are never brought to the post, and no wonder : the very stable management of many is radically bad ; too much attention is paid to trifles, and the essentials, the very life of training, neglected. Some are over-physicked and over-fed, and then over-physicked again ; the bowels, of course, get out of order ; the stamina are weakened ; and the legs, as a natural consequence, fail : others are over-clothed or over-sweated ; and almost all, over-stabled. Shutting the stable-doors close in India can only have one advantage, and that is, nobody can then be aware of the nonsense that goes forward within. How often does training commence on the slight, and perhaps delicately-constitutioned Arab, with two drastic doses of physic ? Before two months are passed over, the bowels become greatly deranged, and the legs bunged : it is then declared, he (which ought to signify the trainer) " went all wrong ;" and this wrong, or rather wronged horse, has to be physicked again, and laid up in bandages for a month, and perhaps blistered, before he can be got rid of. Sometimes a sturdy animal will stand a great deal of mismanagement, and yet appear at the post, and even win, if entered for a race that answers for him and running on a course suited to his make, &c., but this is not gaining by judicious training ; much oftener, however, he fails to show his countenance, having been ruined by a regular adapted process, as the nasty dry coat, disordered inside, over-worked legs, and contracted feet most abundantly testify. A well-made horse, indifferently trained, may beat a bad-made horse well trained ; and one of high caste, indifferently trained, may beat one of not so good caste well trained, &c. &c. It is through these, and various other distinctions, that bungling training is always hidden. Horses, no doubt, will continually go wrong when being fine-drawn in the last dangerous month ; but, unless from accident, &c., it should not occur until that time. It is useless your attempting to train, unless you punctually visit your stables at every feeding and watering hour, (have a good watch, for you should never be more than five minutes out in your time,) then carefully inspecting the grain, grass, water, &c., and always look in the last thing before you go to bed, and the first thing at daybreak in the morning ; for, however good your gora-wallas or jockey may be, you should never lose sight of the proverb, that " He who works with his hands, has seldom too much in his head."

Training in India and training in England are certainly different,* but there is no difference in the prin-

* The Arab, it has been justly said, cannot be trained in India as the English horse is in England : but the remark holds good reversed ; the English racer could not be trained in England as the Arab is in India. The difference

ciples ; and those consist in condensing the greatest
quantity of pure muscle into the smallest possible
bulk, and so gradually to raise the muscular powers
and wind to that degree of perfection that every atom
of speed may be drawn out without any distress being exhibited, and without the slightest damage to the
legs. In effecting this consists the whole arcanum of
good training ; and, by attending to the following, you
may accomplish your end, and be able to cope with

of country, climate, food, and the manner in which the two, from infancy, are
reared, require an alteration of system, and render much of the artificial
means pursued in England unnecessary ; but the English race-horse, notwithstanding his wonderful performances, will, perhaps, not stand more training,
more actual galloping, before he comes to the post than a high caste Arab ; and
yet an English thorough-bred will easily outstrip the best Arab, in either
pace or distance, and beat him in daily journeys, or continuance of labour ;
though, for these two last, the Arab might prove victorious, if on his own
native soil.

Arab blood is a little in disrepute just now, owing to those that have been
exported from this country having been of a very mediocre caste ; but I do
not believe that a thorough-bred, genuine, unblemished Arab horse, and certainly not a mare, of the proper build and stamp, would be objected to—the one
for a stallion, and the other for a brood-mare ; or either to be crossed with
suitable-sized English thorough-breds—by any of the great racing breeders at
home ; and if twenty genuine, high caste Arab horses and mares were now to
be sent to our cold climate, and as judiciously crossed, and well taken care of,
for the next fifty years, as the race now in existence have been from sire to
son during the last half-century, they might equal in size, and surpass in speed,
all those of the present day.

When last in England, my opinion was asked of a late importation from
the Bomb Proof, price twelve hundred rupees, and if I thought he was a *real*
Arab. I replied, to my confiding querist, I thought he was a real Arab, quite
as much a real Arab as a cathammed horse he had purchased of his baker a
few days before was a real English horse : and I recommended that he should
embark that to his munificent donor in India in return, who would then have
a real English horse, and a most equitable exchange, too. An Arab, to be
worth acceptance at home, must either be very showy and handsome, answer-
ing for a lady's park-horse, or else have proved his blood by the very best
performance, displaying besides the cardinal points of a good stallion ; for the
very best performance of an Arab, in India, would be very third-rate at Newmarket. A few of the genuine caste are annually imported to Bombay, but
three parts to seven-eighths bred are what chiefly fall to our lot.

your neighbours ; but if you enter on your sporting
career, intending to train all horses in the same manner, without any regard to their peculiar constitutions
and temperaments, their likings and dislikings, think-
ing the whole secret consists in making them thin,
you will generally succeed, to your heart's content, in
bringing down all the flesh and fat of the body, de-
positing it, unluckily, about the legs and ancles : when
degraded to this state, they should be shut up in
the dark stable ; for such horses, " there is no place
like home."

STABLE AND CLOTHING.

If fresh air and a cool stall are necessary to put a
horse into condition, how much more so must they
now be, when his powers are about to be exerted to
the highest pitch they are capable of attaining ; but,
as the more inducement to rest, and to lie down, a
horse in training has, the better, close up the sides
with tatties that he may not be disturbed during
either the day or night. One single blanket jhool,
made as described at page 84, with the single neck
and head-piece, will generally, during all November,
be quite sufficient clothing ; and these are only to be
worn at night, and during the morning's walk. In
December and January, if it should be cold at night,
the thermometer below fity-five degrees, another
body blanket can be added at nine o'clock. It is
sudden changes from warm clothing to no clothing,
and from warm stabling to cold air, that hurt a horse,
not a cool and uniform temperature. The thermometer, at noon, in the stall, during the cold months,
varies from seventy to eighty degrees.

Fresh air, without a thorough draught ; keeping the stall cool, not cold ; and the horse warm, not hot ; good grooming ; proper clothing ; daily airing of the jhools ; cleanness of litter ; strict attention to the food and water, and punctuality in giving them ; constant regard to the appetite ; careful observance of the dung and urine ; never disturbing while at rest ; stopping the feet every day, and night ; shoeing once in every twenty-five days ; physicking only when actually necessary ; sweating only when actually required ; and enforcing the mildest of treatment,* but at the same time never teasing with kindness, constitute the essence of stable management.

DIFFERENCE OF FORM, ETC.

What description of horse are you about to train ? Is he a slight, or a narrow-chested, or a flat-sided, or a delicate, or a hot fiery horse ; or the reverse of all this ? A powerful-limbed, fine-chested, well circular-barreled, strong, quiet-dispositioned horse : and is he young or old ? for, according as he varies between all these, so must your training vary. Has he been only a short time out of the stables, and just advancing into something of that state we left him in at p. 100, under " EXERCISE," or was he half trained last year, and been kept in tolerably strong exercise, with proportionate hard food ever since ? The latter has a decided advantage ; and if he has been down the

---

* Gora-wallas are seldom known to wrong a horse ; though covering themselves, by mistake, on a cold night with his jhool, and pilfering a little of the evening's feed, are no very uncommon occurrences.

gulph two years, and half trained each year, he has of course a greater advantage still. Racing colts in England, it is true, come to the post at three and four years old, in fine order, most of the great stakes being for young horses ; but a couple of years' extra hard food, with as much exercise as can be given, without rounding the shank-bone or bringing a wind-gall, adds no little to strength and vigour.*

TIME REQUIRED TO TRAIN.

A horse in good hands is deemed capable of proving his utmost speed in five, or, if taken from grass and no exercise, in seven months : many for the Bombay turf, fresh from the Bomb Proof, are brought to the post in three months ; but so short a period is not sufficient, unless they have been in strong and regular exercise for some time previous. Others, again, which have been laid up to fatten and get a decent external appearance, are in this state (only half way to condition) put into training exercise, in the hope of bringing out their full powers in as brief a space, by dint of sweating and galloping :† these, like the former, are almost sure to get thrown over in some way or other, for should their legs prove of that solid texture to stand this hasty training, it is more than their bodies will—they "fly to pieces." The sudden high feeding on grain is also apt to make them foul, or they grow stale, and, if there has been any taint in the pedigree, perhaps sulky into the bargain ;‡ be-

* In India a little more soiling is thought necessary than in England ; and, if so, then a less quantity of physic is needed.

† See the note under "SWEATING."

‡ A good caste Arab will sometimes sulk too ; the General, of 1839 and 40, for instance ; but then the cause, whatever it may be, seldom arises from strong

sides, a three-part bred Arab, though of the most
willing temper, will never stand the training of the
genuine blood. The legs, likewise, sometimes swell
during the day at the commencement of training : this
arises often from debility, and more from the horse
not being ready for a good canter at all, than from
the exercise having been too severe for this stage.
Call, therefore, the first two to six months, according
to the time it may have taken you to putting into
condition ; when you have accomplished that, three
to four more will be ample to carry him up to the
mark.

A DAY'S ROUTINE.

Every morning, precisely at daybreak, your trust-
worthy horsekeeper (if he does not merit that appel-
lation you had better change him, or sleep in the
stable yourself,) is to look quietly in at the stall,
to discover whether the horse is lying down ; if so,
let no noise be made ; there he is to remain till he
voluntarily rises : if standing up, put on the snaffle bridle immediately, for it is just at this time, after the
night's rest, that he will commence nibbling at grass,
one blade of which is hurtful, now that he is going
out to exercise. First, with a perfectly dry towel,
wipe the ointment, given at p. 152, out of the heels,
or the dust and dirt may adhere, and the ointment
become the cause, instead of preventing cracks. One

---

training. The misfortune is, they generally take it into their heads to sulk
the day of the race, by which one would suppose the concourse of spectators
intimidated them, or perhaps reminded them that this is the day of whip and
spur. Gelding will sometimes cure sulkiness, though there should be nothing
wrong with the testicles ; and I should be inclined to risk that operation to
backing an uncertain horse.

gora-walla having been placed on each side, take
off the night-clothes, and brush him down well for
the space of five minutes; then replace one body
jhool and head-piece, &c., or your English set, if you
have them, putting the saddle above. The jockey or
gora-walla is then to mount, ride him to the course,
and walk him about, not at a snail's pace, nor at an
amble, but in the manner described at p. 95, and at
the utmost extent of his walk, for an hour and a half.
The clothes are now to be taken off, the saddle placed
well back, (the work properly of less than a minute,)
and the canter given; after which he is to be walked
till he is cool, then brought into the stall, and the
head tied up *instanter*, one end of each snaffle rein
being buckled forward to the wall, and the mouthing-
bit in his mouth; the heel shackles (with heel ropes
attached, if he is disposed to dance from side to side,)
having been also fastened, the muzzle put on, and
one gora- walla, as at daybreak, placed ready on each
side, take off the saddle, and wisp him down briskly
with dry grass till every hair is smoothed, and the
skin is becoming warm again under the belly as well
as the body; that finished, do the same down all the
legs and fetlocks, till warmth succeeds to the rubbing. The hands are to be used next, to get off as
much hair as possible; the syces must dip them in
water, and heave strongly against his sides, for after
a month all the loose coating ought to be off. One
man will now do, if you cannot spare two, to go on
with the cleaning. Commence first with the curry-
comb, taking care it is not too sharp, and that it is
used very gently if the skin is at all fine or tender,
the curry-comb being only to raise the dust: the
hand-rubber second; and that can scarcely be laid on

too strongly for some horses ; but if the skin and
coat are fine, and the horse restless, that must be
gentle too.   The hair-brush well applied thrice to
the horse and once to the curry-comb, not thrice to
the curry-comb and once to the horse, is to follow
thirdly ; a dry cloth to wipe away all the loose hairs,
fourthly ; and then throw a light blanket jhool over
the body, to be taken off about half-past ten, if the
weather is warm, after he has finished his grain and
grass. Now offer him the small dhool of water ; take
the chill off if it strikes you as cold, or he hesitates to
drink it without, which is often the case in December
and January, in the middle of the day as well as in
the morning, especially if drawn from a well ; then
proceed to the legs, commencing with the hand-rubber, and finishing with the brush.   Lastly, pick the
feet out, and wash them in warm (not too hot) soap
and water ; but above all things, be particularly at-
tentive to drying the heels quickly, not scrubbing
them too strongly, with a coarse towel : when dried,
put on the ointment. The eyes and face may be
washed in the warm water too, with a large sponge,
this being as comfortable to your horse as to yourself. The grain is now to be given : half an hour
afterwards a dhool of water, and then four or five
poolies, nine or ten pounds, of sweet dry grass.*
Half a bedding of litter is also to be thrown down,
(but this may be omitted during the first month,
unless an inclination to lie down in the day is observed,) always putting some of the old well trodden,
that has been dried in the sun, uppermost ; for this
answers three most useful purposes : it prevents

* This is by far too much. Not more than three or four pounds at the
outside ought to be given at any one time.— ED.

any long blades of the fresh bedding running into
the eyes. The sight of two horses I have seen
almost destroyed from this, the thick stem having
nearly cut through the cornea : it is the softest, and
therefore disposes him to lie down ; and not being
fresh, he will abstain from picking at it when he has
finished his allowance of grass. Take away the rem-
nant of the poolies at half-past ten, and leave him undisturbed in a loose state till half-past twelve. Water
is then to be offered, the coat to be brushed, and the
legs to be malished and shampooed. At one, the
mid-day feed, with two or three poolies of grass, and
he is to be left again to himself unapproached till half-
past three or four. The stall at this hour is to be swept
clean, water given, and the afternoon grooming to
take place : the feet and heels are not to be washed
again at this hour, but the morning's ointment is to
be wiped out. About five o'clock put a light single
set of clothes on, (during October and the early part
of November he may go without any at some stations,)
and have him led for an hour, though many, if strong
or fleshy, will do much better ridden at this time also ;
then brought into the stall, well rubbed down with
the hand-rubbers and hair brush, his feet picked, a
little water offered, and the grain given. The bedding is now to be made, a little of the ointment put
in the heels, the clothing changed for warmer, if it
becomes chilly at this time, and as much grass placed
in one corner as you intend he should eat during the
night. At half-past eight give a small feed of grain,
varying from half a mäp up to two mäps, adjust the
clothing, and leave him for the night, as he ought to
have been during the day, in a loose state, unmuzzled,
unheadstalled, and unshackled. Thus you have one

16

day's routine, which is to be adhered to with but little variation so long as he is training.

About one morning in every seven should be a holiday, and Sunday will be a fitting one. Let the walk take place at daybreak, as usual, the saddle being above the clothing ; and whilst out give free scope to his play, and allow him to gape, yawn, move about, and halt at his pleasure. The neck is neither now, nor at any other time, to be kept constrained with a martingale, which impedes the free action of the forelegs, and causes tripping. This annoying rein is sometimes resorted to to keep the horse's head in its proper place, and steady ; but oftener because the rider is unable to keep his own in its proper place, and steady. Unless to a bolter, or a ewe-necked determined stargazer, a martingale should never be used. English young colts, half-broken, may require different kinds of reins and martingales, but a decent rider can dispense with them all upon an Arab.

TRAINING WEIGHT, PHYSIC, EXERCISE, ETC.

You should always train with as near the weight as possible that he is to carry in the race ; never more then an extra half stone, and that is half a stone too much for a slight horse. A strong-legged, straight-spined, high caste animal may not prove the worse for it, but a slighter horse will have his stride shortened an inch in the course of three months, and an inch in every stride will make two or three lengths at the end of a race.* You ought also

---

* There are very few Arabs in India whose owner's weigh above ten and a half stone, that have not their action in some degree hurt ; and a light weight, who is conscious of the nimble active step of a perfectly fresh nag, would detect at once a kind of shortened step, or slight deficiency of spring. By a perfectly fresh nag, I mean a horse that has been taken care of so long as he

to have some idea as to how much flesh your horse can go to training with, so as not to have to sweat off a whole lot, to the detriment of his health, and at the expense of his legs. This is difficult to tell, perhaps, with a new purchase, but a strong-built, good constitutioned horse, will naturally throw up flesh quicker than a slight carcased or irritable one ; and a young horse, (if not quite a young colt,) up to seven or so, will throw it up quicker than after that age ; but whatever description of horse you are about to run, he is to be put well in condition before the training commences ; and if between the age of five and eight, with a large carcase, it is not desirable he should be so plump as one that is rather young, or rather old, slight constitutioned, or flighty ; for these large carcased strong horses, especially just at that age, of five, six, or seven, throw up flesh so quickly that their legs would be in danger, from the great work and sweating required, to draw them out fine. You must endeavour, therefore, at the end of condition (if your object is the turf) to

had a colt's tooth in his mouth, and never had more than eight stone on his back up to five years old. I have mounted numerous " beautiful light going horses" for sale, the property of owners of about eleven stone ; in lieu, however, of fine airy action, they hammered away, in comparison with fresh nags, like so many stone paviers. No man, of course, can be expected to acknowledge this until he has sold his " finest going horse he ever saw." Being a light weight, I would always willingly give three hundred rupees extra for a valuable horse, if he had never been mounted.

A horse frequently pulls up lame from some very trifling wrench or strain, or interfering knock. Halt on the very spot for half an hour, and apply cold vinegar, (a bottle of which should always be taken to the course,) then lead gently home : two days after, you will often find him able to take his canter again, if no subsequent swelling ensues. Further advanced in training, over a hard course, tenderness comes over the feet : poultice for two nights, and put a piece of narrow wax cloth, trebled, between the shoe and the crust : it will remain firm if the crust is rasped level for the shoe.

have more or less flesh on him, according to circumstances.

Presuming, then, that he has been enjoying the cool pendal, devoid of heavy jhools ; that his feet are well open at the heels ; that he is to escape the antiquated and prejudicial drastic purgative · balls, now that he is in good condition, and that you have full three months before the races, commence with one mild drench of physic—the high feeding, and strong exercise, about to be pursued, render this indispensably requisite, as a safeguard against the numerous little ailings that are so apt to arise and cause an overthrow. In accordance, therefore, with the universally adopted precept, that " no horse can run without physic," give the aloes and Epsom salts, &c. ;* and if he belongs to any of the first enumerated class, under " DIFFERENCE OF FORM," he should not purge more than six or seven times, and he must have nothing but walking exercise for the first three days after the physic has set. That over, proceed to the daily canters ; and though he has been in strong exercise before, commence with only a mile and a half : in a week increase it to two miles ; in a fortnight to three, and then quicken the canter, with due regard to the state of his body, &c., never urging him beyond a hand gallop during the first month ; and during the whole time of training he is never to be pressed to his full speed, excepting at the trials ; but the pace is always to go on so gradually increasing, without any irregularity in the distance, that his powers may be arriving at their highest pitch by the commencement of the last fortnight. If you are training for a

* See " PHYSICKING."

long race of three miles, the morning's canter should be nearly four, in order to get "the length" well into him. If for heats of two miles, the canter should be full four, or there is no objection to your giving it of only the length of the heat, walking a quarter of an hour, and then repeating the same. If for a short race, or short heats, the gallop and distance may be proportionably quicker and shorter, but the exercise is never to be so severe as to produce the least distress.

You may put it down as a rule that every Arab, during the first two months of training, should be above his work ; if there is an exception, it is where there are fine, broad, flat limbs, added to a well-formed barrel, and the horse a little sluggish or vicious, then an extra gallop may be taken out of him with impunity, and often with advantage. But the weak points must always be the guiding mark : for instance, when there is a fine round barrel and well ribbed home, yet slight or rather tied-in legs, the latter must be the guiding mark as to the quantity of exercise ; but when the carcase is too small, or flat-sided, with a long hollow flank,—making, perhaps, a rather washy horse—yet the limbs strong, the former must be the guiding mark.

TRIALS.

Towards the end of the second month it will be advisable to take a few trials, that you may be able to judge if he is likely to be qualified for the race you wish. Try a mile and a half with eight stone four pounds, and three days after, the same distance

with ten stone, if he is to run for a welter. After
an interval of another three days, try two miles
and a half with eight stone four pounds, and after
three days more, the same distance with the eight
stone four pounds again. From this you will learn
how he carries weight, and whether he is capable of
running a long or short distance best. In all these
trials push him well, closing the heels to his sides if
of the lazy tribe; but never punish unless he is a
regular sluggard. Continue henceforward taking
trials weekly, or every ten days. At one time start
at score from the post, and keep him to his best pace
the whole way: at another time bound off at a good
gallop, but keep in hand the first half of the distance,
then push him strongly the remainder, always having
every half mile carefully timed: thus you will gain
a wrinkle through what means he is enabled to exert
his pipes to the most advantage, and consequently
when to make play during the race.* In all trials,
unless the horse is of the most willing temper, and
flies by a pull of the ribands and pressure of the calf,
you should have a fresh nag in waiting at the last half-
mile post, to accompany him home; but if you own a
superior known good nag in your stable, which is in
training, it is better to let him start with the one in
trial; there are so few that will exert themselves to
their utmost without a competitor, and it is easy to
tell the rider to hold in the first part, if you wish it.
Previous to taking a trial, or giving a sweat, always

---

* The stride of a well-built running Arab of fourteen hands two inches,
at the top of his pace, on a good turf level course, carrying from eight stone
to eight stone seven pounds, will be found upwards of fifteen feet; and if, when
at this speed, the hind feet overstep the spot the fore ones have quitted,
he has superb springy, and undoubted running action.

put the muzzle on at two in the morning, and the day succeeding a trial or sweat avoid putting him out, for fear of his legs.

THE GRAIN, GRASS, AND WATER.

Bajree and mhut is sometimes used at the commencement of training, but it is not so good as gram. If brought into condition upon it, give it twice a-day for the first fortnight; then once, so as gradually to discontinue it; and it may be crushed a little in the grinding-stone, the same as gram. Gram* and oats, equal parts, would be good, but the oats are seldom procurable. Barley is the only other grain, and a very excellent one it is, but it must not be suddenly introduced. At each feed of gram give half a mäp of barley that has been put in the grinding-stone with the gram, and daily increase it, so as that at the end of two months, one-third barley, and two-thirds gram shall be eaten at each feed. The grain that is relished most will generally be most easily digested; but gram and barley mixed is the most nutritious and best; and with many horses you may go on increasing the barley to one-half. No grain must ever be given new; it should be from eight to fifteen months old, and not more. The grass, of course, should be the very best, the gingwa, having a fragrant small, and stacked after the rains, though a little fresh-dried Huryoli, that has been cut a few days, or a little fresh lucern, may be given at night with advantage; putting it down at nine o'clock, when he has finished his last feed. Gram should be heavy, sweet, and fresh smelling, without holes in it,

* When gram is mentioned, it is always the Chenna or Bengal gram that is meant.—ED.

and a sufficient quantity of it laid in for the four
months, that no change may take place in the quality. When the gram, or barley, are very hard, give
them an extra turn in the grinding-stone, but do not
moisten the grain. If too greedy a feeder, and any
should be voided whole, chop one mäp of Huryoli
grass very small into it at each feed, and also add
one mäp of bran mash,* for the rule is now, in a
measure, to be reversed ; the grain must be proportioned to the exercise, and, therefore, everything must
be tried to make mastication and digestion go on
well. He should love both his food and his work,
then he will thrive. Three drachms of rock or two
of black salt, in every feed, is useful in training to
all kinds of horses : begin with less. You must be
careful to distinguish the difference between a poor
feeder and a little eater : the horse that eats the little set before him with an appetite, increases in
stamina, and keeps his flesh on, is no weak-constitu-
tioned horse, and you should not give to such a one
more than he actually requires. The dung should
always fall in balls at the commencement of training,
and you should endeavour to keep it of the consistence of cow-dung the whole time ; but the high
feeding and strong galloping, and the nature of gram
itself, renders it very difficult, and, towards the last
month, almost impossible to do so. Boiled coltee,
one feed a day, is good for horses that are naturally

---

* If he has a natural dislike to bran, even this handful must not be given,
or it may have an opposite effect, and induce him to swallow down the grain
still more greedily, in order to get rid of the taste of the bran. This would
not be the case, when gram or barley is given while putting into condition all
boiled and mixed with the bran ; then he would be obliged, more or less, to
masticate the grain. A handful of linseed-meal, if not disliked, may be tried
in each feed for this purpose, in lieu of the bran, and it is preferable.

rather lax, as well as others ; or it can be given for the one o'clock feed ; and again at half-past eight o'clock feed ; this, with the cordial ball, will generally keep the dung of a proper consistence, if there is no over-feeding. The dung, towards the later periods of training, is occasionally found, not only a great deal too soft, but slate-coloured, and so slimy and agglutinated, that when lifted up with a cane it will hang on either side without breaking ; hence the horse grows stale : this proceeds from bad stable management in various ways, irregularity, or over-feeding, particularly on gram, over-sweating, or over-work. The cure is bran mashes for two whole days, with four drachms of gum arabic in each mash ; and a little green food in lieu of the dry grass : then the drench of physic, p. 73 ; and this, followed by a few carrots, and the beer tonic, p. 109, daily : boiled sago should also be frequently given afterwards with the *last half* of every feed, and a little linseed meal mixed in the first half, with the gram and barley.

The quality of the water requires as much care as the grain. A change to softer water may not hurt, but from soft to hard infallibly will, and that often too evidently. When it cannot be avoided, three gallons of hot water should be poured on three mäps of bran, and strained off when cold ; or a quarter of a mäp of linseed, and a small lump of ghoor, may be boiled in a gallon of water, and then more cold water added ; either will, in some degree, correct the change; or a little chalk and clay may be added to the water, letting it stand for an hour in the sun. As to training on actual hard water, you might as well try to train on bricks ; a horse will not keep in condition upon it. River water should generally be chosen in

17

preference to well water, as being softer, and ten or
twelve degrees warmer ; but clean well water, if not
harder or colder, is quite as wholesome.   During the
cold weather, water from a deep well, in the early
part of the day, is as warm as river water.   The water
in the cold weather is frequently in the morning too
cold for a horse in training to drink ; but by stirring
your hand round in the dhool for two or three minutes, you may raise it to a proper warmth, without the
addition of hot water, the smell and taste of which,
to many horses, are very disagreeable.   Placing a tub
of water in the stall all day, so that he may drink *ad-
libitum*, is a mistake, arising out of the discovery, that,
when water is always within a horse's reach, and before his eyes, he will drink less than when only watered twice a-day ; but the object is not only that he
should never over-swill himself with water, but also
that it should be drunk at that time that most facilitates digestion.   This tub-system, like the English
one of taking to a pond to water, exercising gently a
quarter of an hour, and then bringing back to the
pond again, may answer very well for some horses,
when putting into condition, but not for training.

QUANTITY OF FOOD, AND HOURS OF FEEDING.

The grain is always to be given in a trough, never in
a tobra ; and if ever he appears indifferent about it, take
it away, and re-examine it : perhaps you are giving too
much, or it may be you fatigued him in the morning.
Never stand coaxing him, therefore, either to eat or
drink ; for there are some horses that, by this means,
may be induced to swallow against their inclination.
See that both are clean and good, but if refused, take
them away till next feeding or watering time.

The more grass that is put before a horse at those times, when it is not left long before him, the better, because he will have the advantage of picking the best out of a lot, and I suppose you do not require to be told that his taste in this respect should have precedence of yours. After morning's feed—as it is all taken away again at half-past ten, and after evening's feed, as you can take away as much as you like, when you look in at nine—it is of no consequence how large a quantity you put down. The grass and water, as a rule, should be very gradually reduced, a little every month ; and the grain as gradually (at the rate of about a quarter of a pound a week) increased ; but the appetite for all must be consulted to a certain extent. If the digestion keeps pace with the appetite, and there is no looseness, well and good ; do not overstrain his stomach in order to see how much he *" really would take in :"* if the appetite is better than the digestion, there must be reduction. The following (supposing he was in good condition when the training commenced) may be considered a fair quantity for a full-sized Arab, of fourteen hands two inches high, actually to swallow in one day and night.

	GRASS. lbs. Of dry Gingwa and Huryoli.	WATER. gallons. five bottles to a gallon.	GRAIN. lbs. Of gram and barley, or partly boiled coltee.
First month, in one day and night..................	9	8	10
Second month, in ditto and ditto...................	8	7½	11½
Third month, in ditto and ditto................	7	7	12½
Last fortnight........	6	6½	13

Remarks.—Gingwa grass, though very fine, is not English hay, neither is gram, oats ; or a little less of the former, and more of the latter, might probably be considered a fair quantity.

Regarding water, the less a horse in training *is inclined* to drink the better, appears an acknowledged axiom : at the same time he is always to have as much as his appetite leads him to take, but not more than three gallons at each watering time.

Thirteen pounds of gram and barley is about seven-teen seers, maps, or powder-canisters' full, when ground.

The Racer must be fed often, yet never till he is hungry, is a maxim in training ; but as much as five maps of ground grain, about three and three-quarter pounds, may safely be eaten at each feed ; and whatever more is required, to the extent of two maps (not beyond), it would be better to give it at half-past eight, to changing the hours to nine, twelve, three, and seven ; the former interferes less with the rest during the day, and the small feed at half-past eight or nine may diminish the wish for grass during the night. Much, however, must necessarily depend on the horse eating largely, and swallowing too quickly. If a large feeder, and quick swallower, and no grass be chopped with the grain, five feeds may be requisite, at nine, twelve, three, six, and nine ; but the first, of nine, one, six, and half-past eight, (the last one always partly consisting of boiled barley or sago,) though not generally adopted, will answer best when properly fed. If you are a determined advocate for the hours of nine, twelve, three, and seven, you should enter upon that system when you commence putting into condition. Feeding at daybreak, even

to the amount of a cutcha seer—the custom with
some turfmen, who always muzzle at night—is not a
good practice, unless for such a voracious feeder as
requires to be fed six times a-day ; and then, after being muzzled all night, it may be necessary. An hour
before would, even then, be better than daybreak.
If an English training groom feeds early in the morning, the exercise does not follow so soon after as it
does in India ; but there are as many little variations
in different stables at home as there are in this country.

MUZZLE, WHEN REQUIRED, LEATHER DHOOL, ETC.

If at any time during training, notwithstanding the old bedding being uppermost, you find
he eats some of it, either during the day or
night, after you have allowed a fair quantity of good
grass, the muzzle, annoying as it is to some horses,
must be used, but not put on till after nine, and then
something must always be given at or before daybreak. In this case, however, you probably commenced training before he was properly in condition ;
for the appetite of a healthy horse is mostly moderate both for dry grass and water, and he can scarcely
contract the habit of feeding too greedily on either
the one or the other, while under this regular regi-
men of training. The circular barreled, large-carcas-
ed, strong horse, is more liable to overeat on grass
than the light carcased ; the last description frequently will not eat enough. Sometimes a horse will eat
half his allowance of evening's grass by ten o'clock,
and not touch it again till just before daybreak, and
then fill himself : this should be discovered, and prevented by the muzzle being put on at two or three

o'clock, when he may not be lying down. Always
give the water four times a-day, allowing the small
dhool once full at each time, with another half-dhool,
if wished for, when he comes home in the evening,
as advised under PUTTING INTO CONDITION. He will
be inclined to drink less, on the whole, in this way,
and thrive the better. You cannot be too particular
with your leather dhool : gora-wallas are always putting currycombs, brushes, and old shoes, in a wood-
en tub ; besides, a tub is not half so nice as an old
dhool, tinged with moss-like green from the continual
use of water. A new tub should have a few shav-
ings burnt in it before being used, and if once taken
to wash the feet, a delicate horse will smell it for a
week.

CORDIAL BALLS, HORSE-BREAD, ETC.

The belly is sometimes a trifle larger than is altogether compatible with training ; the horse may not
be at all too fat, occasionally the contrary, but the
belly droops a little. Feed more liberally, both on
grain and grass, *if* the bowels will stand it, and give
a cordial every other morning ; but even if with this
rather drooping belly he should carry too much flesh,
neither the grain, grass, nor water are to be stinted ;
(over-feeding, which is worse, you have been before
warned against). Give, in this case, six of the alterative balls, p. 74, one every other evening on return
from his walk, and sweat gently once a-week. The
belly will go up of itself, if you are not in a hurry.

If the dung becomes too lax, or you find him getting heavy and out of spirits, and neither caused by
over-feeding ; or if by accident he has been a little

over-fatigued, lessen the exercise a day or two, and give for a couple of successive evenings, at the last half-past eight o'clock feed, one mäp of barley, boiled for two hours, one ditto of sago, and two mäps of bran mash, into which put four drachms of gum arabic and two of rock salt.   Give also the following cordial-ball at daybreak, and a little bajree flour gruel just before his first watering time in the morning.   Cordial ball : —One drachm Columbo root, one drachm gentian, one drachm anise-seed, three-quarters of a drachm of ginger, half a drachm of turmeric, half a drachm of sulphur, one-twelfth of a drachm of bhang, and one-twelfth of a drachm of opium, all finely pounded, and mixed up with the inside of a couple of figs or dates : or boil the figs or dates, skins and all, in a little sugar and butter, then mix in the ingredients.

Cordial balls, two or three a week, or half a one daily, are also indispensable to many delicate horses the last month in training ; and the above is as good a one as at this time can be made up ; yet it is very unpleasant to have to ball a horse continually, however expert the horsekeeper may be in doing it.   A drench is preferable.*   Half, or three-quarters of a pint of warmed beer is the best vehicle for these ingredients, or wash the ball down with the beer.

Horse-bread, though seldom made in India, is beneficial on many occasions during training.   When the muzzle is put on at nine o'clock, and nothing given till feeding-time on return from exercise in the morning, there is a fast of nearly twelve hours.   This is just six hours too long.   Half a loaf of bread, given

* To this I dissent.   As before stated it is always much more annoying to a horse to give a drench than a ball.—ED.

half an hour before daybreak, two hours before the gallop, would be very serviceable to many horses, even when muzzled at ten or twelve o'clock. Three quarters of a pound of gram, or wheat-flour, with three quarters of a drachm of ginger, two drachms of anise-seed, and one ounce of ghoor, baked up together into a large thick ap, can be given instead. The following recipe will make good bread, which the horse will in time grow fond of, if habituated to it by very slow degrees, daily giving a small bit when hungry :—Wheat-flour and gram-flour, of each three pounds ; finely-powdered anise-seed, two ounces ; finely-powdered ginger, one ounce ; ghoor, three ounces. Add the whites of a dozen eggs, well beaten together, and as much beer, well up, as will knead it. Bake in an oven into three loaves, and commence giving when one day old.

BANDAGING.

Training the legs, it appears evident, from the fatness so generally observable about the lower parts, is fully as difficult as training the body ; but if the latter has been properly physicked, yet not over-physicked, the feet kept properly short, and stopped, and the strong galloping not too hastily introduced, the legs may be brouht out as clean and wiry, and the fetlocks as smooth and undented, as during the first canter.

Flannel bandages to the legs are undoubtedly of great benefit, inasmuch as cold applications strengthen the sinews, and keep the legs fine, but the wetting of the bandages every hour annoys the horse and disturbs his rest, and lying down is of greater benefit to

the legs than bandages. Do not take it for granted
that the less a horse lies down in the day the more
he will at night : it is the nature of some horses to
lie down easily, while others, though fatigued, cannot always be induced to do so, even with a dark,
quiet stall, and nice bed. Neat flannel bandages,
kept well wet with cold water, or a little nitre added,
I am a great friend to while putting into condition ;
but, on the whole, it will be quite as well to omit
bandaging in training, unless the state of the legs
seem to require it : which is too often the case, certainly. If bandages are used, do not put them on
again after the walk in the evening.

Dry flannel bandages are used, by those who praise
them, during the whole time of training. They may
be of benefit to some legs ; and they have this advantage, that, if so wished, they may be kept on during
the night ; and the rest is not disturbed by wetting
them during the day.* If worn, they must be put
on a trifle looser than the wet bandages ; but I recommend you to abstain from these, unless you have
some reason for their adoption. Whatever bandage
you choose, be careful to lay the folds even, commencing immediately under the knee, and bringing
each turn as high in front as behind, so that the *bottom of each turn* of the bandage shall be fully as tight
as the top of each turn. Each turn is to descend
exactly one-half of the bandage, yet in such a manner that each looks straight in front. If any part of
the bandage should be tighter than another, it is that

---

* I am an advocate for dry flannel bandages. They promote the insensible
perspiration, and keep the legs of a horse in hard work much finer than wet
ones. They have the advantage also of a horse not being continually annoy-
ed by wetting the bandages, and they can be kept on during the night.—ED.

18

close about the fetlocks, and not immediately under the knee ; an extra piece, of inch-broad flannel, should be tied in front round there to prevent it coming undone, and the same also round the pastern. Dungaree bandages should never enter into a good stable, and a dry dungaree bandage is more likely to cause than to cure a bad state of the legs.

Warm flannel bandages, used for one hour after a severe morning's exercise, (put on after cleaning,) hot water being thrown on them every five minutes, will supple the joints, and prevent swelling ; or, if you prefer shorter work, foment the legs with hot water, as hot as you can bear your hand in, for ten minutes after he is cleaned above ; or let the feet, one by one, stand in the large tub from four to five minutes, with the water *well above the fetlocks*, not forgetting to thoroughly dry each quickly, as it is taken out.

SWEATING.

Sweating would not have to be so much practised if the flesh were only brought to a firm and solid texture before being put into training. A strong dose of physic, and two severe sweats, will, in a fortnight, metamorphose a large carcase into a tucked up, gaunt belly ; but Mr. Green would never attempt such palpable mismanagement as this on a horse that was intended to run to win ; and the legs must be of good timber indeed not to thicken under it. Horses, whose legs have small back sinews, or which are tied in, or are crooked, will, notwithstanding every care bestowed on them, often show an evident inclination, after a good sweat, to counteract Nature's errors in some degree, by throwing out a little more substance

about the hocks and ankles : heavenly creatures like
these were never intended for such wicked work as
this. All heavy sweating is dangerous to slight legs ;
still, sweating must be had recourse to, if the horse is
determined to get fat, when at the same time he is
not overfed : it is an evil, but not so great as having
to physic again. The use of sweating is to take off
the carcase, or neck, any little extra flesh, not deemed
necessary, and which the exercise fails to do ; and
if done at the proper time, and not overdone, the
benefit is often very great ; for, two of the grand desiderata are, to strengthen the legs and diminish the
weight of the body : the continual regular exercise accomplishes the first, and this will effect the
last. A gentle weekly sweat, towards the conclusion of training, is, therefore, necessary for every
horse carrying too much flesh ; it finishes him off, and
draws him out fine ; but with many of the light, high-
spirited, over-willing ones, it may often be wholly
advantageously omitted. If the neck is a little too
fleshy, he should, from the commencement, have a
couple of head-jhools on at the morning's gallop ; the
under one without ears ; but they must be thick indeed to produce any visible effect on this part : the
neck will fine a little of itself as the flesh becomes
firm. If by nature a large bellied horse, and a little
too fat when commencing work, he should always
have one set of body-jhools round him at that time.
Some horses, however, will carry more flesh about
the carcase than others ; and if it is only muscle well
condensed, you perhaps have a trump, and too much
sweating, or extra physic, to draw such a belly over
fine, will often be only running to certain ruin.
Loaded with three complete sets of jhools, a three-

mile gallop, with a couple of half-mile spurts in it, is
as long, and strong, and heavy a sweat, as the most
gluttonous Arab would ever require, if not too rapidly
brought forward. Some turfmen always give the
exercising gallop in one jhool to every kind of horse :
that may do very well in England, but is not so well
suited for India ; it is unnecessary to many, and does
harm to others.

After a sweat, he must be quickly led home,—not
to have other jhools heaped upon him, but all the
lather immediately scraped off with nice bamboo
hoops, not too sharp. The wisping must then in-
stantaneously succeed; or there is great fear of his
taking cold. When cleaned, and the jhool put on,
give the cordial, if you think it required, and then
mix half a wine-glass of ghee, not oil, with half a
wine-glass of brandy, and, immediately the legs are
dried after the washing in the hot water, rub it well
in; about the hocks and ankles particularly. If the
shanks should become sore, rub in the lotion, for
tender shanks, p. 153.

A lot of frothy, greasy, dirty, scurfy stuff, occasionally comes from horses with any superfluous flesh
that have not been sufficiently long in training ; and
some also from others during their first sweat ; so, if
on the second or third sweat he sweats quickly and
with much of this, it is proof he is in a foggy state,
and it must be repeated again in a week or ten days,
giving four or five of the alterative balls, p. 74, one
every other evening, as mentioned before under
" CORDIAL BALLS," &c., if rather too fleshy ; and if
not too fleshy, one drachm of tartarized antimony; and
a quarter of a drachm of ginger instead ; but if he
proves difficult to sweat, (which he generally will by

the third sweating-time, if in condition before the training was commenced, and you are not sweating too hastily,) and that sweat is like water, and he dries quickly after scraping, he is getting into prime trim, and will go on well without any more.*

* To train a horse suddenly up to the!best of his mark the time will admit of, that is not in condition, but all soft flesh, needs a man that has seen a good deal, reflected a good deal, and has great confidence in his own knowledge ; for, as mentioned under, "TIME REQUIRED TO TRAIN," p. 117, he is so very liable to grow stale, or go off his feed, or to injure his legs. After the mild dose of physic, sweating must here be commenced, as well as concluded with, if at all too fleshy, so as to get some of the useless fat out of both the inside and outside, before taking the stronger gallops. When brought home after a morning's sweat, extra clothes, contrary to what is stated above, are to be put over him for a quarter of an hour or more, until he sweats freely in the stall, — in this fleshy case it is necessary, for it acts as a protection against illness ; — and when scraped down and dried, a fresh single set of blanket jhools is to be immediately put on, a small cordial given, and also half a gallon of luke-warm water offered : ten minutes after, he is to be taken out to have another quarter or half mile canter, and then brought in for the regular grooming to proceed. The time for commencing these sweats, the quantity of clothes that he ought to sweat in, the pace that he is to go at, and the length of the sweats, are all difficult affairs to manage properly, for the flesh cannot be taken off too suddenly even in the stall, and the untrained legs will not stand it being taken off in the gallop, on the whole, I would not risk the chance of injury to a favourite horse by this hasty training, however good the stakes might be. If only two months are to elapse before he starts, a gentle sweat every week for the first three weeks, and then a couple of stronger ones the last fortnight, adapting the length, pace, &c., to the size and grossness of the horse, will be near about the proper time, observing that the first sweat should not take place until he can prove his wind,—until he can "blow his nose." After the first two or three morning canters, if he stands panting at the sides, and fails to throw the mucus from his nose, by that peculiar quivering snorting shake of the nostrils, a few days more should elapse before the first sweat is given. Grooms who pay attention to this work, I believe, say the nostrils should always be breathed in three quarters of a minute from the time he is pulled up ; and that some consequence is attached to these minutiæ, I know, for I well remember a groom anxiously looking out for the blow of a fine strong horse, that had been sick for a month, when finishing his first morning's canter, and though it did not occur for a minute or more, it at last came with a fine healthy quaver—a good sign the air passages are clear—and he remarked, "If the tripes only improve, there is no fear of his bellows." A slight horse, when of delicate constitution, will, of course, not have the loud shake in his nostrils of a strong healthy one : and if the horse was thin when commencing this hasty training, the only sweatings must be the last fortnight.

PHYSICKING.

The same kind of remark is applicable here as under " SWEATING." If in good condition, and no soft flesh, when put into training, the one dose at the commencement will generally be all that is required. The shōk that some people have for physicking a month or so before the races, not because the horse is, but because they are afraid of his becoming too plethoric, is the cause of many overthrows and breaksdown. Whatever arguments you may hear to the contrary, this is not the time for preventive physic. The giving daily laxatives also at this stage, and that without a sufficiency of bran mashes, is not only equally censurable, but dangerous and bad, fatal gripes often coming on just when the physic might have been expected to operate.* A craving, large barreled, deep ribbed, strong horse, and that has to run a long race, may sometimes need a couple of doses of purgative physic, besides sweats, during a four months' training, in order to prevent him growing stale in his body, or round in his legs; but a slight, hot, irritable, or weakly one, is not to have every fibre pulled to pieces by drastic physic, even if he does throw up flesh too quickly : three of the alterative balls, p. 74, one every other day, with a couple of gentle sweats, a week between each, will suit much better ; and he will then come to the post in better order, and run under greater advantage than if more purgatives or laxatives had been administered ; besides, it is two to one against physic at this time having the exact effect

* It is incredible what extraordinary things some persons do in training, which had I not witnessed, I should not have thought of mentioning them.

that is wished with a nervous flighty horse ; it very commonly disagrees, or it operates too strongly ; in either case more or less debility ensues, and a month is not sufficient to restore the strength. Should heats have to be run, a pound too much flesh, recollect, is far better, for a light clear-winded horse, than a pound too little. The last description of horses are generally easily purged, and, in lieu of physic, oftener need gruel with four or five cordial balls, or cordial drenches, every week : they should have gentle training, and not be put to trial until within five weeks of running, and then never overtasked.

If a slight sprain, blow, or other injury occurs ; or the space between the shank-bone and suspensory ligament, and between that and the back sinews, should " fill," and there is no time to be lost, a drench of physic may be admissible, as the only means of cooling the leg and preventing loose flesh being thrown up ; and the horse afterwards very gradually brought about by flannel, or *linen* bandages, *single,** being kept on during the day, and wetted every half hour with the sal ammoniac lotion, p. 153. The greatest difficulty, however, always attends the bringing any " go-wrongs" up again, even in the best hands ; and if the sprain has been at all severe, it is useless, as well as cruel, to attempt it, for you run the risk of ruining the leg for life.

As a general rule, then, no purgative physic should ever be administered within six weeks of running. When exceptions do occur, however short time you may have to spare, never be persuaded to ram it

---

* In bandaging for a strain, let the bandage begin at the bottom of the pastern, close to the hoof, and go spirally upwards, instead of downwards.

down the throat without some little preparation, for
if gripes, in training, supervene from this cause, inflammation is generally close at hand.   Bran mashes
should at least be given for one day previous at all
the feeds, and not more than two pounds of grass
allowed until the muzzle is put on at nine o'clock ;
but unless a sprain or hurt has taken place, and the
horse is about to be laid up, more than one day cannot well be spared for bran mashes without his going
somewhat back in condition, for one full day must
also be allowed after the physic has set, so as gradually to increase to the former diet, as any sudden in-
troduction of dry grain into the bowels immediately
the purging ceases is always hurtful, and frequently
dangerous.   At daybreak on the following morning,
water first, the chill being off, and then give the
drench, p. 73, to which you may add three drachms
of Turkey rhubarb,* but as it is of the greatest consequence that a horse in training should purge, and
not be merely sickened with the physic and thus so
many days be lost, if a spoonful even is spilled in the
giving, another should be added, and the clyster
there recommended never omitted : wash the mouth
cleanly afterwards with the salt and water, and if no
strain has been the cause of the physicking, lead for
an hour's walk.   Read "PHYSICKING" in Part II.
for the other precautionary treatment.   If gripes
take place, a quart of warm beer, with three drachms
of ginger, six drachms of anise-seed, and three ounces
of ghoor, may be first tried, not omitting the other

* Rhubarb is found to possess so little purgative action in the horse, that
it is never given by Professional men.   There is nothing equal to aloes, and
nothing better than the aloes ball, when the aloes are good and properly
prepared. — ED.

directions, under " SICKNESS UNDER PHYSIC :" or the following ball, fresh made and soft, to be washed down with a little beer :—Balsam of capivi, half an ounce ; anise-seed, four drachms ; camphor, one drachm, dissolved in half a wine-glass of gin ; oil of anise-seed, one drachm ; the yolk of an egg ; mix. Should the physic operate a little stronger than desired, take chreeate two ounces, anise-seed two ounces ; boil in three quarts of thin rice congee, strain off, and add to the three quarts of congee one ounce of finely-pounded gum arabic, and a bottle of port wine : give a pint, cool, every two hours, allowing some wheat flour gruel also, but no water.

CONCLUSION.

As horses in India are not plated on the morning of the race, shoe three or four days before : you will then see that the shoes fit well ; and always take a couple of extra shoes, with nails and hammer, to the course with you.

The day before running, never give too strong a gallop : a walk will be sufficient, if the slightest disposition to flag was evinced on the previous morning's exercise ; but it is most advisable your training should have been so managed that he should be in that state of trim and freshness to be able to take, and to require, a moderate canter ; but more should not be given.

When stripped for the race, the flesh on the quarters should be as solid as a camel's ; and it should be well on between the last false-rib and the haunch-bone. The carcase should be straight, the belly

19

looking nicely drawn up, and every muscle fully
developed. The coat should be glossy ; the hocks
lean ; the legs and ankles smooth, and cool : and
this is all compatible with the foregoing directions,
which will perfect the wind, and carry him through,
if he can win, as well as if you had attempted a more
mysterious and intricate system.

If you have to start late in the morning, muzzle at
nine, or twelve o'clock, according as you know your
horse, the same as if you were in the first race ; but,
when muzzled early, or starting late, a third of a loaf
of bread should be given a little before daybreak,
about two hours and a half before the running ; some
give half a mäp, or a mäp of ground grain : the bread,
or ap, is preferable.   When the race is run in the
afternoon, as at Bombay, still you should muzzle the
night before, or during the night ; giving the bread,
and a walk in the morning ; only return early, so as
to feed at half past eight, instead of nine o'clock ; and
grant his usual allowance of grain, and also an hour's
eating of grass ; but not more than a gallon and a
half of water at each watering-time : muzzle again at
half-past nine, while he takes his rest till twelve.
At this hour, if eager for water, allow four quarts ;
brush him well, and shampoo his legs, and at half-
past twelve give a seer of ground grain, and also the
third of a loaf of the bread ; or nearly double the
quantity, if he is not to run till after five ; muz-
zling again till three o'clock, when the grooming is
to take place ; and let the jockey that is to ride, give
him a hundred-yard canter a quarter of an hour before starting ; it will stretch his legs, and do him good.

Between heats, wine or spirits are given, with benefit.   Four wine-glasses (thirteen wine-glasses to a

bottle) of sherry or port ; or a wine-glass and a half of brandy, mixed with` two wine-glasses and a half of water, or the same quantity of gin and water, are the proper allowance. Choose from these four according to your fancy ; but take care to give it fifteen minutes before starting. There is always half an hour between heats, so he will have a quarter of an hour's breathing-time to be rubbed down in, before swallowing it. Give it two or three minutes earlier in preference to two or three minutes later ; this is of consequence, in order to have the desired effect ; but do not half stifle him with " blue ruin" the instant the heat is over, or he will be flying under, instead of over, the turf.

If, after a hard-contested race your horse's powers should have been over-strained and his strength exhausted, rub him quickly dry, put the jhool on, and lead him under a tree, or to a cool, shady spot ; then give four drachms of carbonate of ammonia, powdered, and made into a ball with water and linseed-meal ; after which, handrub the legs well, give a little water to drink, and a cold bran mash. Lastly, lead him into a cool, open stable, and leave him in a loose stall, with a large bed under him. Look in an hour or so afterwards, and if the distress should still appear to be great, the breathing quick, the flank tucked up, and the eye red, take away from three to four quarts of blood, and leave him again to himself for twelve hours.

The racer cannot be kept in that excited state at the top of his condition for any length of time : " At the top of condition, on the brink of disease." And if he has to run at other races five or six weeks afterwards, the exercise and food should be moderately lowered for a fortnight, and a few carrots, a little green meat, and evening's boiled food given ; but whether he has been trained up to his full mark, or not, it does not invariably follow he is to be physicked again ; that must depend on the state of the body, and when he received the last dose.

If two months are to elapse, the drench may be given, varying in strength according to circumstances, and followed by refreshing for a few days with carrots, green meat, &c. ; but, if only half that time, it will be better avoided.

Coming out of training, never let your horse down all at once, but always give a gentle canter every other day, for the first fortnight, gradually reducing the grain ; and if after that time you deem physic necessary, give the alterative drenches, p. 74, without any calomel at night.*

RIDING ; ENTERING FOR A RACE ; AND REQUITING

A QUERULOUS VISITOR.

Riding a race is as different from all other riding as a Scotch salmon is from all other fish ; and as many aspirants for a silver cup, unable to afford rac-

---

* On a visit to a racing-stable, at half-past ten at night, containing four horses in training, I was introduced to the following stable-management. The first horse had heel-ropes on, and those so tight that they prevented him lying down. The second, a large and gross feeder, had the muzzle off—if a little hard piece of leather with circumference scarce sufficient for a dog's mouth can be termed a muzzle—fortunate, therefore, it was off, for the animal would have been stifled by morning. The third was half-strangled, from the tightness of the neck strap of the head-stall. The fourth was smothering under two heavy jhools, and purging away from over-feeding ; yet the old, careless griffin of a master had been successful the year before. Who shall despair to win after this ?

ing establishments, both train and jockey their own
steeds, let me advise you not to give up your own
natural-formed seat for one you have never tried before. Do not stick your back up like an angry cat,
striving to imitate William Buckle, or any other celebrated rider ; but keep your middle person from the
waist to the knees firm, yet flexible, grasping well
with your thighs, and resting the weight mostly in
the saddle, not in the stirrups ; and if you have occasion to use the spur, apply it as far under the belly
as the legs can reach. The management of the arms
is even of greater consequence : you may have as
strong a seat as a first-rate hog-hunter, and yet ride
a horrible race, from not keeping a steady unjerking
pull (not a dead pull) on the mouth. The man who
has trained the horse is the only individual who can
direct the most advantageous way in which he should
be ridden ; though the person that has daily acted
as jockey, if not a goose, must, of course, be able to
form some opinion likewise. If you are about to
ride a hard-mouthed horse, always put a bit and curb
on ; and this should have been done in training : for
if in taking his exercise-gallops he once runs away,
he will be continually attempting the same trick : for
having now got to know his speed, he will be on the
look-out to break away with you in any part of the
race, perhaps swerve, or bolt ; and he will rarely strug-
gle honestly when challenged for the rally in ; but,
while he should always be prevented from all chance
of running off, you need not go into the other extreme, and throw him out of his stride, either at
starting, or during the race, by an endeavour to
restrain him too much when from over-eagerness you
see he will not suffer it ; it is better, in these cases,

notwithstanding any instructions you may have received as to lying by, to allow the horse partly to
make his own race : you can try to ease him a little as
this over-eagerness subsides. In riding a match, a
good caste horse against an indifferent caste one, always, after the first hundred yards, rate him well
the whole way so as to make him fairly shut up by
the time he arrives at the distance post ; for his object, if he is up to it, will be (thus over-matched) to
make a waiting race of it.

You cannot expect to carry off all you start for
the first season of your novitiate : added to muscle,
bone, blood, make, a good constitution, good training,
and good riding, you must use the greatest discrimination as to entering for a long or a short race, or long
or short heats, and also to the weights. Some horses
will fly with eight stone, yet prove very sorry with
ten stone. Some will carry the ten stone well enough
for a single race, yet fail in heats. Besides this, the
course being hard or soft, light or heavy, dry or wet,
up hill, down hill, or level, all and each make a wonderful difference in performance. There is not a
horse in existence who, in some race or other, will
not gain an advantage from one of these causes.
Straight pasterns and tender feet, for instance, are
not adapted to a hard course, nor slight legs and
slanting pasterns to a heavy one ; so, however confi-
dent you may be in having the best horse, never be
too sanguine as to gaining : the best horse is rarely
the best for all descriptions of races, weights, and
courses.

Many beginners are much dissatisfied at strangers
or acquaintances running down their horses. No-

thing is so favourable.   I never wish to hear a horse
of mine praised, unless on the day of sale.   If a man
tells you the neck is too thick, say yes, and the nostril is a little too closed : if he declares the quarter to
be short, say yes, and rather wanting muscle ; and,
for every point he complains of, you name another.
By good management, neither too acquiescing nor
too differing, you may turn to good account a querulous visitor of this kind, and lighten him of a gold
mohur for each of his mistaken notions.   These first-
sight, guess-work observations, half to three parts
wrong on an average, are frequently changed by the
utterers themselves in a week, and although your stud
may not be perfection, yet, as all must be judged by
comparison, it is not improbable that his and many
others are much worse ; consequently, instead of being discomfited, always give plenty of encourage-
ment to whoever intrudes his critical remarks, strictly
coinciding in their general correctness ; and when the
first pause occurs, ask, (if you know your horse,)
what odds he will give against the ill-proportioned
one ?   If he takes the bet kindly, do not be in a
hurry ; wait a day or two, then offer to double it : in
this way you turn the tables on him genteelly.
Every person has a right to look at your horse going
his rounds, and also at rubbing down afterwards,
when done on the public course.   A bystander can
never dive into the real state of his condition by a
few minutes' superficial glance at the external appearance ; it is more likely to puzzle and mislead,—
so rather court than avoid inspection here.   Your
" dark" horse will not grow lighter by this little
piece of complaisance ; but if ever you admit either
stranger, acquaintance, or friend inside his stable for

half a second without being present yourself, it will
be useless your denying your relationship to our
" useful" friend at p. 203.

STOPPING FOR THE FEET.

Equal parts of tar and kidney mutton fat boiled
together, and first laid over the frog only, then cow-
dung over the whole. A piece of sponge, or thick
numbda, cut the shape of the sole, and kept over it
by two transverse slips of bamboo fitting under the
shoe, and wetted with hot water every three hours,
should be used occasionally instead of the cow-dung,
as it gives a nice soft pressure to the sole ; a little of
the tar stopping being always previously laid over
the frog, if deficient, to encourage its growth and
save it from rotting.

OINTMENT FOR THE HEELS, AS A PRESERVATIVE
AGAINST CRACKS.

One pound of hog's or mutton-kidney fat, boiled
down to the softness of ghee ; two ounces of sugar
of lead, well mixed in afterwards. The heels to be
very slightly smeared over after washing at nine in
the morning, and after being cleanly wiped out on
return from walk in the evening. Whenever the
slightest crack appears, always poultice for one day
with a little fat, linseed, bran, and a mashed turnip,
carrot, or piece of melon, all boiled together, omitting
the canter on the following morning : after which,
equal parts of finely-powdered burnt alum and cala-
mine powder, mixed, should be put on the cracks

morning and evening, at the same hours as before, having first washed them with warm soap and water. The former ointment is not to be omitted.

LOTION FOR TENDER SHANKS.

The leg, from the knee to the fetlock, often becomes very sore after sweating or galloping on hard ground, and he flinches when being hand-rubbed, which he never did before. Having fomented each leg for five minutes, as high as the knee, in a tub of rather hot soapy water, and *gently* dried them, warm and rub in *gently* with flannel, morning and evening, the following lotion :—Boil four ounces of bruised poppies, and four ounces of nim leaves, in four quarts of water ; strain off two quarts, and add three ounces of camphorated spirits.

SAL AMMONIAC LOTION.

Four ounces of crude sal ammoniac (almost always procurable in the bazaar), and one ounce of sugar of lead, dissolved in three pints of vinegar and one of water.

Cough Ball —

2 Ck? Assafœtida

1 do Goor

1 do Ginger Powdered.

Make into 15 Balls & give 3 a day,

[20] hour before feeding time. —

PART IV.

TREATMENT OF A FEW DISEASES.

No one but a skilful professional man can possibly treat a quarter of the diseases of horses properly ; and it often requires great experience, and the most able scrutiny, to be able to discern, or sometimes even to guess, what is the matter with a horse, or in what part he may be lame. This Part, therefore, while adapted to as full a practice as the most learned amateur can ever safely venture on, is written merely to prevent your outstripping the bounds of prudence : but these remedies must occasionally be resorted to, for, under inflammations and affections of the feet, &c., when assistance cannot be obtained, to do nothing, is to let the horse either die or be ruined. Remember, however, " prevention is better than cure ;" and if you diligently read over Part III. once in every month, and follow in that track, you will have little need for Part IV. But I must here again remind you, an Arab horse is not an English horse, nor is India England ; and consequently, I advise you to adhere as strictly as possible to the directions I lay down, and not foolishly to alter the quantities of physic, or substitute other ingredients, or give them at different intervals than those prescribed, without first consulting some per-

son who is capable of fully explaining to you the nature of the illness, as well as the virtues of the phar-
maceutical compound.

In all diseases of the sudden acute kind, a horse's
fate is decided in less than one-half the time a man's
would be ; consequently, you cannot be too prompt
in rendering relief ; at the same time, never commence with either lancet or physic till you have formed some idea of the nature of the malady ; the grand
art consists in " giving the proper medicine, in the proper dose, and at the proper time ;" so rather stand by
the animal for half an hour with the book in your
hand, watching the symptoms as they gradually present themselves ; for there are few amateurs who would
not very frequently save their horses, if they would
only wait and discover the disease, before commencing with their ever-ready fleam and dirty aloes; after
which it often becomes impossible to tell what the
complaint really is ; and hence the horse is lost.

CLASS I.   Sickness under Physic.
            Overpurging.
CLASS II.   Gripes.
CLASS III. Cold.
            Sore Throat.
            Influenza.
CLASS IV.   Strangles.
            Swelling of the Glands under the Jaw.
CLASS V.   Fever.
CLASS VI.   Inflammation of the Lungs.
            „   of the Bowels.
            „   of the Liver and Spleen.
            „   of the Stomach.

Class VI.   Inflammation of the Heart.

     „   of the Kidneys, the Neck
              of the Bladder, and
              Bladder.

     „   of the Feet.

     „   undiscoverable.

Class VII. Red Urine.

       Bursantee.

CLASS I.

SICKNESS UNDER PHYSIC

is caused, firstly, by the ball breaking in the mouth, and half of it, perhaps, sticking there for a couple of hours ; secondly, by the physic being too strong ; thirdly, by the horse not having been sufficiently prepared, or by having been suffered to drink too much cold water, or to eat too much, or to other bad management.

Symptoms of the first :—The horse looks dull, hangs his head, and the saliva is black with the aloes. Treatment :—Give whatever remains of the ball, adding another drachm or two to it ; for, at least, that quantity is generally slobbered away before it is discovered ; and wash the mouth out with salt and water.

Symptoms of the second :—Looks dull, and hangs his head, as before ; generally coming on towards the evening of the day the physic is given. Treatment : —If you think you have given too strong a dose, keep him perfectly quiet, with a bed to lie down on. By not giving any exercise, and only very little grass and water when it commences to work, it will, perhaps, not operate more than is desired : if it does, see " OVER-PURGING."

Symptoms of the third:—Looks dull, hangs his head, lies down gently, and occasionally, though seldom, rolls, throwing himself on his back, and yet without appearing griped. Pulse, natural. Treatment :—Leave this state alone too : it will sometimes occur, even when the horse has been properly prepared, and the physic good ; but if the uneasiness continues for an hour, or more, throw up a clyster of warm salt and water. At other times, all the symptoms of severe gripes come on, and you must be quickly on your guard. Back-rake immediately ; then clyster with two ounces of soap and two ounces of common salt, in a gallon of thin warm rice congee. Then drench with one drachm of oil of peppermint, or three drachms of finely-grated ginger, and one ounce of Epsom salts, in a quart of thin warm rice congee ; and throw three gallons of hot (hot enough to burn and make him flinch, but not scalding) water over his loins and belly. The whole of this, excepting the back-raking, to be repeated every hour ; trotting *gently* in the interval.* If, after three hours, the symptoms should not be alleviated, and the pulse should rise beyond sixty, take away three quarts of blood, continuing the above treatment. Should the physic be operating, or immediately it begins to do so, there must be no exercise ; the Epsom salts must be left out of the drench ; and the clyster be composed of one quart of thicker congee, with a teaspoonful of laudanum in it.

* Trotting in such cases I disapprove of.—ED.

If a horse purges more than twenty times, he must be considered over-purged ; and, if unattended to, inflammation may succeed.

Treatment :—Continue the gruel, as directed under " PHYSICKING," till you have given it six times ; then change to the following : four drachms of prepared or common chalk, three drachms of gum-arabic, one drachm and a half of catechu, and one drachm and a half of anise-seed, well mixed in a pint of arrowroot, or thick rice congee : give this every four hours. The legs to be, also, well hand-rubbed every four hours ; and, in the interim, bandaged up as high as the knees in flannel or grass ; and, if the weather is cold or damp, the jhool and head-piece to be put on. He should have a large soft bed, but be muzzled, if inclined to eat; and not a particle of grain, grass, or water given. After three drenches of the above, that is, after twelve hours, if the purging remains undiminished, add to it a quarter of a drachm of opium and a quarter of a drachm of alum* and give the same, also, by clyster, increasing the quantity of arrowroot in the clyster to a quart. There will be no danger of fatal inflammation, and very little of the bowels being injured, if this treatment is fairly adopted ; but if you allow the over-purigng to go on for twelve or eighteen hours, and then suddenly stop it with over-doses of opium or catechu, you will, most probably, as suddenly stop his breath at the same time. Should the purging, after another twelve

* Half a drachm of the former and a drachm of the latter may be added with advantage.—ED.

hours, still continue unabated, the distress appear great, and the legs and ears cold, he will be in much danger : blister the belly, take away three quarts of blood, and give the medicine, both by mouth and clyster, every three hours.

Blister for the belly.—Half a pound of flour of mustard, one ounce of spirits of turpentine, two drachms of finely-powdered Spanish flies, and half a pint of linseed-oil ; to be made into a paste, and spread on dungaree a foot square, with a jhool underneath it ; or else spread on the inside of a sheepskin, and kept close to the belly for two or three hours, by bandages tied over the back.*

On recovering from violent over-purging, a seer of well-boiled ground grain, (gradually increasing to two,) one mäp of bran mash, and three drachms of gum-arabic, should be given at each feed for a week ; wheat, or bajree flour gruel, sweetened, always at the first watering time in the morning ; only two gallons of water at each drink, and that with the chill off ; very little grass after each feed ; a little dried lucern, of the previous day's cutting, is best ; and for the first three days, not moved from his loose stall.

But inflammation may also come on from the badness of the aloes, (if the stuff sometimes procured from the bazaar can come under that name,) or from improper ingredients being mixed up, or from the physic being given when the bowels were overloaded ; as well as being caused by over-purging, and the then deadly sudden stopping of the purging with strong astringents. The symptoms are the same. A quick small pulse, from fifty to eighty, and scarcely to be

* It ought, however, first to be well rubbed in for twenty minutes.—ED.

felt; heaving at the flanks; distressed countenance, and eyelids very red : the feet also become cold, and the hind leg, up at the stifle, sometimes trembles violently. Treatment :—Bleed four quarts, or more if the horse looks as if he could stand it : blister the whole of the belly, tying the jhool over it : put each foot in water, as hot as he can bear, for ten minutes, drying each quickly as it comes out ; then rubbing till well warm, and bandaging half way up to the hocks and knees in flannel.* Clyster with thin, warm rice congee, if the bowels are not open ; and drench, also, with a quart every hour. Put on warm clothing, if it is cold weather : but the irritation having been so great as to produce inflammation, he generally dies.

CLASS II.

GRIPES

are caused by drinking cold water, especially when heated by exercise ; or too much water immediately after feeding ; or by exercise, immediately after feeding ; or by over-feeding. By green food with the morning's dew on it ; or too much green food suddenly given ; or too much, even when accustomed to it. By change of grain. By the cold air. By want of exercise. Also, when the attacks are frequent, perhaps by some occult disease existing in the bowels.†

---

* Instead of half way, it ought to be up to the hocks and knees in flannel.—ED.

† Gripes are more often caused by indigestion than any thing else.—ED.

Symptoms.—The pain comes on quite suddenly ; he paws the ground ; looks round to his sides ; rolls, and rolls over ; tries to strike his belly with his hind feet ; and breaks out into a perspiration : gets up again in a few minutes, shakes himself, and not unfrequently begins to eat. Almost all these exist, in a greater or less degree ; and, after a short interval, they all return. The belly is sometimes tremendously swollen ; I have seen it like a bullock's struck dead by lightning, and he groans heavily.*

GRIPES.

Distinguishing Symptoms between it and Inflammation of the Bowels.

The ears, and legs, and feet are scarcely ever cold till after the perspiration breaks out ; and, when rubbed dry and warm, they do not become cold again till after he breaks out into another sweat. In inflammation of the bowels they are always cold, and though good friction will make them warm, they quickly become cold again.

The pain decreases after a trot ; and when brought back to the stall he often stands quite quiet for two or three minutes, as if perfectly recovered. In inflammation, the pain increases after a trot. There are, also, short intervals of ease during gripes, but none during inflammation.

* This inflation of the belly is from the presence of gas emitted by undigested and fermented food. The best remedy is, one ounce aromatic spirits of ammonia, and four fluid ounces of solution of aloes given in a pint of warm water, with copious clysters.—ED.

In gripes, he often rolls quite over : in inflammation very seldom.

In gripes, he frequently commences picking at grass : in inflammation, I believe, never.

Rubbing the belly relieves the gripes : it increases the pain in inflammation.

The pulse is generally natural at the commence- ment of gripes, becoming fuller and quicker after a couple of hours or so, but not rising above sixty. In inflammation, it is never natural, but much accelerat- ed at the commencement of the disease ; not full, but small, and scarcely to be felt, and rising in four or five hours to eighty or ninety, or more.

Gripes, are not so often mistaken for inflammation of the bowels, as inflammation of the bowels for gripes.

Treatment.—Gripes from bajree and mhut. These are generally easily cured. Three drachms of finely- powdered black pepper in a quart of hot, (do not burn his throat,) greasy mutton broth.*

Gripes from curby.—Three drachms of finely-pow- dered black pepper, and a quarter of a drachm of mustard, in half a pint of warm ghee.

Gripes from green meat.—Two drachms of finely- powdered black pepper, a quarter of a drachm of cay- enne ditto, and one ounce of tincture of opium, in a pint of warm congee.

Gripes from cold water.—Four ounces of sweet spirits of nitre, and one drachm of finely-grated gin- ger, in a pint of warm milk.

Gripes when severe, or the belly is greatly swollen. —Six ounces of linseed-oil, three ounces of spirits of

* The treatment recommended in the last note is preferable.—ED.

turpentine, one ounce of tincture of opium, three drachms of finely-powdered aloes, and one drachm of oil of peppermint, mixed.*

Gripes when the horse is known to have worms.—Three quarters of a pint of linseed-oil, and three ounces of spirits of turpentine, mixed.

Gripes when the horse has sore throat or influenza.—Three quarters of a pint of linseed-oil, one ounce and a half of sweet spirits of nitre, and one ounce and a half of tincture of opium, mixed.

Gripes when the bowels are very costive.—The same as that for worms.

Gripes when the bowels are well open, or loose.—One ounce of tincture of opium, and one drachm of oil of peppermint, or three drachms of ginger, in half a pint of warm congee.

Gripes which come of themselves.—One ounce of onion juice, in half a pint of warm ghee ; or three drachms of aloes, and one ounce of tincture of opium, in half a pint of warm water. Or half, or three quarters of a pint of brandy, gin, or rum, in a pint of warm water.

Should the first dose of any of these not relieve in twenty minutes, always back-rake ; after that, clyster,† repeat the drench, and throw hot water over the loins and belly, and continue doing these last three every hour, till cure takes place, trotting gently in the in-

---

* The aromatic spirits of ammonia and solution of aloes will be found preferable to this also. If there is not evident relief in two hours, the aromatic spirits of ammonia without the aloes ought to be repeated, and copious clysters of warm water and soap every half hour.—ED.

† Clysters ought always to be administered from the first appearance of internal pain.—ED.

terval ; but always give the same dose twice, or, if
you like, thrice, before changing to another. If it is
a severe case, and no relief obtained after three doses,
that is, after two hours and a half, take away three
quarts of blood.*

The first clyster, may be two ounces of spirits of
turpentine, and two ounces of onion juice, in a gallon of thin warm congee. When it is time for the
second, for the bowels have not been opened, the clyster every hour should be four drachms of aloes, or
eight ounces of Epsom salts, with six ounces of ghoor,
in a gallon of thin warm congee ; but if he has dunged freely, and the pain should still continue, each
clyster should consist of two ounces of tincture of
opium, in only a quart of warm congee.

Do not forget to change the clothing, if any has
been on, that has become damp with the perspiration.

Doubtful Symptoms.—If the symptoms are not very
clear, and you are frightened lest it should be inflammation, give half a pint of linseed-oil, and two ounces of spirits of turpentine, mixed, which repeat, in
half an hour, with one ounce of tincture of opium†
added ; and let the clyster be two ounces of soap, and
two ounces of salt, in a gallon of thin warm rice
congee.

For the first twenty-four, or, if the gripes have
been severe, the first forty-eight hours after recovery,
give only one mäp of boiled grain, and two of bran

---

* See " BLEEDING," p. 62.

† Half a drachm of unadulterated or purified opium, is reckoned equal to
about one ounce of the tincture. If you have none of the tincture ready,
macerate the half drachm in a small wine-glass of brandy.

mash, at each feed ; the water with the chill off, and very little grass.

Gripes in India are very common, and the cordial quart of Hodgson, with three drachms of finely-grated ginger, six drachms of anise-seed, and three ounces of ghoor, is, after all, the most grateful cure : and one that is generally at hand. In giving it, you may omit the little point of mistaken politeness, you so generously offer to your friend at dinner, begging him "not to wait," but to swallow it down, fixed air and all, the instant it is poured out. You are now only treating the inside of a horse, and that un- der disease, which, having too much wind already there, will not be cured by another quart being thrust down his gullet. Pour the beer into a clean cooking- pot ; then put in the ginger, anise-seed, and ghoor, and stir it round whilst on the fire warming : in this way the stimulants become properly incorporated with the beer.

CLASS III.

COLD.

A thorough draught, or letting a horse stand still when heated by exercise, are almost as frequent caus- es of cold in this country as in England. Stripping off the jhool in the cold weather, and then taking him out of the warm stall to be led for his morning's walk, or, at the gora-walla's option, to stand still, common sense must tell you will chill ; and suddenly bringing a horse from the open mydan, in cold wea- ther, into a close Bombay stable, has an equal tendency to produce cold or inflammation. During the months that are very cold, if you purpose riding at daybreak, and your horse is used to a comfortable stall, always keep as much clothing over the saddle as he had on at night, until brought out, and then, when you mount, give a trot for the first quarter of a mile. This may appear over particular ; but, on getting out of bed in January, at daybreak, walk out yourself without dressing.

Symptoms.—The same as in the human being.

Treatment.—Decrease, and boil the grain, and mix one mäp of hot bran mash with it, or more, if he is fond of bran ; decrease the grass also, giving lucern or green grass instead ; take the chill off the water by boiling a handful of linseed, and a lump of ghoor in three quarts of water, then adding to it two gallons of cold : clothe him a little warmer than usual if it is cold, but let the stall be open, well open, and cool, not damp. If he coughs, put a drachm of antimonial powder, and three drachms of nitre in two wine-glass-es of hot water, and then mix with three ounces of the simple oxymel, and give it twice a-day, before his morning's and evening's mash, which must now have less boiled grain in them ; and do not exercise him beyond a walk. If the cold is very bad, he must not be moved from his loose stall, but clysters of warm soap and water used every other day. In some of these severe colds, when the pulse is much quick-ened, the glands below the ears perhaps swollen, the skin dry, and the running from the nostrils thick and plentiful, taking two or three quarts of blood is necessary, giving six ounces of Epsom salts in a pint of thin warm congee, every morning and evening,

until it begins to operate.* Should the cold and
cough not be of this severe acute kind, but remain
hanging on him ten days or more, and the pulse be
under forty-two, leave off the antimonial powder,
&c., and resort to the mild beer tonic stimulant, p.
109, once a-day, in the morning ; giving also half a
drachm of asafœtida in half of one of the fried vegetable bringals, every afternoon. A little of the Bam-
boo-ke-puttah, is also useful in this case.

Simple Oxymel.—Two pounds of honey and a pint
of vinegar, simmered together over the fire.

If a horse takes cold, and, instead of becoming feverish, remains cold, perhaps slightly shivers, which
sometimes happens, the hot instead of the cooling
treatment may be begun with. A pint of warm beer,
with two drachms of ginger and one drachm of camphor dissolved in it may be given, which repeat in
twelve hours, the grain being boiled, and mixed
with a hot mash.

A horse is seldom the better for having a cold
hanging on him a week or ten days, and nothing is
more annoying than hearing a favourite one cough-
ing ; therefore these easy directions should not be
neglected : besides, as colds of all kinds (both feverish colds, when the pulse is quickened, the skin dry,
and the breath hot, &c. ; and those when the pulse

---

* The following treatment is better ; half a drachm of digitalis, one drachm
tartar emetic, one drachm aloes, and three drachms of nitre made into a
ball, given morning and evening until the faces become softened, after which
the aloes ought to be omitted. The glands below the ears and the throat well
rubbed in with the following liniment. Liquor ammonia two parts, spirits of
turpentine one part, and olive oil three parts. The head well steamed twice
a day and a hood put on. Clysters of warm water and soap every morning.—ED.

is not quickened at all, and the running from the nostril remains thin `and watery) are so liable to lay the foundation of rheumatism, or leave the horse more or less debilitated, and pre-disposed to take on other disease, the beer tonic, p.· 109, should always be given every morning for a week after the cold has gone off; or when given during a chill or lingering cold, be continued for a day or two longer.

For a horse in training, or that is sufficiently in vigour and spirits to work off a slight cold in his exercise, three quarters of an ounce of nitrous æther in half a pint of warm beer, may be given, for three successive nights : or four drachms of nitre, one drachm of black pepper, one drachm of anise-seed, quarter of a drachm of opium, and one ounce of honey or ghoor, to be put in the half pint of beer. A hot bran mash should be added to the evening's grain, for these three nights, and the bowels also once opened by a clyster consisting of one and a half ounce of soap and three drachms of aloes, in a gallon of warm water.

SORE THROAT.

Severe cold, or a cold neglected, may have. sore throat connected with the cough, which is sometimes a serious affair.

Symptoms.—The food is not properly swallowed, but lumps of grass are often quidded out again. The water is not freely gulped ; he sips and slavers in the dhool ; it, in fact, hurts him to swallow it. The discharge from the nose is thick ; mucus is coughed up, and the cough is so painful that he sometimes stamps

22

with his foot. There is a wheezing noise when he breathes, and the glands below each of the ears are often swollen.

Treatment.—Take away *two* quarts of blood ;* in this case never more than three. Blister the throat. Give half a drachm of digitalis,† one drachm of antimonial powder, and three drachms of nitre, dissolved in two wine-glasses of hot water, and then mixed in three ounces of the simple oxymel, p. 168, three times a day. As much warm bran tea‡ as he will drink should also be given, and the dhool held up as high as the chest, that he may not be distressed by lowering his head. Not more than half a seer of boiled grain must be put into each bran mash, but lucern or green grass should be put in the trough as high as his chest. Dry grass irritates the throat ; so, if no green meat is to be had, more boiled food, as turnips, carrots, &c., should be allowed instead. He must be left to his loose cool stall, with a bed, and well jhooled at night and the early part of the morning, if it is the cold weather. The digitalis is to be discontinued after three days, and the antimonial powder and nitre, after six. The bowels must be opened by clysters every other day, consisting of one ounce of soap, and four ounces of Epsom or common salt, in a gallon of warm water.§

---

* See "BLEEDING," p. 62.

† The treatment the same as recommended in Note at page 168, with the addition of bleeding if the horse is in high condition, also blistering the throat sharply.—ED.

‡ See "BRAN TEA," p. 71.

§ Clysters of warm water and soap ought to be used every day.—ED.

fortunately, is hardly know in India ;* but severe
colds and sore-throats are not uncommon, both in the
hot and cold weather ; and if these were properly attended to and taken care of at their commencement,
and the horse, on recovering, neither over-fed, nor
allowed to drink too much gruel, which often brings
back the complaint in all its force, requiring a second
bleeding, added to the greatest care, to save him from
danger, we perhaps should see nothing resembling it.
The real epidemic may, however, some day be trans-
ported here : it is said to be very infectious, and that
when it does visit a neighbourhood, many cases will
occur about the same time.

Symptoms.—At the commencement of the disease,
the coat is a little rough, the breathing somewhat
hurried, the eyes inflamed, and the throat sore ; hence,
the swallowing is difficult, the food and water being
sometimes returned through the nostrils : a discharge
also takes place from them, as well as from the mouth,
and the legs are swollen.   Fever is present, and great
weakness.   The pulse varies, being in some patients
only fifty ; and in others, ninety ; depending on the
degree of fever.

Treatment.—*If* the pulse is full or wiry, and above
fifty-five, and the membrane inside the nostril red,
bleed three quarts ;† ‡ and *if* the dung is hard, give

---

* So far from this being the case on this side of India, it appears almost
yearly in an epidemic form. I have repeatedly, year after year, had from two
to three hundred on my sick list with this disease.—ED.

† See "BLEEDING," p. 62.

‡ Bleeding ought to be resorted to with great caution, unless the horse is in
high condition, and the inflammatory symptoms run high, it is likely to do more

three-quarters of a pint of linseed-oil, with a drachm
of ginger in it.   Clyster with a gallon of warm water,
and four ounces of Epsom, or common salt.   Insert
a seton in the chest, and also at the top of the neck,
and blister the throat.   Foment the legs with hot
water, and keep the stall cool.   The following morning, if the pulse still continues full and quick, and the
membrane inside the nostril is redder than usual, bleed
again three quarts ; but no more purgative physic is
to be given.   If a second bleeding is not required,—
or, if it is, then, after twenty-four hours, give three-
quarters of an ounce of carbonate of ammonia, and
three-quarters of an ounce of nitrous æther, twice a
day, at eight and four : also, two drachms of nitre,
one drachm and a half of gentian, one drachm and a
half of colombo-root, and one drachm and a half of
ginger, twice a-day, when the stomach is a little empty, at twelve and six :* these last balls may be washed
down with a half pint of beer, or a quarter of a pint
(a wine-glass and a half) of port wine, mixed with a
wine-glass of water.   Clysters, if the bowels are not
open, and hot fomentations to the legs, must be used
every day ; and if the legs continue much swollen,
they are to be scarified.   The first twenty hours,
while the physic is in his inside, feed on sweet fresh

harm than good.   Prostration of strength and debility is so great and rapid,
that every drop of blood is wanted. The following treatment I have generally
found successful. The bowels gently stimulated with from two to three drachms
of aloes, and daily clysters of warm water and soap. The throat sharply blistered and the head steamed twice a day with boiling water poured on hay, and
the following ball given morning and evening until the mouth is slightly
touched. Calomel one drachm, linseed meal four drachms made into a ball
with Venice turpentine. After all inflammatory and febrile symptoms
have subsided, mild vegetable tonics to be given.—ED.

    * Instead of the nitre I would put a drachm of camphor in each of these
balls.—ED.

bran mashes and *a little* dried green food : after that, as it is the real epidemic, liberally on gram-flour gruel —three quarts, three times a-day—boiled gram with bran mash, boiled carrots, fresh lucern, &c., and also thin gruel for drink—not water. Continue this for a week or ten days, when improvement or death will most probably have taken place ; if the former, lessen the medicine daily, and be careful to keep the bowels open with clysters.

CLASS IV.

STRANGLES.

Strangles occur between the age of one and five, oftenest about three. There are three kinds of it. Strangle fever, without any abscess ; true strangles with the abscess under the jaw ; and bastard strangles, when the abscess bursts inwardly ; but they are not so common in India as in England.*

Symptoms.—A slight fever, dulness, and disinclination to eat or drink occasionally comes over colts at two or three years old, either with, or without any cold, which keeps them weak and sickly for some weeks ; and no abscess forming in the channel to mark the complaint, we are at a loss to account for the ailing : it may possibly be the strangle-fever. When an abscess forms in the channel under the jaws, then he has the true strangles ; and it is most desirable that it should form, ripen, and be discharged ; for the constitution is then said to be renovated by it. There is

* All colts have strangles in India as well as in England.—Ed.

always a nasty discharge from both nostrils, with a chocking kind of cough. When the abscess forms and bursts inwardly, it is called bastard strangles— though other forms of the complaint, and when it hangs long upon the horse, also come under that name. Sometimes during the strangle-fever and abscess, or, perhaps two, will form, not under the channel, but in some part of the body, such as the thigh, groin, &c. : this, fortunately, rarely occurs, as it renders the complaint very puzzling. True strangles, from mismanagement, may run into bastard strangles, and that into glanders ; but bastard strangles has never the good luck to run into true strangles.

Treatment.—The strangle-fever, either with or without a cold, is to be treated the same as under " COLD," feeding on warm bran mashes, green food, sliced carrots, &c. ; and if there is sore-throat, the same as under " SORE THROAT." The true strangles is to be treated the same ; but as the bleeding delays the abscess forming, he is not to be bled, unless the ears and legs remain cold, which shows that the lungs are becoming slightly affected. A tobra (not the one he eats out of) should be kept constantly half full of bran mash, and hot water poured on it every hour : the head being held over ; this will promote the discharge from the nostrils, and be of great benefit ; but if the breathing is difficult, this cannot be borne. Immediately the abscess begins to form, the liquid blister is to be rubbed over it, and when soft and pointing, opened with a lancet ; but the matter is only to be very gently pressed, never forcibly squeezed, out. A poultice, kept continually warm, is then to be applied over the whole channel for two

or three days ; after which, a little Friar's balsam, or
tincture of aloes, is to be daily squirted into the sore.
Should the abscess burst of itself, enlarge the opening. When the abscess bursts inwardly, still promote the discharge from the nostrils with the tobra
of hot mash, feeding on green food and mashes. If
the abscess forms in any other part, instead of under
'the channel, treat the same. After the strangles are
over, a mild dose of physic is always requisite, followed by the " BEER TONIC," p. 109.*

SWELLING OF THE GLANDS UNDER THE JAW.

After five years old, a tumour sometimes forms in
the centre of the channel under the jaw, without being accompanied by fever. A warm poultice should
be applied till it becomes ripe, when it is to be opened, as before mentioned, with a lancet, and healed
with the Friar's balsam.

A large hard swelling occasionally remains in the
middle of the channel, the effect of strangles, cold,
&c. Blister it, and if not lessened after a month,
repeat the blister, or rub in the discutient lotion. If
the glands below the ears remain hardened, treat
them the same.

----

* The treatment here recommended is judicious, but the best plan of
steaming the head is putting some hay into a bucket, pouring boiling water
over it, placing the bucket under the horse's nose, and covering up the horse's
head with one end of a blanket or cumbly, and the other end hanging down
and enclosing the bucket.—ED.

CLASS V.

FEVER

is as common among horses as ourselves, and the after effects of it equally debilitating. More horses, I am inclined to believe, die from the effects of fever than from attacks of any of the acute inflammations ; and for this reason, the danger is so often overlooked for the first three or four days, until inflammation of the lungs or bowels is approaching ; then death is too near for bleeding or physic to be of any avail.

Symptoms.—The three principal and distinguishing symptoms of fever are, the great disinclination to exercise, the almost total loss of appetite, and the coat feeling dry and hot, and generally rough also, about the ribs. There is a peculiar soostiness all over the animal, but no expression of pain. A direct cold fit sometimes first occurs, as with us, and this comes on quite suddenly. The mouth is dry, the breath foul, and the tongue pale. The pulse may be quickened, or it may be weaker, or almost natural ; but, during the fit, the legs, like the body, are more or less cold. When the cold fit is over, a warm one frequently succeeds, and a slight perspiration. In this state he remains, the fever often returning on the following day, and near the same hour. He is also generally flatulent, and the bowels are costive, but occasionally they scarcely at all alter, and the difference of warmth in the feet, some hot and others cold, often not at all remarkable until the fever has existed some days : but if at all thin before, the falling off in flesh and great prostration of strength, will be clearly manifest in forty-eight hours.

Treatment.—During the first cold fit, (not when the warm one has commenced,) if a quart of warm beer, with three drachms of ginger, or a pint of port, and a pint of hot water, with a little spice were given, a jhool put on, and the horse gently trotted in hand for a quarter of an hour, (or let the trotting go on while the wine or beer is preparing, only be quick about warming it,) the fever might be nipped in the bud, and no more seen of it. Three horses I have cured in this way ; feeding on bran mashes and green food the following two days. If unfortunately not observed at the onset, (which it rarely is, except by a man who lives half the day in his stables,) bleed* five or six quarts if the horse is fat and the pulse much quickened ; but if the pulse is not much quickened, or not above fifty-five, never bleed, for the horse will frequently sink 'under it. Always backrake, then clyster. Give half a drachm of calomel, one drachm of emetic tartar, and one drachm and a half of aloes, made into a ball, and ten hours after, another ball of the same.† After ten hours more, give half a pint of linseed-oil, or six ounces of Epsom salts in thin congee ; and if the dung is not softened, repeat it after another ten hours : nothing more, however, than three or four extra evacuations are allowable ; purging is strictly prohibited. If the pulse was high and bleeding has been resorted to, half a drachm of digitalis, one drachm of emetic tartar, and three drachms of nitre, are now to be given, morning, noon, and evening, in about three ounces of warm water‡

* See "BLEEDING," p. 62.

† Instead of giving linseed-oil or Epsom salts, I would continue the ball until the fæces become softened.—ED.

‡ This ought to be given in a ball, and the digitalis continued until the pulse becomes intermittent.—ED.

but leave out the digitalis after two days, or three, at most. Two drachms of cream of tartar may be given once in the day, as a cooling drink, when the digitalis is left off. The food must be warm bran mashes, with a little green grass or lucern ; a little thin gruel occasionally ; and the water have the chill off. Clothe warmly, if the weather is cold, making a large bed. The emetic tartar and nitre are to be left off when the appetite returns, and he becomes a little lively ; but if the attack has been at all severe, you must not think of mounting him for a month at least, not even for a walk. Beer tonic, p. 109, should be commenced a week after recovery.

CLASS VI.

INFLAMMATION OF THE LUNGS.

Before commencing with inflammatory diseases, I must caution you against taking away a little blood, as a preventive when inflammation is coming on : this will render the disease very confused to you, whatever may be the case with a professional man. Wait an hour or so, until the disease fairly shows itself ; the symptoms will then be fully developed, and you will know what part is attacked ; and one full bleeding at the proper time, with the other treatment steadily pursued, will generally make a safe and speedy cure.

After an attack of inflammation of any vital part, it will take a fortnight, and often a month, before the horse can be again mounted. Boiled food ; a little sweetened gram flour gruel in the morning before the

first watering-time, and green grass, lucern, or carrots, are always needed to recruit the strength ; but
nothing is more dangerous than surfeiting with any
kind of food after these attacks, in order to raise the
condition quickly. Starvation, that is, as far as keeping the horse hungry, is the only safe system for ten
days after recovery : the muzzle must be used at
night if the appetite increases too quickly ; but if, on
the contrary, the appetite should flag, and the spirits
not revive in that time, the beer tonic, p. 109, should
be immediately resorted to ; and even if the recovery
is perfect, still, after ten days or so, a few mild beer
drenches should be given. There is no disease in
India, whether cold, fever, inflammation, or any other,
for which blood has been abstracted, and whether
the appetite is regained or not, that tonic stimulants,
of some kind, are not beneficial afterwards ; and the
beer tonic, in proper quantities, is as good as any ; the
danger consists in commencing it too early.

INFLAMMATION OF THE LUNGS is caused by sudden
changes from cold to heat, rarely, it is said, by the
contrary ; by over riding ; by drinking cold water
when hot, &c. It occasionally comes on quite suddenly : at other times the horse may have ailed a
day or more previous to the attack.

Symptoms.—Veterinary writers have fortunately
given us two symptoms, which mark this disease so
clearly, that by common attention we can generally
discover it : always, I may say, if not complicated with
any other disorder. "The legs and ears are cold ; of
a deathy coldness ; and the horse persists in standing,
or, if he lies down, it is only for two or three minutes." The pulse is oppressed, rising to seventy or a

hundred, and often imperceptible. The inside of the corner of the nostrils becomes of a dark crimson colour, the nostril itself being expanded, and the breathing greatly distressed. He appears stiff all over, and gently but anxiously turns his head round to his sides. Sometimes there is a cough ; sometimes none.

Treatment.—Bleed six to eight quarts,* three to four (according as the horse is large or small, fat or thin) from each vein, *at the same time*† and it is particularly recommended in this inflammation to bleed from a large orifice with a broad-shouldered lancet, that the blood may flow freely and quickly. The bleeding over, back-rake ; then clyster with one ounce of soap and four ounces of Epsom salts in two gallons of water, and give three drachms of aloes in half a pint of thin congee.‡ Soak the feet and legs in hot

---

* See "BLEEDING," p. 62. Bleeding a particular quantity may appear to veterinarians equally as objectionable as giving a particular quantity of any medicine. Bleed, they say, till the pulse rises, &c. &c. I once saw a man bleed, and take a teacupful away, when he said the pulse rose. Bleed till the pulse rises, is about as useful a piece of information to many people as what I once received from a surgeon I had written to regarding a horse that was dying from an inflamed vein ; first, said he, "dissect it out." Bleeding a given quantity may, in some cases, be bad ; but a quart too much or too little is better than a gallon too much or too little, and a certain quantity must be laid down. I have done the same with the dangerous medicine digitalis, &c.; for an acquaintance of mine once gave hellebore to a horse (strictly according to some professional book, he said) till the head drooped. It was done, however, too effectually ; the head drooped for ever.

† The bleeding ought to be continued not only until the pulse rises, but till it falters.—ED.

‡ This is dangerous treatment. If purging ensues from the aloes it is certain death. I would rather give very small doses of aloes, combined with digitalis, tartar emetic and nitre. The aloes to be discontinued immediately the faces become slightly softened. Not a particle of aloes, however ought to be given until the inflammation has been somewhat subdued by the bleeding. The sides and briskets ought to be sharply blistered, and copious clysters of warm water and soap administered twice a day.—ED.

water, then rub them well till dry, and bandage them up● the knees and hocks in thick flannel bandages, or cover them round thickly with dry grass. If it is cold weather, put on a warm jhool ; but the horse must remain in as cool a place as possible ; if in a stable, every door and window should be open. In six hours after the bleeding, should the breathing still continue laborious, the ears and legs cadaverously cold, and he still stand in that peculiar stiff position, with the forelegs rather wide apart, open both veins again, and take from each another two or three quarts, and give half a drachm of digitalis, one drachm of eme-tic tartar, and three drachms of nitre, made into a ball with linseed meal and liquorice water, or put them into a drench. Two ounces of the simple oxy-mel,* are also to be given once every eight hours ; and clyster every day, for three or four days, if the bowels are not open, with one ounce of soap and four ounces of Epsom salts, in two gallons of warm water. Nothing must be given to eat for the first forty-eight hours but *cold* bran mash, (boiling water poured on bran, and allowed to stand till it is cold,) a handful of green meat occasionally, and the water with the chill taken off. The digitalis must be left out after two days ; *i. e.* after six doses, and the emetic tartar and nitre after three days.†   Beer tonic (page 109,) to be commenced a week after recovery. If you blister

---

* See p. 168, for the "OXYMEL."

† A horse I had was attacked with violent inflammation of the lungs at six o'clock in the afternoon : he stood stiff as a post until two the following morning, when he fell, to all appearance, dead, and cold as marble all over. I was dining out, and did not return till that hour, but a veterinary surgeon was at hand. He was bled in both veins, back-raked, and clystered. Five hours afterwards, both veins were opened again: the horse recovered, not-withstanding the severity of the attack and the neglect of the first eight hours.

the sides, the proper time for it is an hour after the
first bleeding ; but never do this in the hot weather,
nor during the rains, unless it is cool.

INFLAMMATION OF THE BOWELS.

is common enough everywhere.   The causes are, cold
suddenly applied ; cold wind blowing on a horse's
belly, picketed outside, that has been accustomed to a
stable ; or a draught of wind when under physic ;
drinking cold water, when hot ; costiveness, unat-
tented to ; which last is often produced by gora-wallas, when *en route* by themselves, not searching for
good water.

Symptoms.—The horse lies down, apparently without much pain ; after a few minutes, gets up, and
then lies down again.   The breathing is a little
quickened ; the pulse, at the commencement, increased to sixty or seventy ; and the ears and legs
rather cold.   In the course of an hour or two all
these symptoms rapidly increase ; the pain of the
belly becomes very great, which is fully evinced on
pressure ; the pulse rises to eighty or ninety, and the
ears and legs get much colder.   His haggard countenance is often anxiously turned towards his flanks,
as he groans and rolls ; but he seldom tries to strike
his belly with his hind feet, as in gripes.   The bowels are always costive ;* the belly is sometimes swollen, and the urine, if passed, is in small quantities,
and with pain.   The mouth is hot and dry ; and the
eyelids red, looking gorged with blood.

* This is not always the case.   Inflammation of the intestines is sometimes
accompanied by severe diarrhœa.—ED.

Treatment.—Bleed* fròm six to eight quarts ; three to four quarts (according as the horse is large or small, and fat or thin) from each vein at the same time.† The bleeding over, back-rake, and clyster with six ounces of Epsom salts, dissolved in two gallons of thin rice congee. Foment the belly with hot water for half an hour, while a blister is preparing to be applied, about a foot square.‡ Give half a pint of linseed-oil, which repeat every seven hours till an evacuation takes place ; but no purging is allowed here any more than in the previous disease ; merely the removal of the costiveness, so as to cause a softened state of the dung.§ The legs must be well hand-rubbed to restore the circulation, and then bandaged with flannel or tied round with grass. A jhool, if it is cold or damp, should be put over the body, but the horse kept in a cool place. Warm bran mashes, with two drachms of finely-powdered gum-arabic in each mash ; linseed or bran tea; thin gruel, and a little green grass, is all the food allowed for the first three days. If the bleeding has been properly performed, and none of the other treatment omitted, the force of the disease generally yields in six or eight hours ; but if after that time the inflammation should not be subdued, and the symptoms of uneasiness and pain continue as at first, bleed again two or three quarts from each vein, and draw the firing-iron over the belly two or three

---

* See " BLEEDING," p. 62.

† The bleeding ought to be continued until the pulse falters. If the horse drops so much the better.—ED.

‡ The blister ought to be well rubbed in, to the belly and sides.—ED.

§ If there is constipation, I would at once give a dose of Aloes, guarded with Opium.—ED.

strokes, a little behind the blister. The costiveness must be fully removed before the inflammation will subside ; but immediately the dung is softened, no more physic is necessary, nothing but a soothing congee clyster.*

INFLAMMATION OF THE LIVER, OR SPLEEN.

The first of these is much more common at many stations than the preceding disease. The causes are, the climate, added to not giving physic, or giving that which is of no use, when, from a foul habit, there has long been evident necessity for it.

Symptoms.—Are somewhat between inflammation of the lungs and bowels. The pulse increases as the disease advances, and rises to seventy or a hundred. The horse will sometimes stand, but not with his forelegs so fixed and apart as when the lungs are affected. The eyes, mouth, and nostrils are always more or less yellow ; but the legs are not so particularly cold. The bowels are always costive, unless the inflammation is very trivial, and then there may be a slight looseness. The head is, generally, being continually turned to the side that is affected, and which, if pressed on, near the middle of the false ribs, will be painful.

Treatment.—Bleed† from six to eight quarts. Blister the side you think affected, about the middle of the false ribs for about a foot square, six inches above

---

* A handsome Arab, that had gone through a morning's parade without the slightest sluggishness, was attacked with inflammation of the bowels when led to his stall. The bleeding, &c., having been delayed for twelve hours, he died on the following morning.

† See " BLEEDING," p. 62.

and six inches below the finish of the ribs ; back-rake, and clyster with six drachms of aloes, dissolved in a gallon of warm water; and give one drachm of calomel, one drachm of emetic tartar, and one drachm and a half of aloes, made into a soft ball, every six hours, until the dung is well softened; but if the bowels were relaxed from the commencement, which is the case sometimes, though very rarely, bleed not more than from three to four quarts, and give one drachm of calomel, half a drachm of opium, and one drachm of chereeta, every twelve hours, for three times; after which, a pint of linseed-oil, and a pint of congee, mixed. Diet to consist of warm bran mash ; water with the chill off; and, after twenty-four hours, a little dried, green grass. On recovering, you must rigidly attend to the leading paragraph, CLASS VI., p. 178, for a relapse is very likely to occur ; to prevent which, a does of physic should be given about three weeks after, consisting of one drachm and a half of calomel over-night, and four drachms of aloes in the morning.

Inflammation of the spleen seldom takes place. Symptoms and treatment the same as "LIVER."

INFLAMMATION OF THE STOMACH

may also be said to be very rare, and not to be distinguished from inflammation of the bowels. Symptoms and treatment are the same as in that disease.

INFLAMMATION OF THE HEART

is another very rare disease, and more resembling inflammation of the lungs. If a horse dies of the lat-

24

ter, the former may be found inflamed ; the same
as when a horse dies of inflammation of the bowels,
the stomach on dissection may also be found inflamed :
but, as primary diseases, they are both allowed to be
very rare.

INFLAMMATION OF THE KIDNEYS ; THE NECK OF THE
BLADDER ; AND BLADDER,

are caused by cold ; continued rain dropping on the
loins ; over-riding, or strain of the loins ; not allowing the horse to stale, if he requires it, whilst riding ;
long feeding on musty gram, &c.

Symptoms of inflammation of the Kidneys, the Neck
of the Bladder, and Bladder, are the same.—The
mouth is hot and dry ; the pulse greatly increased ;
and the head anxiously turned towards the flanks, as
under other inflammations : but here there is often
observed a stedfast gaze towards the affected part ;
the head being turned over the body, and the muzzle
almost put on the loins, instead of slightly directed
towards the belly. The most distinguishing symptoms, however, are the hind legs. He stands wide
apart ; straddles broad when walked ; and shows great
pain, by shrinking when the loins are pressed on.
The testicles are occasionally drawn close to the body,
and then let down again. He strains to stale, and
the little that is passed is high-coloured, or bloody ;
but he is not so continually lying down and getting
up again as when inflammation of the bowels is just
taking place.

Treatment.—Bleed,* from six to eight quarts, three

* See " BLEEDING," p. 62.

to four from each vein, at the same time ;* back-rake ; clyster with four ounces of linseed-oil, and four drachms of aloes, mixed in four quarts of thin warm rice congee. Give a drench of physic, consisting of four ounces of linseed-oil, and four drachms of aloes, in a pint of thin congee. Put a mustard poultice† over the loins, laying the same on the inside of a sheep-skin, if at hand. A blister is not allowed ; so if the mustard poultice cannot be had, foment the loins every half hour with nearly boiling water, and keep them well warm during the intervals. Cover up with a warm jhool, if in cold weather : hand-rub the legs, and bandage them up to the knees in flannel, or grass ; but keep the horse in a cool place. When the physic has operated, half a drachm of digitalis, half a drachm of emetic tartar, and two drachms of finely powdered gum-arabic, made into a ball with linseed meal or ghoor, should be given once in every eight hours : the digitalis to be left out after six doses, and the emetic tartar and gum after ten. Warm bran mashes ; water with the chill off ; and, after twenty-four hours, a little dried green grass may be allowed for the diet. Clysters of plain warm congee should be used once in every eight hours during the day of the attack, in order to foment and soothe the inflam-ed parts. On recovery, treat as under leading para-graph, CLASS VI., p. 178. Should the hindlegs re-main stiff for more than a fortnight after the disease is subdued, put a charge over the loins.‡

---

* The bleeding ought to be continued until the pulse falters.—ED.

† Mustard poultice :—Mustard-flour and linseed-meal, equal parts : mix them together with an equal quantity of hot vinegar.

‡ Charge :—Pitch, one pound ; tar, one pound ; bees-wax, quarter of a pound ; rosin, two ounces ; heat them together, and, when a little cool, spread thickly-

INFLAMMATION OF THE FEET

is caused by hunting, or hard riding, or driving over
stony ground ; by severe training, particularly if the
course is hard ; by washing the feet in cold water
whilst hot, or, *vice versa ;* when in a high latitude, by
putting the horse into a hot stable, and bedding the
feet up in deep hot grass the instant of return from
the cold air ; or, by inflammation being transferred
from the lungs, or any other organ, to the feet.   The
two fore-feet only are generally attacked, but sometimes all four.

Symptoms.—The pulse becomes greatly increased ;
the inside of the nostrils red ; and the countenance
distressed, as in other inflammation ; but the horse
is here evidently very uneasy on his legs, and when
he lies down the muzzle is often rested directly on the
affected feet, which are always found intensely hot ;
and the arteries on the sides of the pastern throbbing
distinctly.   These last symptoms are what we are
told to rely on, as the distinguishing marks of this
complaint.   He occasionally breaks out into a sweat,
but never attempts to paw with his feet, or to kick at
his belly ; and when down, though he may groan quite
as much as when any of the previously mentioned vital organs are the seat of attack, yet he never rolls.
Under any other inflammations also that had existed
only an hour or two, the horse would be able to walk
without exhibiting any pain in the extremities ; but
in this, the fore-feet are lifted up and put down again,

over the loins, strewing over flocks of short tow immediately it is on.   This
will stick fast for six weeks, or two months ; during which time the horse
must be well walked ; but not mounted.

similar to a man suffering from broken chilblains, and having a boot on ; notwithstanding, you will seldom discover the disease till all the symptoms become fully marked.

Treatment.—Take the shoes off very gently, filing away the clenches, and slowly withdrawing each nail separately, for the pain is intense. Thin the sole all over as well as you can, cutting away small chips from the crust also, with the drawing-knife, and then filing even. You must do this when he is down, if he is unable to stand to allow it. Bleed three quarts from each affected foot ;* if you cannot get that quantity, take as much as you can, and then bleed six quarts from the neck vein. The bleeding over, put the feet into warm poultices of bran and linseed meal. Back-rake, clyster, with warm soap and water, and give the mild aloetic salt drench, p. 73 ; also one drachm and a half of emetic tartar, two drachms of nitre, and two drachms of cream of tartar, morning and evening, for three days, dissolved in half a pint of warm water. Make a large soft bed, that he may lie down as much as possible ; but, for the first three days, the diet must be only bran mash ; water with the chill off, and occasionally a handful of green grass. On the following day after the attack, if the inflammation has not subsided, bleed again, three quarts from each foot ; and if the horse is fat, change the warm poultices to swabs of cloth, which wrap round the hoofs, keeping them well wet with two ounces of nitre dissolved in a quart of the coldest water. On the third day, if the inflammation still remains, the pastern, round about the coronet, is to

* See " BLEEDING," p. 62.

be blistered ; but unless the blistered part is well
covered up with a cloth, and also something put
round the neck to prevent him getting at it with his
mouth, he will tear it off, and the pastern will then
for ever remain denuded of hair.

INFLAMMATION UNDISCOVERABLE

would not be so common, if people would only take the
trouble to read over quietly the different inflammations in the stable, in presence of their horse when
reported sick ; yet some, who do take that trouble, are
often in such a fright, if the horse is valuable, or in
such a hurry, that they fail in catching the symptoms
indicative of the part affected.

If the lungs are the seat—the purple nostril ; the
stiff fixed standing, with the forelegs rather apart ;
and the deathly claylike coldness of the ears and legs,
are the principal distinguishing signs.

If the bowels—the redness of the eyelids, when
turned down ; the lying down and getting up again ;
and coldness of the ears and legs.

If the liver—there will be yellowness about the
eyes, added to the other symptoms of inflammation
of the bowels : and if you here make a mistake, the
treatment for this will possibly cure the other, although, of course, not so well, nor so safely, as purging is dangerous when the bowels are the seat.*

If the kidneys—the stradling of the hind legs, and
shrinking on pressing the loins.

---

* Not when your Aloes are good, and guarded with Opium.—Ed.

If the feet—they are hot, instead of cold; the muzzle often resting on them when lying down, and the great disinclination to stand.

The note at the bottom of the page, however, ought to serve as a guide and warning, to convince yourself that inflammation really does exist in some part before you commence to cure.*

CLASS VII.

RED URINE,

in India, must be considered as arising more from some little derangement in the digestive functions, than as a primary disease of the kidneys ; and what would alarm in England, is here allowed to pass almost un-noticed. The native remedy is ghoor and ginger, six drachms of each, mixed, and given daily, for three

---

* A horse that had been for some months having only very gentle exercise, was taken out and galloped after a hog. On return to his stall, he immediately lay down. The alarmed master, without feeling the pulse or asking any body's opinion, took five quarts of blood. The poor animal not being much refreshed by this, a friend recommended he should be clystered and physick-ed. The horse, after this, getting more "gureéb" still, they both allowed that it was a most extraordinary case, but that, as he appeared so near dead, bleeding again could not do harm, if it did not do good. At this stage, as I lived close by, my advice was solicited. I had seen the horse on his first return : his case was plain enough—a little overgalloped when not in wind, and brought home hot. Out of pity for the poor brute, I undertook to do all I could, saying, I had a bottle of Elixir lately sent me from London, just adapted for these obscure cases. I then mixed some sawdust, red-ink, and blue-paint, in a quart of sour claret for the master to smell at, and putting the sufferer, half-dead from treatment, into a loose open stall, with a large soft bed, washed his mouth out with the Elixir of warm water, and left him with a little green grass till the following morning. The horse survived ; and the owner gave me a gold mohur for a pint of the mixture ; and his hunter, from henceforth, went by the name of, Impostor.

days ; and if the pulse is not increased beyond its natural standard, half of this may be tried. If there is too much excitement, a pint of the dhye (sour milk) sweetened with a small lump of ghoor, and given every morning, would be preferable. Some boiled food, with a little bran mash, and dried green grass, or lucern, should never be forgotten.*

Red urine, as a disease of the kidneys, or from inflammation, must be treated of separately.

BURSAUTEE.

Various are the remedies that have been employed for this disease, and it is rather unconsolatory to find, that no veterinary surgeon, at either of the Presidencies, has yet condescended to favour the public with a paper on the subject. If, then, we are to be doomed to grope out a cure ourselves, I cannot too soon add my ideas to those of other amateurs, who have already written for our benefit in the " Sporting Magazine ;" such recommending the madar, blue vitriol, &c.

In accordance with its name, the months of June, July, August, and September, generally the two middle ones, are the periods at which this disease breaks out. The worst cases are always low, damp, and " feverish," situations. It rarely occurs in a bad form in the Deccan ; a dry " liverish" climate, like this, is one of the most effectual ingredients in the cure.

---

* Bloody urine where there is no disease of the kidneys, is generally caused by indigestion. I have seldom found the following fail in effecting a cure. Aloes one drachm, Nitre four drachms, made into a ball with honey or treacle. One to be given morning and evening until the faces become softened.—ED.

When a horse is predisposed to break out with bursautee, and it happens to be at an unfavorable station,
and he is at the same time neglected, the usefulness
of the animal is then destroyed for seven or eight
months, and he will too often retain the scars, and
loss of hair, for ever. It being my opinion, that the
cause lies in a constitutional predisposition, which
cannot be discovered till the complaint appears, and
the only likely safeguard, against its breaking out
severely, being a dry climate, I shall proceed to recommend a trial of that which in most cases will be
found to expedite the cure. On the first appearance
of the disease give a mild, warm drench of physic,*
consisting of aloes and Epsom salts, with a drachm
of ginger, in rice congee.† Three days after the
physic has set, give half of a common masallah ball
daily, for three days, then omit one day, and commence with two grains of cantharides, one drachm of
ginger, one drachm of gentian, or chreeate, and one
drachm of anise-seed, in a ball ; this to be given every
evening, after the last seven o'clock feed. After six
days increase the cantharides to four grains, and after
twelve days, to six grains. After eighteen days, if
the appetite improves, increase the cantharides to
eight grains. After twenty-four days, discontinue
the ball altogether for three days, and then commence
again with the first quantity of only two grains, increasing to the second, as before, and so on through
the whole monsoon.‡ The food during this time,

* See " PHYSICKING," p. 66.

† I would rather give a ball, consisting of aloes and ginger. —ED.

‡ Instead of the foregoing, I would give the following ball morning and
evening. Cantharides five grains, Dinioclide of copper half a drachm, Gentian

whether the horse is fat or thin, is to be boiled sago, boiled barley, boiled oorud and sheeps' heads,—try everything to induce him to eat the sheeps' heads, or in default, any strong meat broth,—and the more black salt he will *willingly* eat with his grain and bran mash the better.

If the horse is gross, and unable to take much exercise, from the largeness of the sores or swelling of the limbs, still liberal (not over) feeding on this kind of diet cannot be dispensed with : you must muzzle occasionally at night. Lucern and green grass, cut the day before, I am also friendly to in small quantities. Keeping the horse in a dry loose stall, well littered at night-time, is of course to be remembered, and as much walking, or gentle trotting exercise should be given, morning and evening, as possible, for which you may as well take off the shoes. The external application for the sores (and to apply which, you should endeavour to obtain the assistance of a clever native farrier) is the native poultice :—

Leem ke putta, as much as the size of an egg.
Chitrawal ke putta,   ditto.
Vikmar, as much as two peas, or two gram.
Fulkeree, a quarter of a rupee weight.*
When the sores are small, four tea-spoonsful of the

two drachms, Pimento one drachm. The Cantharides to be discontinued for a few days, when the secretion of urine becomes increased.—Ed.

* I have seldom found the following applications fail in effecting a cure, when the Cantharides and Dinioclide of copper ball is given at the same time. The sores to be touched every second morning with the following escharotic solution, with a feather, until they look healthy. White wine vinegar two ounces, three and a half drachms, Bisulphate of copper, two and a half drachms, Sulphuric Acid three drachms—and dressed morning and evening with the following ointment. Carbonate of Zinc one ounce, Venice Turpentine one ounce, Suet six ounces. The feeding throughout to be liberal.—Ed.

koorkum-ketail, half a tea-spoonful of finely-powdered
blue-stone, and half a one of alum, all mixed, will frequently dry them up. As a preventative for the en-
suing monsoon, I should recommend the same treatment to be commenced with on the 1st of May, and
carried on to the 1st of July, but not increasing to
the eight grains of cantharides, unless some symptoms
of breaking out again show themselves, in which case
you may gradually go up to ten grains.* The cure,
of course, consists in eradicating all tendency to the
disease from the constitution, as the sores would
generally heal of themselves by October or November.
Many persons are advocates for the application of the
hot iron, or the caustic madar, to the sores, and giving large doses, internally, of blue vitriol in solution.
It is not for me to say anything against this treatment
in severe cases to those who understand how to use
these remedies, but there is no more analogy between
bursautee and farcy than there is between a common cold and glanders.

WARRANTING.

CAVEAT EMPTOR, at p. 253, says, "It is known that
horses have secret maladies, which cannot be discovered by the usual trials and inspections; therefore
the buyer requires a Warranty of Soundness, to guard
against such latent defects." I have taken the liberty
of extracting a great deal of the language, that
follows, down to the line at p. 265, finishing with the

---

* I prefer the ball given in the last note at page 193.—ED.

words "knowledge of the seller," from the above
author, and converting the same to my own purpose;
for which plagiarism I offer every apology. The
arguments and recommendations, however, in various
parts of "Caveat Emptor," in support of Warranty,
are not exactly applicable to India, nor can I agree
with them even for England, being opposed to warranty in every shape; so, with all due deference to
the ability and the pleasantry displayed in the writings
of that author, I am about to advise you to swamp
all warranty, for these reasons :—

1st. If you sell a horse to-day that either has a
slight cold on him, or catches one during the time of
sale, and that cold, from improper management or
neglect, degenerates into a chronic cough, the purchaser may, perhaps, declare he had a chronic cough
on him at the time of sale, and bring evidence to prove
the horse coughed the minute he came out of your
hands, and has coughed every day since : if warranted,
in law you *might* be liable, and have to take him back.

2nd. If you sell a horse, that should die two
months afterwards of chronic diseased lungs, and a
veterinary surgeon was to declare, from appearances
on dissection, that the horse must have been diseased
for a period of three months, and, consequently, must
have been so at the time of selling : if warranted, in
law you *might* be liable, and have to refund the
money.

3rd. If you sell a horse that, four or five months
previously, had put out his hip, strained his shoulder
or back sinews, or had been lame from navicular disease ; and a fortnight or so after purchase, he again
puts out his hip, strains his shoulder, or back sinews,

or becomes lame again from navicular disease : if warranted, in law you *might* be liable, and have to receive him back.

Caveat Emptor, p. 304, quoting from Lord Ellen-
borough says : " I have always held, and now hold,
that a warranty of soundness is broken, if the animal
at the time of sale had any infirmity upon him which
rendered him less fit for present service."

1st. Again, if you sell a horse perfectly fresh and
unblemished, and that horse, a week afterwards,
throws out a spavin : if warranted, in law you *might*
be liable, and have to receive him back.

2nd. If you sell a horse perfectly fresh and unblemished, and that horse, a month afterwards, becomes
blind from ophthalmia ; and the purchaser proves that
the sire and dam of that horse were blind from that
cause, it is an hereditary disease : If warranted, in law
you *might* be liable, and have to receive him back.

Caveat Emptor, p. 313. "Where, however, the
proof of pedigree and hereditary disease : are both
accessible, it seems clear that a constitutional taint is
unsoundness."

From the foregoing two sets of examples, with the
quotations from law at the bottom of each, and which
have been brought to bear on exactly similar questions, you may judge of the difficulties you might
occasionally be placed in, as a seller, by warranting.
I have used the word *might* throughout them all,
nothing regarding horseflesh in law being positively
certain, for so much depends on particular circumstances. " Unsoundness itself is sometimes sufficient
"to break a warranty ; at other times there must
" have been knowledge of the unsoundness. Most

" cases are questions for the jury, rather than of law.
" No legal contract can be founded on fraud, and
" wilful deception amounts in law to fraud." This
is plain enough ; yet, if you take your case to law, the
chances are always nearly equal, whether it will be
decided for or against you ; " not from any defect in
the law, but because both buyer and seller have
always proofs of the shameful transaction."

Suppose you gain your cause : if you have been a
seller, your horse may be returned to you half-ruined ;
and if you have been a purchaser, you are always
bound to return a horse in as good a state as he was
when taken from the seller's hands.   Here is a second
affair that may upset your first, and cost you another large sum.   Avoid law, if possible, and never
enter into any discussion : " your character, if you
have any, will not be enhanced by embroiling yourself in a quarrel with a cheat ;" but in order to prevent disputes, as well as litigation, never warrant, nor
ask for a warranty.   Do not commit yourself either,
by saying, " He is sound as far as I know :" this is a
qualified warranty, and the purchaser may maintain
assumpsit upon it, " if he can show the horse was unsound to the knowledge of the seller."   Such might
be fair in some cases, but very unfair in others, and
it might lead to great disputes ; for every man who
really knows a horse, must be fully aware there are
not ten in every hundred that can strictly, professionally, and legally, be called sound.   This, therefore,
should be your only warranty :—" There's my horse,
his price is——rupees, ready coin ; you take him with
all faults and diseases ; I allow you a quarter of an
hour's inspection, and I will send him over when you
send the money."   There are even objections to al-

lowing a man to try your horse. A friend of mine had a chesnut Arab for sale. A purchaser called to inspect him ; he appeared to suit ; was sound, wind and limb ; fresh, unscarred, and four years old ; price 1,200 rupees. " I like him much," said the purchaser ; " might I throw my leg over him ?" " Yes," said my friend, " ride up and down here as long as you wish, in my presence." He mounted ; walked, trotted, and cantered ; the action was good in every respect. You imagine, perhaps, the horse was sold. No, he now discovers two objections ; he did not want a chesnut, he wanted a grey ; and he did not like to go to so high a price as 1,200 rupees. The chap ought to have been forced to take him. I wonder how an imposition of this kind would be decided at law ? If fifty heavy men were to play this trick on a slight blood Arab, his action, of course, would be none the better for it.

Having recommended you, as a seller, never to warrant, and consequently, in equal fairness, as a buyer, never to ask for a warranty, there is the greater reason in the latter case for you to proceed with caution, and if distrustful of your own judgment, to have a friend with you. When, therefore, a horse is brought out for inspection, if the appearance, figure, limbs, &c., do not satisfy, make your *congé*, but do not abuse another man's property when at sale. If you are pleased, and fully certain that it is a horse you want ; that the colour and price will suit, and that you have got the money ready to pay, take ten minutes' examination or allow your friend to do it for you, then solicit five minutes for a walk, trot, and canter ; in a quarter of an hour let your decision be final : *if undisturbed* by the owner, this is ample. In

England the case is different ; there it is always advisable for an inexperienced person to have a new purchase submitted to a veterinary surgeon besides, for
a couple of hours, a day, or two days, as he may think
necessary. Half a guinea is all you have to pay, and
this, with your own, or your friend's eyes, to boot, is
abundance of warranty. Some persons, however,
expect too much from a veterinary surgeon. A
professional man can only tell you of any disease or
remains of disease, or fault in the build, which is
likely to produce disease or strain. He cannot tell
you, merely by looking, if a horse is subject to gripes,
rheumatism, or inflammation, unless some outward
sign or symptom remain. He cannot tell you if a
horse has ever been sprained, unless there is enlargement, mark as of blister, or something externally to
denote it. He cannot say either if one horse is more
liable to become blind, throw out a curb, spavin, or
splent, than another, unless there is some visible sign or
malformation, or he knows the sire and dam, or grand-
sire and dam, had these defects ; and then he may
say, " These diseases being often hereditary, or this
build being faulty, they are more liable to occur in
your horse." Beyond this, no uninspired veterinary
surgeon can caution you. When a recruit presents
himself before the surgeon of the regiment, on enlist-
ing, do you suppose the surgeon could tell if he had
fever last year, or sprained his leg last year, unless
some evident weakness or enlargement remained ?
How can he tell if he is subject to gripes ?

Buying a horse blind in both eyes, it is said you
cannot return him as unsound. Caveat Emptor, p.
274. " But it has been held that a warranty against
visible defects is bad in law, the purchaser being

expected not only to possess ordinary skill, but to
exhibit] ordinary precaution." But a large splent
extending on to the back sinews, a large spavin,
large curb, or contracted, foundered foot, anchylosed
pastern-joints, are all as visible defects as blind eyes :
they are palpable defects, yet they constitute unsoundness : but "law is law."*

Much has been said against dealers in England, and
dealers in India too. I have seen some black tricks
in both countries ; notwithstanding, I think, in the
long run, dealers are as much sinned against as
sinning. In either country, every man is bound to
be wide awake, or, as the judge says, expected, not
only to possess ordinary skill, but to exhibit ordinary
precaution ; and experience tells me to trust a dealer
quite as soon as a gentleman.†

---

* The whole of this Chapter on Warrantry is most judicious and correct. —ED.

† Addison's definition of the word gentleman is "a term of complaisance,
sometimes ironical." And gentlemen, and passers for gentlemen, are as often
mysticall mixed up togetherin one house, as thorough-breds and passers
for thorough-breds are in the same staple.

At a dinner-party of eight, some few years ago, the conversation turning
upon horse-flesh, I happened to let fall my ideas of the little general honesty
existing in any part of the civilized world, in selling a horse. My *vis-à-vis*
exclaimed, "Impossible ! no gentleman would ever attempt to pass off an unsound horse." Five more of the party chimed in to this most creditable speech,
so well calculated to delude the unwary, leaving only one of the same opinion,
or, rather, who acknowledged the same opinion, as myself. Clearly seeing
that I had got into company with either knaves or fools, most probably a little
of both, I thought more nourishment was to be gained at this house for the
body by drinking, than for the mind by talking, so I allowed the subject to
drop. Three months had not elapsed, when my *vis-à-vis*, the "impossible"
gentleman, asked me to look at a horse of his that had been sprained, and
blistered, but was still lame. The horse had a ringbone on one pastern, besides something else internally wrong in the foot of the other, arising, most
probably, from concussion ; so I pronounced him incurable under eight

Every novice in horseflesh is satisfied with his new
hobby for a week. A horse, however badly bred, or
faultily built, if only in good external condition, will
always catch his eye before a thin one ; and bog-
spavins, thorough-pins, capped hocks, and windgalls,
as well as the round shank-bones and dents, are all
less likely to be taken notice of when the nag is in
plump order ; many having a bone-spavin, a contracted long foot, or founder, have I seen pass through
three or four hands, each new possessor alike uncon-
scious of anything wrong : these treasures, whether
latent or patent, not being always discovered till the
horse is hunted, or suddenly becomes lame. Kind
Griffins, then, for whom this volume is chiefly written, I most fully exonerate, and acquit you of the
charge of intentionally deceiving ; yet, for reflecting
on your judgment, and for daring to assert, that if
you want knowledge you must begin with " BLUNT
SPURS," I know you would like to see me "regularly bitten." Friends, impose upon me with every
fault and infirmity the horse is subject to ; from the
day this book issues from the press, I know I must
be considered fair game ; but if you have the slightest
compassion for a man who has endeavoured to save

months,— very probably, not then. "What shall I do?" said he. "Write on
half a sheet of paper," I replied, "that the horse has been lame for two
months—is thought to be incurable—and that he is in the market for sale."
The man burst out laughing. He afterwards tried to get rid of him, but
failed ; for I took especial care that none of my acquaintance should be deceived by such an apostate as this. He then sent him to a dealer, who refused to sell him as sound. At last, he handed him over to a friend to dispose
of, from whom he received nearly the full amount of his original cost. I
did not discover the unlucky wight that was imposed upon ; but, fancy this
hypocrite crying out, "Impossible !" Here lies the honest distinction between
a man wanting to buy, and one wanting to sell.

your limbs, as well as your money, I implore you, never ask me to buy

A CHEAP HORSE.

SHARP SPURS HAVE FINISHED HIM.

Always on hand, for sale, at

MR. GREEN'S REPOSITORY,

BOMBAY BOMB PROOF.

RUPEES.

A good horse	400
A very good horse...	500
A superior horse...	600
A very superior horse...	700
A first-rate hunter	800
A very handsome horse...	900
A superb horse, carrying a magnificent head and tail	1000
A perfectly fresh officer's charger...	1100
A high caste, five-year old horse, without any blemish...	1200
A racer	1300
A handsome racer	1400
A three mile welterer	1500

It was my original intention to have sent this Treatise forth with a brief exposition of every complaint and accident the horse is subject to, which I had divided into thirty-five classes, under a hundred and fifty heads, but at present I am prevented doing so : at some future period these may possibly be added. On the request of an old acquaintance, not to fail to subjoin a few lines on red urine, and bursautee, I have dwelt a little on these two diseases, though out of their place.

I have now to acknowledge my thanks to Professors Spooner and Morton, of the Royal Veterinary College, for their very great kindness in perusing the foregoing before publication ; Mr. Morton has, also, most obligingly undertaken the trouble of seeing the whole through the press for me ; and if there are any little points not in strict accordance with the views of these scientific gentlemen, they are, perhaps, of no great importance. I can, however, assure you my manuscript received due praise, especially for the forcible expounding and illustration of the Foot and Heel ; and I therefore am entitled to expect the work will soon realize me half a fortune ; in order to succeed in which, I am about to change half my name. In conclusion then, critical gentlemen, I respectfully caution you to "Ware Name,"* and if you do not liberally patronize these pages, drawn out by the head of Blunt Spurs, you may yet get punished with a heel, and be brought to the ground by

SHARP SPURS.

* "Ware horse," I suppose, you know, is the caution given in England to the bystanders, when a horse is brought out for sale.

ADDENDUM.

HINTS ON THE EDUCATION OF A HORSE, COMPILED
FROM THE WORKS OF VARIOUS AUTHORS.

INTRODUCTION.

A HORSE in India when purchased from a Dealer's
"Lot," has in almost every instance been backed, and
probably has been ridden for years. Many persons
are satisfied, provided the horse will go quietly along
a road, and think that putting him through a course
of instruction in a Riding School, is not only unnecessary, but actually injurious. There are others,
however, who can appreciate a horse that has been
taught to be "generally obedient;—light in hand;—

to carry himself well ;—to walk, trot, steadily and quietly, and always in hand ;—to rein back freely, and close steadily to either hand ;—to canter to both hands, and change leg ;—to go about on the forehand, and haunches," &c.,—but who may not know, how to teach a horse the accomplishments they desire, and it is for their use, that I have thrown together these *hints*, extracted from various authors ; but principally from " Adams on Horsemanship," " Horsemanship by Captain Richardson," and "Training of Cavalry Remount Horses" by Captain Nolan.

By Monsieur Baucher's *Méthode,* recommended by Captain Nolan,* " The horse is gently used, the progress is gradual, but certain. For a few days he is ridden on a snaffle, with a loose rein at a walk and a trot. He is then bitted, and a few simple lessons teaches him, to yield to the feeling of the rein, and the pressure of the leg,—then he is collected and got in hand, not by pulling and sawing at the horse's mouth, but by gradual pressing him with the leg, till he raises himself off the bit, and gathers himself up at a walk, then he can be controlled, and put together, to any extent required, by the judicious use of the spur. As all this is done at a halt, or at a walk, the horse undergoes no fatigue. Reining back, then perfects the horse in the use of his limbs, and in unqualified obedience to the rider's hand and leg. This once attained, a few lessons will teach the animal to canter, change leg, passage, and pirouette ; the horse becomes a perfect charger in a very short time, without having, in any way suffered from his breaking, indeed ! without having been over-tired, or over-worked, during the

* Nolan on Cavalry Tacticts.

whole of his education, and from his mouth having been gently dealt with, it remains fresh and good, instead of being hard and callous."

The Instructor should possess, activity and firmness, the greatest possible coolness, good temper, and patience ; he must gain the confidence of his horse ; unless he does this, his work is one of brute force, and opposed to all the instincts of an intelligent animal. Horses are by degrees made obedient, through the hope of recompense, as well as from the fear of punishment ; mere force and the want of skill and judgment, tend to confirm vice and restiveness, punishment therefore should never be inflicted on a young horse, except for decided restiveness and downright vice ; even in that case, so soon as the horse moves forward, he should be treated kindly.

Care should be taken not to over-fatigue the horse, nor to wish to obtain too much at once.

THE LONGE.

Many persons mistake the meaning, or intention of longeing a horse, and suppose it is only to tire, fatigue, and worry a horse into subjection, the design is to make him familiar, and accustom him to be handled.

It is not recommended to longe a young horse, particularly without a rider on his back, if it can be avoided, as he is apt to rush round the ring, and strain himself ; the longe is however useful, and often necessary with refractory horses, but the use of it, should be made the *exception*, and not the rule.

The young horse, having a plain snaffle in his mouth, with side reins, fastened to a roller, to which there is a crupper attached, and a cavesson on his head, the noseband of which should be three inches above the nostrils, and not fastened too tightly, is led into the school, (which it is desirable should be an enclosed space ;—as the colt will work kindlier, when enclosed by walls, than in an open space, where he would be striving to enlarge his ground, or disengage himself ;)—care should be taken to see that the crupper is properly fitted, and that the hair of the tail be not doubled up, or entangled with it, and that the reins are of a proper length : the colt's head should not be confined too much, nor drawn down too tightly ; —the inward reins in longeing, should be a few inches shorter than the outward reins ;—so as to allow the rider of the horse, if mounted, to see his inward nostril.

A skilful person, will, single-handed, longe a horse in many figures ; and by heading with a whip, change him without stopping, and longe him in a figure of 8';—a horse should only be longed at a walk, till he circles without force. At first you will require an Assistant, who should lead the horse round the ring, while you keep in line with his forehand ; if you get before it, it will tend to check the pace, and if you get behind the shoulder, it will excite the horse to increase the pace, and cause him unnecessary alarm ; when the horse has become accustomed to the place, the Assistant had better be dispensed with, as the fewer there are about a horse, the better.

In longeing to the left, the whip should be carried in the right hand ; and in longeing to the right, it should be carried in the left hand—the arm extended, the lash trailing on the ground ; so that the whip may be readily thrown towards the hind quarter of

the horse to urge him forward ; but, the proper place
to strike a horse is 'on the belly : study to keep the
colt at a strictly regular pace, first at a walk, and then
at a trot. When the colt has been longed to the one
hand, for a sufficient time, draw him quietly to the
centre, speaking to him and caress him ; have in
your hand a little sugar, or gram, to give him, but
keep the whip out of sight, or let it fall at once upon
the ground. Alter the length of the side reins, and
put the horse round to the other hand. Do not let a
lesson exceed half an hour.

When the horse has become tractable, you can
teach him to change from the one hand, to the other,
without a pause ; the side reins in this case, being of
course of equal lengths. In longeing to the left ; when
you wish to turn the horse to the right, pass the whip
over into the left hand, retaining the cavesson as before ; seize the tape at the length of the arm, with
the right hand, and, giving the word " change," draw
the horse round to the right, at the same time throwing the whip in front of the horse, to check his
forward movement ; and cause him to turn, and pass
round to the right ; retain the whip in the left hand,
and the tape in the right. To change from right to
left ; grasp the tape as before directed, at the length
of the arm, with the left hand, and draw the horse
round ; at the same time, throw the right arm out
to the right, with the whip extended ; to check the
horse, and make him pass round to your left.

MOUNTING.

Place a saddle on the horse, and with a plain
snaffle in his mouth, and a cavesson on, lead him

into the school, and walk him round a few times ; then* " stand in front of the horse, raise the line with the right hand and play with it, speaking to the horse at the same time to engage his attention, whilst an assistant quietly mounts ; no one else should be allowed near, as the more people there are round a horse, the more alarmed he is, and the more difficult to manage ; as soon as the man has mounted, turn your back to the horse, and move on, leading him round, do not pull at the bridle nor look the horse in the face, but turn your back to the horse, and he will follow."

" In mounting a young horse, place the left hand rather high up on the mane, and with the right take hold of the pommel, *not* the cantle of the saddle, you can thus always swing yourself on to the horse's back ; whereas, if your right hand is on the cantle, and the horse springs forward, or turns round, in trying to pass the leg over the horse, you must let go your hold with the right hand, and thus lose your balance and are thrown off. By the other way, you hold on with both hands, the saddle is open to receive you, and you can swing yourself into it in spite of any thing the animal may do to prevent you."

The rider should have a whip in his hand but no spurs on,† " and his legs must not press the sides of the colt, if the colt begins to kick and plunge, you must keep a firm hold of the cavesson, and the rider must preserve his seat by balance alone ;—there must not be the least violence, nor noise."

When the alarm of the colt has subsided, proceed to longe the colt with a rider on his back.

* Training of Cavalry Remount Horses by Captain Nolan.
† Horsemanship by Captain Richardson.

" In urging the colt to walk, the rider should bear slightly on the mouth with both hands, at the same time that the pressure is made with both legs. Avoid upon every occasion to allow him to amble, or break from a walk into a trot. If he starts, or shies at objects, caress him and take instant measures gently to quiet his alarm." *"The first point to gain is to get the young horse to go forward and to go willingly, after which you can proceed to bend the horse's head first to the one hand, and then to the other. The rider should not play with the snaffle rein, but merely draw it gently to the side he wishes to bend the horses' head to, (of course always having a feeling with the outward rein ;) and if the horse follows the indications of the rein only a few inches, his head should be brought straight again with the outward rein ; this should be done first at a halt, and then at a walk.

To teach the horse to follow the indication of the rein, you should ;—when given on the inward rein, draw the horse gently towards you with the cavesson, and ease off the line, when the indication is given on the outward rein ; thus the rider can be assisted by a judicious use of the cavesson, in making the horse 'change,' and 'pirouette,' &c. so soon as the horse is teachable, the assistant and the cavesson, should be dispensed with.* " Begin to *collect* the horse both at a walk and at a trot, raise the horse's forehand, by keeping the snaffle in constant play, and do not allow the horse to lean upon your hand ; practice the horse in changing from hand to hand, and in circles first large, and then in smaller ones ; feel the

---

* Training of Cavalry Remount Horses by Captain Nolan.

horse up, with both reins at every step, and if the
horse is sluggish, make use of the whip upon the
horse's shoulder, and work him well up to hand ; but
be particular, not to have a dead pull on the horse's
mouth."

* " It must always be borne in mind," Captain
Richardson remarks, " that the fineness of a horse's
mouth, is not produced by lacerating the gums of
the horse.   The delicate, and beautiful skin which
covers them, is never so tender and sensitive, after
abrasion, as before.   The mouth of the colt has to
be formed to the usage of the hand ; as the hand is
the medium of the will of the rider, it is by very
gentle and correct indications of the hands and of
the legs, that the education of the horse is to be carried
on, and perfected, not by ponderous bits and rough
treatment ;" great care should therefore be taken in
selecting a bit.   † " The best for all purposes is a light
one, with the cheeks of an average length, the mouth-
piece merely sufficiently arched, to admit of the horse's
tongue passing freely underneath it ; the width should
vary according to the breadth of the horse's mouth.
A bit of this sort is quite sufficient to bring any horse
under control, for it is a mistake to fancy, that the
opposition a horse offers to the rider's hand, is caused
by the peculiar shape of the mouth, or that one horse's
mouth, is by nature, much more sensitive than
another.   The jaw-bone of every horse, is covered in
the same way ; whether a horse be light or heavy in
hand, cannot therefore depend upon the quantity of

---

* Horsemanship by Captain Richardson.
† Training Cavalry Remount Horses.

flesh between the bit and the jaw-bone, though many suppose this to be the case ; but the fact is, it is not the horse's mouth that is hard, but the rider's hand that is in fault." "If the horse has never been taught its yield to the pressure of the bit, and to bring his head in, he will, should he have a severe bit in his mouth, set his jaw against it, to alleviate the pain he suffers ; and thus, he adopts a way of his own, which he will ever after recur to, in similar circumstances." The bit should be placed in the horse's mouth, so that the mouth-piece be one inch above the lower tusk, the curb chain laid flat, and fastened to that tightness, as to admit of one finger being passed, between it, and the horse's jaw.

BENDING LESSON.

*"The balance of the horse's body, and his lightness in hand, depend on the proper carriage of the *head* and *neck,* and to these two points, first direct your attention. They should always precede, and prepare the horse by their attitude, for every movement about to be executed ; and the rider has no power over the animal, until he has rendered both these points, susceptible of every impulse communicated by him. It stands to reason, that if they do not lead in all turns, and changes of hand, &c., if in any circling, they are not bent to the circle, if in reining back, the hand is not brought home, if their carriage is not always in keeping with the different paces, the horse may execute the movements required of him, or *not,* as he pleases ; for his resources are still at his own disposal."

---

* Training of Cavalry Remount Horses by Captain Nolan.

" A young horse generally attempts to resist the bit, either by bending his neck to one side, or the other, setting his jaw against it, carrying his nose high up, or low down, he must therefore, by bending him to the right and left, be taught to arch his neck, and to bring down his head on the reins being felt, and thus be rendered manageable. As a general rule, when the horse champs the bit, it is a sign that he no longer resists the action of the hand. It is of the utmost importance that the horse never be allowed to take the initiative." Always oppose the raising of the horse's head,—always lower your hands and bring it down. The horse being brought into the school, see that the bit is properly placed in the horse's mouth ; and the curb chain so, that you can pass a finger under it; place yourself on the near side, in front of the horse's shoulder, facing inwards, the feet a little apart, to give you more power."

" Take the off bit rein in the full of the right hand, close up with the ring of the bit, between the fore finger and thumb, the near rein in the same way with the left hand. Thumb nails towards each other, and little fingers outwards, bring the right hand towards the body, extending the left one, from you at the same time, so as to turn the bit in the horse's mouth. The strength employed must be gradual, and proportioned to the resistance met with, taking care at first, not to bring the horse's nose too much in, or too close to the chest, which would make the bend very difficult ; if the horse reins back, continue the pressure, until he finding it impossible to escape, from the restraint imposed upon him by the bit held thus crossways in his mouth, stands still, and yields to it."

" When the bend is completed, the horse will hold his head there without restraint, and champ the *bit*, then make much of him, and allow him to resume gently his natural position, but not to throw his head round hurriedly."

" Practice this in the same manner to the left. To prepare the horse to ' Rein in,' take the near snaffle rein in the right hand, and the off rein in the left, at about six inches from the rings, cross them behind the horse's jaw, and draw them in, till the horse gives way to the pressure, and 'reins in' then make much of him."

You should now mount the horse, and bend the horse's head to the right and left.

" *To the right,* by passing the second finger of the right hand through the bit and snaffle reins low down, so as to have the reins short on the off side ; then draw them gently towards you, till you get the horse's head completely round to the right, in the same position as in the bend dismounted ;—when the horse champs his bits, allow him to resume his natural position."

" When bending the horse's head *to the left,* pass the right hand over the left one, and placing the forefinger through the near reins, proceed as before directed."

" Next teach the horse on the reins being felt, to arch his neck ; and there remain steady, till he be allowed to get his head away again."

" To ' rein in' turn the little finger of the bridle hand towards the horse's head, lowering the hand as much as you can and keep it there; with the right, (nails down) take hold of the bit reins, close within the grasp of the left hand, and shorten them by degrees, drawing them through the left. When the horse resits much, and holds his nose up, keep the reins steady ; do not shorten nor lengthen them ; the legs closed, to prevent the horse from running back ; he will remain perhaps a minute, or more, with his nose up, and his jaw set against the bit, but will then yield, bring his nose in, and champ the bit ; make much of him with the right hand, loosen the reins, and after a second or two, ' rein him in' again. This practice gives the horse confidence, for most young horses are afraid of the bit, and if frightened at first by a sudden jerk of the reins will never after go kindly up to hand."

"HOW TO TEACH A HORSE TO OBEY THE PRESSURE OF THE LEG."

* " *To circle the horse to the right, on the forehand.* Apply the left leg well behind the girth, very quietly, and without touching the horse's side with the spur, press against him, till he takes a step to the right, with his hind legs ; take the pressure of the leg, from him, and make much of him ; then repeat the same, and get another step from him, and so on till he has turned about ; the horse should not rein back ; but his fore legs remain steady, and his hind quarters, circle round the fore. At first you may feel the *left* rein, and use the whip very gently on the horse's side, near to where the leg is applied, but care must be taken never to hurry a horse ; if done by degrees he will soon understand what he has to do."

* Training of Cavalry Remount Horses by Captain Nolan.

"The leg opposite to the one which presses the ' hind quarters' to circle round the ' fore,' must be kept close to the horse, to assist in keeping him in his place, by communicating a forward impulse, whilst the other leg communicates the impulse, which makes a horse step from right to left, or left to right ; and in order that the pressure of the one, shall not counteract the effect of the other, the leg applied to make the horse step to either hand, should be further behind the girth, than the leg used to keep him up to hand. Both legs should be close to the horse's sides at all times, the pressure on either side should be increased, as occasion requires. In circling to the other hand, *vice versâ.*"

CIRCLING ON THE HAUNCHES.

*" By circling the horse on the ' fore-hand,' you have taught him, on applying the leg, to move his haunches to either hand, and as he has thus learnt to obey the leg, you can, by making use of it, prevent him from moving his hind legs, to the right or left, and can now teach him to circle on them."

To " circle on the haunches right about ;"—bend the horse's head a little to the right with the bit ; pass the right hand over to the near snaffle rein, apply the left leg as far behind the girth as possible, to keep the haunches steady ; make the horse step to the right, by feeling the outward snaffle rein, and passing at the same time both hands a little to the right, keep the horse up to hand, with the inward leg.

At first the horse must be halted, and made much of, three or four times during each turn,

---

* Training of Cavalry Remount Horses by Captain Nolan.

and if his haunches are thrown out, they must be brought back again by applying the outward leg ;— thus gradually led on, the horse will learn to go about to both hands, on his haunches ; when the horse is broken, it will be sufficient to carry the bridle hand to the side, you wish to turn to."

THE USE OF THE SPUR.

* " The *spur*, is not only used to inflict punishment, when a horse refuses to obey the pressure of the leg ;—but, it is also, combined with a good hand, a most powerful agent in bringing into subjection the most intractable, and in infusing spirit into the most sluggish animals ; it requires great prudence, and a thorough knowledge of the horse, to use the spur so as to obtain the proper results.

"The object is to unite the horse's powers at the centre of gravity, that is, between the *fore-hand*, and *haunches ;* and it is by the combined use of the hand and leg, that we attain this.

" Suppose your horse at a walk bearing the weight of five lbs. on your bridle hand ; when you close your legs to him, you will feel the effect of the impulse communicated in the additional weight thrown on your hand, and this weight augments, in proportion to the impulse given.

" On feeling this additional weight on the bridle hand, do not give way to it, but keep the bit hand low and steady, and play with the right snaffle rein ; the horse finding the bit an insurmountable obstacle, will by degrees learn, instead of throwing his weight

* Training of Cavalry Remount Horses by Captain Nolan.

forward when the impulse is given by the hand, to throw it back, and bring his haunches under him ; but should you, instead of closing the legs, or using the spur gently, put both spurs into his sides, the horse would throw so much weight forward, from the great impulse received, that he would probably pull the reins out of your hand ; your object would thus be defeated in the beginning ; and the horse having burst from control on the first application of the spur, by throwing his weight forward, would ever after do the same. It is of great importance therefore, that the spur be used with judgment, and a knowledge of the horse's temper, so that the impulse communicated to the horse with the spur, should not be stronger, than what you can easily control with the hand.

"Increase by degrees the use of the spur, until the horse will stand its application without throwing any weight on the hand, without increasing his pace, or without moving, if applied when standing still."

REINING BACK.

*"Reining back should not be commenced until the horse is well bent, and obeys the pressure of the leg ; during the reining back, the horse must be well in hand and well balanced ; as he can then make an equal use of all his fore legs, and raise them equally from the ground.

"Having a steady feeling of both reins, apply both legs to the the horse, to make him lift one of his hind legs ; at the moment of his doing so, double the feeling of both reins, which will oblige the horse to recov-

* Training of Cavalry Remount Horses by Captain Nolan.

er his balance, by stepping backwards, and thus, the first motion in reining back, is produced; give the horse his head, and make much of him ; at first a few steps backwards, is all that should be required from the horse, increasing by degrees ; if he bring his hind legs too much under him, ease the hand, and apply both legs to make him regain his balance forward ; for this reason always apply the leg first, and then an increased pressure on the reins, because if you feel the reins first, the horse throws his weight back, and it stands to reason," as Captain Nolan observes, "that the more weight he throws on his hind legs, the less able he his to lift them."

"The horse must never be allowed to hurry, or run back out of hand, nor diverge from the straight line ; should he do so, place him straight, by bringing his haunches to the right or left as may be required."

SHOULDERS IN.

The horse having learnt to follow the indications of the hand and obey the pressure of the leg, can now be taught the 'Shoulder in,' at first a few steps only being required of him.

Separate your reins, take one in each hand, and hold them rather short ;—bring the inward hand down, letting the wrist rest just above the hip, draw the horse's head round, at the same time advance the outer hand, to admit of the horse freely bending, press him with the inward leg and he will move diagonally, the outward hand by light touches, animates the horse, and guides him, in the direction you wish him to go.

PASSAGING.

After a few lessons at the shoulders in, proceed to the half passage, and passage ; that is, to teach the horse to move sideways. The motion of the horse's legs in passaging is the same as that in shoulders in, but the head is turned differently. In the passage the horse looks the way he is going, and moves di·· rectly to either side.

The horse being well balanced the feeling of the reins corresponding with the pressure of the legs,— supposing you are going to the right, lead the shoulders off first, by a double feeling on the right rein, at the same time, apply an increased pressure with the left leg,—the horse will cross his legs, and move sideways to his right. After a few paces stop, and make much of him ; should the horse not readily obey the leg, apply the whip gently on the horse's shoulder, and flank.

PACES.

The Walk.—The walk is the least raised, the slowest, and the most gentle of all the paces, but it should be an animated quick step.

* "Before moving forward, the horse should be light in hand, the head brought home (and not with the nose stuck out) the neck arched, and he should stand evenly on all his legs."

"In urging the colt to a walk, close the legs and communicate a sufficient impulse to carry him forward, but do not ease the hand, because if you do, the head and neck may relapse into a position which may defy the control of the hand.

* Captain Nolan.

29

" You should always have a light feeling of both reins, and when the horse bores on the bit, keep the hand steady, use both legs, which, by bringing his haunches under him, will oblige the horse to take his weight off your hand."

* " Avoid upon every occasion to allow the horse to amble, or break from a walk into a trot ; if he starts and shies at objects caress him, and take instant measures gently to quiet his alarm."

† " *Trot.*—A horse trots when he raises the " off fore and near hind leg," or "near fore and off hind," from the ground at the same time. Begin the trot in a very careful and quiet manner, and do not proceed to extend his pace, until he has become well collected in the slow trot.

" The hand must be constantly at work to retain the head and neck in their proper position, without counteracting the forward impulse communicated by the leg ; thus the horse will acquire regularity of pace, increased speed, and that safety, which is natural to the horse that is well balanced and light in hand.

† *The Canter.*—" Is a repetition of bounds, during which the fore hand raises first, and higher than the hind quarters.

" The horse being properly placed, light in hand and well balanced, throw the weight more on his haunches, by increasing the pressure of the legs, and restraining him with the reins, and according to the hand you wish to strike off to, throw the weight of the horse to the opposite side. He must not be al-

* Horsemanship by Captain Richardson.
† Training of Cavalry Remount Horses by Captain Nolan.

lowed to canter with either fore-leg leading at his own will, but must be made to do so at the will of the rider.

To canter with the right or off fore-leg leading, the extra bearing must be made upon the right rain ; and at the same time the pressure with the left leg must be increased. If the horse refuses to strike into the canter by the pressure of the leg alone, then use the spur instantly, or strike the horse with the whip on the left shoulder. If the horse still hesitates, pass the whip behind the back and strike the near hind quarter. To canter with the left or near fore-leg leading, make the extra bearing upon the left rein, with the pressure of the right leg or spur. Teach the horse to strike off on the circle first, than on the straight line after that, try him at changing leg.

"A horse may canter false, disunited with the fore, or disunited with the hind legs. If the horse in cantering to the right leads with the near fore, followed by the near hind, he is cantering false. If leading with the near fore-leg, the off hind leg remains further back, than the near one, he is disunited ; in such cases, close both legs to the horse, to bring the haunches under him ; feel both reins, but the hand you are leading to the stronger, to bend the horse's head slightly in that direction ; throw the weight off the leg he is required to lead with ;—which will enable him to throw it forward *and* to canter as required.

TO STOP A HORSE.

* "The horse being accustomed at the pressure of the rider's legs to bring his haunches under him,

---

* Training of Cavalry Remount Horses by Captain Nolan.

when you wish to stop, close both legs, and throw your body back, keep your hand low, and increase the bearing upon both reins, by drawing the arm back. If you do not use the legs, but merely pull at the bridle, you may by strength of arm, stop the horse ; but it will be entirely on his fore hand, and the horse would be under no control. As soon as the horse has obeyed the check, and remains still, ease the reins."

LEADING.

In leading you should never be further forward than your horse's shoulder, with your right hand hold his head in front of you, by the bridle, close to the mouth, and if necessary touch him with the whip with the left hand.

APPENDIX.

Mode of constructing an open Circus or School.— Enclose a circle of a diameter of from 42 to 50 feet with thick planking, or a mud wall, 3½ feet high, with folding doors to be made to open inwards ; and outside this, about three or four feet from the planking, have a mud wall built six feet high ; so that the horse cannot see over it.

Prepare the ground as follows :—

Dig up the whole of the earth within the circle, a foot in depth ; hollow the centre about six inches, into the shape of a saucer, replace the earth with a few inches of good mould, free from stones, cover the whole with about six inches of straw, or old bedding, which has been well saturated, over the straw, place three inches of good mould, and have the whole well trodden down, so as to form a good foundation ; the sides sloping upwards to the wall :—over all, put some cart loads of saw dust, or tan.

LONGEING WHIP.

The longeing whip should be 13½ feet long, the handle being 5 feet, and the thong 8½ feet ; made of hide, or leather split at the end.

THE END.